DARKNESS RISING

DARKNESS SERIES

Katie Reus

Cover art: Jaycee of Sweet 'N Spicy Designs
Editor: Julia Ganis
Author website: https://www.katiereus.com

Darkness Rising/Katie Reus. -- 1st ed.
KR Press, LLC

ISBN-13: 9781635561128
ISBN-10: 1-63556-112-4

eISBN: 9781635561111

For Kaylea Cross, one of the most authentic people I know. Thank you for always being in my corner, cheering me on, and believing in my success long before I believed it was possible. You've been with the Darkness crew and me since the beginning and I thank you for all your support.

Praise for the novels of Katie Reus

"…a wild hot ride for readers. The story grabs you and doesn't let go."
—*New York Times* bestselling author, Cynthia Eden

"Has all the right ingredients: a hot couple, evil villains, and a killer action-filled plot. . . . [The] Moon Shifter series is what I call Grade-A entertainment!" —Joyfully Reviewed

"I could not put this book down. . . . Let me be clear that I am not saying that this was a good book *for* a paranormal genre; it was an excellent romance read, *period.*" —All About Romance

"Reus strikes just the right balance of steamy sexual tension and nail-biting action….This romantic thriller reliably hits every note that fans of the genre will expect." —*Publishers Weekly*

"Prepare yourself for the start of a great new series! . . . I'm excited about reading more about this great group of characters."
—Fresh Fiction

"Wow! This powerful, passionate hero sizzles with sheer deliciousness. I loved every sexy twist of this fun & exhilarating tale. Katie Reus delivers!" —Carolyn Crane, RITA award winning author

"A sexy, well-crafted paranormal romance that succeeds with smart characters and creative world building." —Kirkus Reviews

"*Mating Instinct*'s romance is taut and passionate . . . Katie Reus's newest installment in her Moon Shifter series will leave readers breathless!"
—Stephanie Tyler, *New York Times* bestselling author

"You'll fall in love with Katie's heroes."
—*New York Times* bestselling author, Kaylea Cross

"Both romantic and suspenseful, a fast-paced sexy book full of high stakes action." —Heroes and Heartbreakers

"Katie Reus pulls the reader into a story line of second chances, betrayal, and the truth about forgotten lives and hidden pasts."
—The Reading Café

"Nonstop action, a solid plot, good pacing, and riveting suspense."
—RT Book Reviews

"Exciting in more ways than one, well-paced and smoothly written, I'd recommend *A Covert Affair* to any romantic suspense reader."
—Harlequin Junkie

"Sexy military romantic suspense." —USA Today

"Enough sexual tension to set the pages on fire."
—*New York Times* bestselling author, Alexandra Ivy

"*Avenger's Heat* hits the ground running...This is a story of strength, of partnership and healing, and it does it brilliantly."
—Vampire Book Club

"*Mating Instinct* was a great read with complex characters, serious political issues and a world I am looking forward to coming back to."
—All Things Urban Fantasy

CHAPTER ONE

Greer stretched out on the hard-packed snow, her thick jacket providing a barrier between her and the ice. Not that she really needed it. As a dragon shifter she was practically immune to most of the elements.

The sun was bright in the Montana sky this morning, bathing her face in a perfect glow as she relaxed in the snowy meadow, though no warmth compared to the fire pumping through her blood.

Things in the clan were interesting right now, and though she was almost always on call as one of the healers, she took a couple mornings a week for herself to fly and be alone. Dragons weren't like wolves in that they needed their pack. Well, for most dragons.

For her it was different. She needed her clan and she loved them. Dragons didn't tend to live in the same house or mansion or whatever as their clanmates, whereas wolves could all live in one giant place and be perfectly satisfied.

As she shifted slightly against the snow, she sensed something before she felt it.

A rumbling.

Was this...an earthquake? Here? She knew there were tectonic plates all over the planet so it wasn't completely out of the realm of possibility. And sometimes she felt it deep in her bones when there were rumblings far beneath the earth's surface. And this was definitely a rumbling.

She stood, bracing herself to potentially take flight as the ground trembled and shook beneath her.

To her left an explosion of rocks, debris and snow burst through the air before arcing out in a riotous cascade as it fell back to the earth.

Gasping, she took a step back. *Oh. My. God.* This was *not* an earthquake.

A dragon burst out of the ground, its skin a shimmering waterfall of colors in a very familiar pattern. His wings glittered under the morning sunlight, a kaleidoscope of gold and bright violet that slid into a pale lavender. His movements were almost liquid, his wings appearing as if made of smoke more than solid substance as he began circling in the air.

She knew a dragon who looked like that but she shelved that knowledge for later. Because this wasn't him. No, this was a dragon who'd been in Hibernation. And who knew how long this dragon had been asleep, but she needed to make sure it didn't reveal itself to humans.

She raced along the snowy plateau, waving her arms as the dragon continued circling overhead in the sky, stretching its beautiful, multicolored wings, flapping hard and powerful. When the beast saw her, it circled toward her and...*shot fire* at her.

She froze for a millisecond before instinct kicked in. His fire landed half a football field to her right, melting all the snow around it. Snapping to attention, she took a deep, steadying breath and centered herself. Holding her hands in front of her chest, she gathered all of her healer's powers into a bright green ball of energy. Not something she did often, but self-defense required it.

She launched the sparking ball of energy straight at the dragon. It wouldn't kill him, but it should knock him down. Then she was going to knock some sense into this arrogant beast.

And unlike him, she didn't miss. Her energy slammed into his face, knocking him off his path. But…he shook it off as if she'd barely grazed him.

Oh no. It was time to run. Or fly.

She'd started to do just that, calling on her inner dragon, when the giant, beautiful beast swooped down directly toward her, moving so quickly she didn't have time to flee.

Without thinking, she stalked toward him and smacked him on the nose. "I can't believe you shot fire at me!" she snapped.

That was just bad dragon etiquette. Yet now that she'd had time to think about it, she realized he hadn't been attacking her, because the fire had gone so wildly off course. And considering the strength she could feel rolling off this stranger, she didn't think that was accidental. If he'd wanted to hit her, he would have. She was immune to dragon fire—as were all dragons—for as long as their bodies could withstand it anyway. But he shouldn't have been immune to her healer's fire. That was something she was going to worry about later.

In response, the male shifted to his human form in such a fluid, quick transformation it took her breath away. She'd only seen a few ancient dragons change forms like that.

Now the male stood in front of her, staring at her with electric, mesmerizing amber eyes. In that moment she froze, trying to decide if she should run or stay.

Then he tilted his head to the side ever so slightly and she forced her eyes to remain on his. This male was a predator, likely a warrior, that much she could sense. It wouldn't do her any good to turn her back on him.

Finally he spoke, but in a language she didn't understand—which made her pause.

She was part of the Petronilla clan, and one of their gifts was understanding every spoken language. It was one of those biological survival things woven into their DNA. It was simply part of who they were as a clan.

"I don't understand you," she said to the male.

His hair was long, the soft dark waves falling right to his broad shoulders. From what she could see, his chest was incredibly built and muscular. She wasn't going to look any lower—that was bad manners. She couldn't help staring into his eyes, however. He had the kind of face that would make angels cry.

And he was on her clan's territory. Which was the real issue right now.

Though to be fair, he must have been sleeping far beneath the surface so he would have no clue he was on her Alpha's territory. She turned slightly and pointed back to where her four-wheeler was. She often came out here with it, then stripped and shifted and took to the skies. She just hadn't gotten around to the shifting or flying part today. She'd been enjoying basking in the sun. Now it looked as if flying was going to wait.

He reached up as if to touch her face but she gently caught his wrists and pushed them back down.

They didn't know each other and she hadn't given him any privileges yet.

He said something again, growling low in his throat as he leaned forward and sniffed her. Actually sniffed her.

Okay, then. This dragon must have been asleep for a long time because that was very bad manners. She just hoped he wasn't as ancient as Mira and Prima, because while she loved the "twisted sisters," they were like feral animals half the time. Every time Greer looked into their eyes, there was no civilization. They were simply putting on a veneer for everybody. She loved them, yes, but they were far more in touch with their dragon side than she was. Sighing, she turned and headed back to her four-wheeler, looking over her shoulder at him.

The male paused, watching her curiously, but ended up stalking after her, his bare feet quiet against the snow. He didn't seem bothered by the cold or his nudity, which for the most part was to be expected with dragon shifters. And males in general. They seemed to have no problem showing themselves off.

He stared at the four-wheeler, frowning as she slid into the front seat. She started the engine and then patted the seat behind her.

He simply lifted an eyebrow and shook his head, murmuring something in that language she didn't understand.

Sighing, she gave it a little gas so he could see it move. Then she patted the seat again. She needed to get him back to her Alpha's place, and arrangements would have to be made. They'd have to find his people, and more importantly, make sure this dragon understood that they were not out to humans. Not only that, for all she knew, he knew nothing of technology—and given the way he was looking at her four-wheeler with disdain, she figured that was a good bet.

He shook his head again.

"Seriously? It's not like this thing is going to hurt you," she muttered. "You're a freaking dragon." Sighing, she turned off the engine and got off the vehicle. And when she stripped off her jacket, his eyes lit up with interest.

Of course. God save her from all males.

She motioned for him to turn around. For a moment he acted as if he didn't understand her but she could see a hint of something in his eyes, something wicked and sensual. And she really shouldn't feel anything at all for a complete stranger. Especially one who practically crackled with danger and energy. This was not the type of male for her. She respected warriors, but...no. She was a healer.

She made the motion again. Normally she didn't care about nudity, but she wasn't stripping down in front of some stranger. Especially since he was watching her with barely concealed hunger.

Finally, *silently*, he turned, giving her his back. And a very bitable backside.

Damn it. She'd given up trying not to look at him and the man was huge everywhere. *Everywhere.*

Shaking those thoughts off, she moved with the speed of her kind and stripped, tying her clothes into a neat little ball before shifting to her dragon form. Then she made a little whooshing sound with her wings. He turned then and for the first time since his appearance, he smiled. A real smile that made him go from dangerous and sexy to panty-melting divine.

This was not good. She was not going to be attracted to some random stranger who'd arrived on her clan's territory out of the blue. Nope.

He shifted again in a flash of color and light and then he was next to her in dragon form, almost twice her size. She only knew a few dragons who were this large. She was large by normal dragon shifter standards but this guy was a whole other level.

She couldn't just leave him here but she was still a little nervous about bringing a stranger deeper into her clan's territory. But she had no choice.

As they took to the skies, she didn't fully camouflage herself because she wanted him to be able to see her. So she half camouflaged herself so that she was a shimmering shadow of movement as they flew over a mountain pass. He took her lead and did the same, and when they reached the exterior of her clan's most internal area where all of their homes were, she wasn't at all surprised that three of the sentinels surrounded them, not making any threatening movements but escorting them until they reached an area just outside where their homes and shops were.

It was where her clanmates liked to play random sports including soccer, football or just flat-out attacking each other for fun. Because that was what dragons did.

She immediately shifted into human form and dressed. The other males of her clan did as well. But the newcomer didn't.

He eyed the males, his dragon eyes a mix of ambers and greens. His giant muscled body was tense, his wings folded tightly against his back. He looked ready to attack at any moment, which was not good. She was going to give him the benefit of the doubt because she'd basically attacked him with a ball of energy and he hadn't tried to hurt her.

And because the most primitive voice in her head told her that he could have. It was easy to miscommunicate with others when you didn't speak the same language—and when you were an apex predator by nature, sometimes you simply attacked first and asked questions later. Something she wasn't going to let happen now.

She stepped toward the male but Dagen, one of her favorite sentinels, stepped forward trying to block her.

"Greer." He moved quickly, never giving the beast his back.

She moved so she was standing next to him. "It's okay. He speaks a language I've never heard and I can't translate it. He's just woken from a Hibernation."

Dagen's eyebrows lifted.

"He hasn't been aggressive toward me." *Not really.* She wasn't going to tell the others about him shooting warning fire at her.

Without waiting for his approval, because she sure as hell wasn't asking for his permission, she stepped forward and placed a gentle hand on the new dragon's snout. "You need to shift to your human form now," she said even though he wouldn't understand the words. She just hoped he understood the tone and meaning.

Because by now they'd started to attract a crowd of other dragons. Hell—dragons, wolves, and other shifters living among their clan. And some humans.

Among them was Prima, who let out a startled shout and started racing toward them.

The dragon saw her, and immediately shifted to his gorgeous human form.

To Greer's surprise the big male raced at Prima, and Greer tensed for a battle but the two simply embraced in a bone-crushing hug.

Then Prima punched him on the shoulder once—hard—and he did the same to her as they started talking and... That was definitely Gaelic. Scottish in origin maybe—not Irish or Welsh. Or she didn't think. Her brain computed that confusing language but it was different than the one he'd been speaking before.

Her dragon unleashed her claws inside, not liking the sight of this male naked and embracing another female. Which was beyond stupid. She didn't know him and she didn't care about him. *Simmer down*, she ordered her other half.

It took her a moment to realize that both Prima and the male had turned to her. He said something she didn't understand and Prima hurried over to her and wrapped an arm around her shoulders. "This is Greer, our healer," she said in Gaelic.

Or Greer was pretty sure that was what she said. Some of that language was confusing.

"How do you know him?" Greer asked, keeping her gaze on the male—who was unabashedly staring at her. She wasn't sure if she liked it or not. *Liar, liar.* She liked it—she just didn't want to. She'd had enough experience with a warrior for many lifetimes. She wasn't going down that road again.

"He's an ancient like me and Mira. He was known as the Dragon of War many, many millennia ago. I thought he had died," she added in English. "Mira will be quite happy he is alive."

She tore her gaze from the male and focused on Prima. *The Dragon of War?* Hmm. "Why is that?"

The tall, beautiful female stood in the way most warriors did, at attention and ready for battle. Her long, jet-black hair was a hot mess though, all tangled and filled with...leaves? She'd probably been battling with someone in human form and, as usual, had forgotten to tie back her hair. "He is one of us. We had thought our kind had all died." Her answer was as simple as that.

Okay, then. "Will you keep an eye on him while I get Conall and Rhea? I need to let them know about this newcomer."

"I'm sure they know about his presence by now."

"All the same, it's protocol. I found him, I need to let my Alpha know."

Prima grinned, her dragon in her gaze. "Ah, yes, protocol. So very important."

"Oh, and he wouldn't get on my four-wheeler. I need to send someone back to grab it."

"I'll have someone take care of it," she said as Greer started walking away.

Before Greer could blink, the big male was in front of her—still naked—and intentionally blocking her way.

"Where are you going?" Though she only understood part of the question and inferred the rest, his tone was commanding and kind of obnoxious.

She looked over at Prima instead of bothering to answer him. "Tell your friend I don't answer to him." As a healer she was used to a certain amount of respect and she didn't appreciate him being all up in her personal space. Even if he was quite possibly the sexiest male she'd ever come across.

"I go where you go," he said, drawing her gaze back to those bright eyes. Again, she only understood part of the ancient Gaelic but it was enough.

Before she could respond, one of the younger males walked up to them and held out a bundle of clothing to the stranger. "My man, you need to put some clothes on and cover your junk," he said.

Though she doubted the dragon understood the words, the male took the clothing and put it on.

And for the first time since he'd burst up through the ground, she felt as if she could breathe again. Because that body needed to be covered for her sanity.

Especially since a few of her female clanmates had been eyeing him hungrily.

Not that she cared. *I don't.* They could have him, for all she cared.

She was a healer. She wasn't going to get tangled up with a male who'd been known as the Dragon of War.

CHAPTER TWO

Reaper watched as the tall, beautiful dragon shifter turned away from him, her copper-colored hair falling along her back in waves. He'd been asleep a very long time but he hadn't been thinking of females or sex when he arose. No, he'd been thinking of fire—of war. Something deep in his bones had awoken him, telling him change was coming. Something cataclysmic on the horizon.

And his dragon was ready for battle.

Now, however...this female had his thoughts on a different trajectory. She was beautiful, yes, but her scent called to him on a primal level. It made him think of sweet summer rain and the vastness of the stars scattered across the sky. It made him think...*mine.*

"Who is she? Other than a healer?" he asked Prima in a language he was fairly certain was understandable only to her. She was one of the fiercest warriors he had ever known before his Hibernation. Perhaps a bit unhinged during battles—but the best warriors were.

"Healer is all you need to know. So show some respect." Prima turned back to him as the female walked away.

Oh, he would respect her. He would respect and worship her body if she allowed him. The thought both annoyed and intrigued him because he had been awakened with a purpose. For war. He did not have time for carnal pleasures. He had no time for the tall female with the perfect ass, deep green eyes and... *No more.*

"What language do you speak with the healer?" he asked Prima in the language of his people. There were many other shifters—and not just dragons—watching them curiously and he wanted to keep as much of this conversation private as possible. "And what year is it?"

She answered him even as she released one of her dragon claws and sliced her palm open. Then she grabbed his wrist roughly and did the same to him, scoring his palm.

If it had been anyone else he would have attacked, but he knew how this female thought. She was long-lived like him. They had been ancient even back when they'd gone into Hibernation. She did not like explaining herself. Something he understood.

As she put their palms together, she started chanting in a language that made the beautiful healer stop in her tracks and turn around.

Her green eyes flared with curiosity, her head tilted slightly to the side as she stared at their palms. Good. He did not like the sight of her walking away.

He wanted to order her to stay with him. His dragon half practically demanded it.

When Prima was done, she drew her hand back, her palm already healed. His was the same. Then she spoke in her current language. "We speak English here. Well, it is one of the many, many languages. I have given you the gift of my clan. You should be able to understand most languages on the planet now. I have a feeling that is going to come in handy for you later."

"Thank you." He nodded respectfully. Her gift was an incredible one, and something he would not forget. "You are the Alpha of this clan?" For dragons, the Alpha wasn't always necessarily the strongest. Usually, yes, but dragons in general were *all* strong. The Alpha tended to be the best leader for the time period.

She gave him a horrified look. "No. But my nephew is. Come."

She fell in step with Greer who gave them a sideways glance.

"Greer, this is Reaper. It is a shortened version of his original name, which is too long and complex for most to say."

"Reaper," he said, testing the sound of it on his tongue. He liked it. And it had the same meaning as his given name. He was a reaper. A warrior. It was why he had been woken up. Though it made no sense that he was so attracted to a female like the one on the other side of Prima. A healer of all things.

Greer. A beautiful female who had all the muscles in his body pulling taut as he imagined taking her...

No! he ordered his most primal half. He would not be sidetracked by a female.

Liar, his dragon whispered. *She is ours.*

"Reaper?" She snorted softly and muttered something under her breath.

"You mock my name?" What the hell was this?

Greer didn't even look at him but instead spoke to Prima. "If you're okay taking him to see Conall, I have patients to see to. I think he'd be okay with me breaking protocol."

He could scent her lie. So it was likely she had no patients, but clearly she did not want to be around him and he did not understand why. When he'd been topside, he'd had his pick of lovers. He'd been greatly sought-after by females.

Prima nodded and patted her cheek gently. "Of course. I'll come see you later."

Smiling softly, Greer nodded once and then veered off on a side street—without giving him a backward glance.

Go after her.

He moved so quickly he had not been aware he even meant to. Moments later he was standing in front of the surprised healer. "You will come with us." What was wrong with him? He knew that ordering her was stupid but his tongue was not listening to reason.

She stared at him in shock. "Excuse me?"

"You will come with us. I go where you go." *Stop talking,* he ordered his damn dragon. But there was no listening to reason. Probably because he agreed with his dragon. He wanted to be wherever this female was.

Greer turned around toward Prima. "Handle this, please. Or I will."

He felt Prima's strong grip on his upper arm, tugging him with her as the healer sidestepped him and continued on her path—damn, that ass was perfection.

He rolled his shoulders, ignoring the obnoxious beast in his head telling him to run after her and make more demands. He would do no such thing.

"Can you pretend to be civil?" Prima murmured so quietly only he could hear as she tugged him in the opposite direction. "That was insane, even for you."

"She should be with us," he grumbled, but did not push it. Glancing around, he took in the square and rectangle-shaped homes. They were large enough for dragons but quite uniform. "What is this place?"

"There is much you have to learn about," Prima said. "This right here is a neighborhood of sorts. It is shifter-only and the humans in this time period don't know about us."

That surprised him. "They do not?"

"No. We are the thing of their nightmares. In fact, they think actual dragons are myths. Not just dragon shifters."

He snorted derisively. "Humans," he muttered. When he'd been alive, they'd been afraid of everything. It seemed some things had not changed.

"That attitude will not get you far around here," Prima snapped, a spark of energy flaring in her eyes.

"Apologies…" Though he was not really sorry. "Have humans changed since I lived topside?"

She paused and shook her head. "No. There is goodness in a lot of the humans but they are destroying the planet. They argue over everything and seem to fear what they don't know, what is different than them. I fear for us, and fear for where we live. Mira and I have talked about potentially retreating to a different realm. Some of the Hell realms are quite beautiful despite the name."

Interesting. Again, he saved this information for later. "I have many questions about this world, but first tell me about the healer. Is she spoken for?" Because right now, Greer was all he could seem to focus on.

Now Prima gave him a pitying look. "She is single. But I do not believe you are her type. If you are looking for simple sex, I'm sure you will be able to find it. Plenty of it in fact."

He lifted a shoulder, and made a noncommittal grunt. He had always bedded female warriors. Females who liked sex as rough as he did. Yet he sensed the healer would be different. He did not know what to do with these strange new sensations inside him. So he ignored them.

As they strode down the paved street, he asked, "How long have you been awake?"

She lifted a shoulder. "A few months. A year. What does it matter?"

"So not long, then."

"Not long at all. Truthfully I thought all of the ancients like us were gone."

"No, they are not. I feel it in my blood. We are all beginning to wake up."

Her expression turned serious then. "All of the ancients?"

"I simply know what I feel in my blood." And he needed to find a couple of very specific ancient dragon shifters. They needed to prepare for what was to come. His blood was telling him war was on the horizon so he needed to search out warriors he had fought with before.

"This is our Alpha's house." Prima pulled out a small rectangular thing and pressed some of the buttons on it. "They are all out back sparring."

He wanted to ask what the rectangle thing was but held back. He had far too many questions and he'd been asleep for a very, *very* long time. Besides, the only answer he had truly cared about was whether the healer was spoken for. And she was not.

Priorities.

Prima opened the front door of the Alpha's home and they strode through it, her steps filled with purpose. He glanced around at the interior, finding it interesting. It was all very...polished. Civilized. Framed images of things hanging on walls of different colors. Smooth furniture of wood and some stone. Interesting.

He followed her down a spacious hallway into a large room that smelled of spices and food. Then she opened another door onto a wide-open outdoor space. He recognized little Arya and Dragos—who were not so little anymore. But their scents were the same. That did not change with age.

Surprised, he glanced at Prima. "The Alpha is your brother's child?"

"Well he's mine too," Arya said, striding up to him. "Considering I carried him inside me."

He vaguely remembered a little wisp of a female with pale hair, dark eyes and a fighter's heart who had turned into quite the warrior if he had to guess judging by her faint scars, scent and attitude alone.

"You are blessed to have a child." It was not always easy for shifters to procreate, especially dragons.

"We have three."

His eyes widened slightly as he looked between her and Dragos—who simply watched him with a warrior's intent gaze. "Blessed indeed."

She sniffed once and gave Prima a look he couldn't quite define. A bit challenging. "Want to spar with me next?"

"Not today. But I will kick your ass tomorrow for certain," Prima answered.

Arya sniffed again and gave them her back but not before he saw a pleased grin. "Maybe think about running a brush through your hair," she tossed over her shoulder. "You've got leaves and dirt in it."

Prima simply shrugged and held out a hand toward the two shifters battling against one another with blades. "That is my nephew and his mate."

They were both incredibly fast. The female was slender and quite small for a dragon. Her skin was a pale brown and her dark hair was braided into an intricate crown on her head. A scent lifted on the wind, strange yet familiar.

"Quit sparring and come meet another ancient," Prima finally said, impatience bleeding into her words.

"Greer found him in the mountains, which I'm sure you're already aware of."

At the female's words the two Alphas stopped and turned toward him but did not drop their weapons. Instead they strode toward him as a cohesive unit. Yes, definitely an Alpha couple. They hadn't stopped to greet him; they'd waited until they were ready, as Alphas would. He could respect that.

"You are a wolf?" he said to the female. Surprise filtered through him so much that he asked such an obvious question when the truth was right in front of him.

"No shit, Sherlock."

He did not like her tone. "My name is Reaper, not Sherlock."

The female's face split into a wide grin and she laughed. "Oh, this is going to be interesting."

"You have a problem with non-dragons?" The male Alpha's voice was carefully neutral, but his dragon sparked in his gray eyes. As the son of two strong dragons, this one would be battle-hardened as well.

"No. But in my time different shifter species did not mate." Or it was rare. "I was simply surprised."

The male's eyes glinted with silent warning. "Times are different."

"A warrior is a warrior." Though he had always thought dragons superior to all shifters. "You are both quite young to be the Alpha couple." Especially the female.

"Man, this one really doesn't censor himself," the she-wolf said, grinning. She held out a hand. "I'm Rhea."

He took her hand, shook it once and was surprised at the power he felt flowing through her. She was quite young, maybe a few hundred years old at most, but would grow into her considerable powers fully in time. Even though he had already stated his name, he said, "Reaper."

"Conall, would he be able to speak to you privately?" Prima asked after he had also shaken the male's hand. "He's just woken on our land and this world is going to be a shock to him."

The male nodded at his aunt, then he and his mate headed toward the back door. "Follow me."

Reaper wasn't exactly surprised when Prima came with him. Moments later they were inside a large room filled with many shelves and...things. No jewels or gold, however. His own hoard was buried far beneath the earth—and he'd stashed even more of it away in an icy cavern far from where any humans lived. Or at least, no humans had been there prior to his Hibernation. Considering how weak they were he couldn't imagine they'd gotten there in his years gone.

"Who are your clanmates?" Conall asked, getting right to the point as he shut the door behind them.

"I was never part of a clan. Not officially." He'd led men, had fought in wars. After his parents died—also warriors—he had cut ties with his clan. They hadn't been like him. Dragons were fighters by nature, but his clan hadn't been full of warriors. They'd been…weak, in his mind. He recalled far too many petty arguments over clan meals. "I was a warrior."

"You were a fucking *general*." Prima shook her head slightly. "We called him the Dragon of War."

"Jeez, no wonder you two are friends," Rhea muttered, looking at one of those small rectangular things similar to the one Prima had.

"But there are others I need to get in contact with," Reaper said. "Ancients like myself. I believe they are awake. My blood tells me so anyway."

The Alpha nodded as the Alpha female started talking into the rectangle and walked away from them, going to stand by a window. "I can help you if I have names. And any information you have on them."

Reaper relayed the names of the warriors he needed to speak to. Ones he knew to be great fighters. "Brennus of the Zmey clan, Cynbel of the Patmos clan, and Cale of the Cearrach clan."

"It will take some time, but I believe we can find who you are searching for. If they are even awake."

He nodded once, curious as to how they would search for the other dragons. "How long will this take?"

Conall lifted an eyebrow.

"I am not pushing you." Okay, that might be a lie. He wanted to know when. He sensed that war and destruction were coming, that he needed to be ready. But he would not tell them any of this. It was not their business and he wasn't sure he trusted them even if they were related to Mira and Prima. In fact, maybe because of that.

He adored the females—and wondered where Mira was because normally she was not far from her sister—but clan came first for the two females. Always. As much as they respected him, he was still an outsider to them. "I would just like a time frame." He almost said please but it was not in his nature. He was used to giving orders.

"A couple days. A week at the most."

He wasn't sure how that was possible. It would take time for word of his awakening to travel. He looked over at Prima, who simply nodded as she absently pulled a couple leaves from her hair.

"They have something called phones now. And the internet. Trust me. They will find the others."

Her words were sincere and Reaper had no reason to distrust her. And right now he wanted to see the healer again and wasn't sure how to make that happen. But he had an idea. A sneaky one. "When you woke did you need to see the healer?" He was careful with his words, not wanting them to scent a lie on him.

"Sort of. My awakening was not an easy one."

"I think I should perhaps see one of the clan's healers," he said, looking back at the Alpha. "Only if you would allow me to?"

"You guys are really big on formality." Rhea had tucked her rectangle away into a pocket and rejoined them.

The Alpha gave his mate a soft smile before he looked back at Reaper. "We have two healers. I'll take you to see the one you've already met."

"I'll do it," Prima said. "I need to talk to Greer about something anyway."

Yes, he liked the sound of her name. Greer. It was simple and unique. He did not like the way she had snorted when they had been introduced. There was nothing wrong with his name.

Reaper. It was time to reap the benefits of awakening in this time and place. Starting with the gorgeous and annoyingly aloof female healer he couldn't stop thinking about.

CHAPTER THREE

Greer hurried down the stairs when she heard a knock on her front door. It was fairly rare for shifters to knock at all. They only knocked if the front door was locked—which she'd done today. Something that was out of character for her since she was one of the clan's healers. And with Victoria, her fellow healer, just having had her baby, Greer had taken over all the duties even though Victoria had insisted she was fine. And she very well was fine, but she deserved this time with her mate and new baby. Still, Greer had wanted some warning if someone very specific decided to come to her house, hence the locked door.

As Greer reached the front door, she scented *him*.

Reaper. The male who had thought he could tell her what to do. As if he had the right.

Just the thought of him bothered her even as it aroused her. But she was quite gifted and she covered up her scent, smothering it and the strange feelings he evoked. She didn't care for bossy males. Keeping her expression neutral, she opened the door to find him and, of course, Prima.

"Is everything okay?" she asked, addressing Prima. If she didn't look directly at him, it seemed to help. Sort of.

"I think my friend should see you. He's been in Hibernation for a long time, and my own awakening was not an easy one. I would feel better if a healer looked him over and I did not want to bother Victoria."

Putting away her personal baggage, she went straight into healer mode. Stepping back, she gestured with her hand. "Of course, please come in. Have you eaten anything?" she asked him. Because Prima was right. He should be looked over by a healer and fed. And she was ashamed she hadn't thought of that already. "I'm sure you must be starving."

When he looked at her, his eyes a mixture of amber and green, she saw his dragon staring back at her for a long moment. In that span of seconds, she was aware of how very ancient he must be. Looking into his eyes was like looking at the moon, stars and planets. There was far too much depth in his gaze, as if she was peering into the distant past.

Just as quickly, he blinked and the man stared back at her. "I am hungry." His voice was a deep rumble and there was something in his tone she couldn't quite put her finger on. As if maybe he wasn't talking about food at all.

Except food was all she was offering.

"Come this way." Her kitchen was spacious, able to accommodate twenty dragons easily. "Please sit at the island," she said, moving toward her refrigerator. It was always stocked courtesy of Maeve, one of their chefs, mainly because people were always stopping by.

"I'll do that." Prima practically shooed her away from the refrigerator. "You scan him and make sure he's okay. I'll get him food."

She didn't like the flush of awareness that slid through her as she moved closer to the giant dragon.

Some part of her was drawn to him even as she wanted to run away. What the hell was that? She'd never experienced this before, the electrical sensation flowing along her skin, her healer's energy dancing just under the surface.

It was probably a case of curiosity. But that didn't explain the pull she felt, the raw sexual awareness she was desperately trying to keep locked up. She'd never had to force herself to stay in professional mode, but for the first time in her long existence she had to do just that. Her dragon was curious about this male, wanting to lean in and run her nose along the column of Reaper's neck, to nibble on his ear—but she shoved the urges back.

As she sat in front of him on the barstool, she was careful not to touch him. Though it was hard to ignore that their knees were only an inch apart as she situated herself. Part of her was almost afraid to actually touch him again, to feel his warm skin under her fingertips. When she'd grasped his wrists out on the wide-open stretch of snowy land, there had been an arc of electricity she'd felt straight to her core. It unsettled her. "I need to scan you with my healer's gift. Is that okay?"

"You may touch me anywhere and any way you choose." His voice was a deep, sensual rumble.

She blinked, her cheeks heating up at his roughly spoken words. "I don't actually need to touch you, I just need to... You'll see." She reached out gently, putting her hands above his head and around his face before she moved slowly down to his heart. She didn't need to go any lower than that, simply holding her hands in place as she allowed her healer's sense to push outward, scanning him for any type of injuries or illness.

Fire and strength radiated from him. So much so that it shocked her.

He was healthy from what she could tell, his body a finely honed weapon. Which she shouldn't be noticing right now, and she was ashamed that she did. But it was hard to ignore his broad shoulders and the sharply defined musculature underneath his shirt—not to mention the pale scars along his forearms and around his neck. They seemed to be everywhere and she wondered if they extended to places she couldn't see.

Abruptly, she dropped her hands. "I can officially give you a clean bill of health." Shifting the chair back to get some much-needed space, she pulled in a breath, not that it helped. Being this close to him rankled her in a way she didn't quite understand. Her dragon was fully awake, rubbing up against her insides, wanting to know who this male was. If she didn't know better she might think it was the mating pull. But there was no way that could be true.

Healers almost always mated with healers, or if not healers, then those with similar qualities. Her dragon could not be attracted to this warrior who took lives.

Even Victoria, who had mated with Drake, had mated with a male so sweet and kind even though he was a warrior. Drake had withstood Hell for over a thousand years and came out with a pure heart. This…made no sense.

"Are you sure? Maybe you should check again?" His tone was perfectly neutral but there was a wicked glint in those amber, green-flecked eyes.

She narrowed her gaze. "You are fine." Oh, yes he was.

"He's looking for someone," Prima said, drawing her attention toward the other female who'd laid out a bunch of food for Reaper on the island. "A few someones in fact. Perhaps you could check with some of your healer contacts and see if they know where these dragons are."

"You're searching for your clan?" she asked as she looked back at him, taking another subtle step away. Though it was kind of a silly question. Of course he was searching for them.

"No."

She blinked once. *Okay, then.* Sighing, she looked at Prima again. "Give me the names and I'll check with my contacts in the dragon community as well as among the wolves and some humans I know. Perhaps they will be able to find who you're looking for."

"You speak with humans?" He seemed shocked by this.

"Of course I do. I have human friends and I have healed many humans over the centuries. They are a part of this world as much as we are."

He made a scoffing sound that made both her and her dragon sit up straight in irritation.

"You have something against humans?" Her tone was perfectly polite and civil, but he was doing a good job of pushing her buttons.

He lifted a broad shoulder. "Humans are weak. Mortal." He said the last word as if it were a sin.

"Newsflash, buddy—we're mortal as well. We don't live forever." So much for staying cool about this. But he'd found one of her hot buttons.

He lifted a big shoulder again and she was annoyed with herself for noticing how broad and muscular he was. "Their lives are over in the blink of an eye. I have no interest in knowing humans."

"You think you're better than them?" She should really stop pushing but he was pissing her off.

"Of course I am." He said it in such an imperious manner that Prima choked on air and stuck her head back in the fridge. "I am an ancient dragon with many kills and wars to my name. Humans are weak."

"What you are is obnoxious." First he'd tried to tell her what to do and where to go and now he was insulting an entire group of people?

"Excuse me?" He straightened in his seat, his expression offended.

"You're the most maddening dragon I've ever met! I know a human who survived a Hell realm and she's one of the bravest people I've ever known. You, on the other hand, are a maddening...jerk...fuckface!" Her words were all twisted because she was so angry she couldn't come up with an actual insult. She couldn't remember the last time she'd actually called anyone a name. Not even in her head. But this male made her crazy.

He paused, watching her as he digested her words. "You would like to fuck my face? I find this idea pleasing. Very pleasing." He practically purred the last few words. "I will lie down right now and let you—"

"Stop!" She turned and stormed out of the room because she didn't trust herself not to do something stupid, like launch a ball of healer energy at him. She just couldn't look at his stupid, obnoxious, handsome face any longer. Those smug, sexy lips— Nooooooooooo. No, no, no.

As she reached the foyer she nearly ran right into Dragos, who took one look at her face and turned right back around. She couldn't believe she was letting Reaper drive her out of her own home, but she was keyed up, her energy sparking at her fingertips as if she was a dragonling with no control.

And the idea of actually fucking his face? Why did she like it so much? Even thinking about straddling that sexy, oh-so-handsome face and letting him tease her with his tongue? "No!"

What. The. Hell.

Oh no. No, no, no. This could not be what she thought it was. No way in hell. She needed to get far away from him, and fast.

* * *

Prima howled in laughter as the sexy healer stomped out of the room.

"You find this funny?" Reaper demanded.

"Yes, I really do. You have been awake less than an hour and you have already angered the sweetest dragon in our clan. You just told her you would like her to fuck your face and offered to do it right here. To quote some of my younger clanmates, you've got problems, my friend."

He *did* have problems. Many of them, and they definitely included the sexy female he had just inadvertently angered. "I do not understand why she likes humans," he muttered. "It makes no sense."

"If that is your takeaway, you really missed the point of your conversation with her. Look, you have been asleep a long time. I know you think you are attracted to her—"

"I *am* attracted to her," he snapped. There was no sense in denying it. He was desperate to taste her, especially after that show of fire and anger. And the image of her sitting on his face while he pleasured her made his entire body hard.

"Fine. But she is a healer. And you are, well, you are Reaper. It would never work. So forget about her. I will find you some females who would love to fuck you if that is what you require. In the meantime, let's talk about why you are awake."

He stilled. "What do you mean?"

"Don't play games with me." Prima's expression was deadly serious.

He couldn't afford to piss her off, and the truth was he did not want to lie to her regardless. "I…am not sure why I woke up. My blood tells me that things will be changing soon. That war might be coming." He still had much to learn about this world if that were true.

Still frowning, she started piling food onto a plate for him. Then she slid it into…

"What is that?" he asked.

"A microwave. It heats up food—but you can't put certain things in them or they'll catch fire. I learned that the hard way… What else does your blood tell you? Because this world is constantly at war, even now."

He lifted a shoulder. "It simply tells me to be ready to battle. That fire and war are here." He was a dragon. He would survive. The strong always did. "Where is your sister?" he asked instead of commenting.

Prima shook her head as the microwave made a dinging sound. She opened the door and pulled out the plate. "She is in another country hunting down a male. Sort of."

"Sort of?" He inhaled deeply as she slid the plate in front of him. The scents were…different. Some were pleasing, others new to him.

"Everyone thought I'd gone mad all those centuries ago but in reality I think Mira has. She is helping a male and other shifters with…something."

"Mad?" He'd gone to sleep before the twins had so he wasn't sure what she referenced.

She started finger-combing her mess of tangled hair. "It was nothing. I was simply tired of the world—tired of the pettiness of humans."

He grunted and picked up what was definitely a cooked bird wing of some sort. He popped the whole thing in his mouth and found the bones crunchy. Whatever it was seasoned with was delicious.

"In public don't eat the bones," Prima said absently as she pulled out her small rectangle again. She frowned as she looked at it.

"Why not?"

"Humans will think it's strange. They just eat the meat."

He shrugged and ate another one. Humans had weaker teeth and digestive systems. He was a warrior. Crunching bones satisfied him on a deep level. "What is that thing?"

"It's called a smartphone. Or just a phone. We send messages to others with it."

"Messages?"

"Yes. Across the globe in seconds."

"That is impressive."

"It is. And it is how they will locate your friends. Tell me more about why you want to find Brennus, Cynbel and Cale."

"I fought with them over the centuries. They are ancients and awake." He wanted to search out familiar fighters, to prepare for what was to come. "Oh, I must find Arthur as well." He had forgotten about that male, and his blood told him the ancient was definitely awake.

Prima paused at the mention of the ancient Celtic dragon. "I always wondered what it would be like to fuck him."

"Arthur?"

"Yes."

Reaper shook his head. Arthur and Prima would likely tear each other apart.

"You trust them?" Prima continued.

"I know them." That was different than trust though. He wasn't sure he trusted anyone. Not truly. The twins and a handful of others being an exception. Mainly because there wasn't a malicious or calculating bone in Prima's or Mira's bodies. They were the best kind of dragons, far more in touch with their animal side than human. But Brennus, Cynbel, Cale and Arthur? If he had to pick who he trusted of those four, Arthur would win. The male wasn't calculating either.

"Hmm." Her rectangle—smartphone—dinged again. She looked at it, frowned again.

"Is everything okay?"

"I don't know. It's Mira. She doesn't like that all these ancients are waking up, or what you told me about fire and war."

"You told her?"

"Of course."

He should not be surprised. "Even if she doesn't like it, there's nothing to do but embrace it. Nothing is written in stone, regardless. Besides, we are dragons."

And only the strong—the dragons—would survive. He did not have much hope for the humans, however.

CHAPTER FOUR

Greer knocked on the already open door to her Alpha's office. Conall was leaning against the front of his desk, arms crossed over his chest as he talked to his mate about something pack related.

They both smiled when they saw her. "Shut the door behind you," Rhea said.

"What's up, guys?" She'd been summoned here, which was very rare. They weren't huge on formality in their clan except on certain occasions that called for it. And the summons she'd received had definitely been official.

"What do you think of this new ancient?" Conall asked, getting right to the point.

It had been almost two days since she'd had to see Reaper—yep, she'd been avoiding him. A weird little tingle went down her spine at the mention of the newcomer, but she ignored it. "He's obnoxious."

Rhea laughed lightly. "I swear, he seems just like Mira and Prima."

Conall nodded once. "I agree. And I have found some of the dragons he is looking for, in New Orleans."

Good. Then he could leave and she could be done with him. And all those strange sensations that flared to life when he was around could disappear with him. She was a healer, calm by nature, but around him her insides were a riotous storm, wild and out of control.

"Good," she said simply. She wasn't sure why she was here at all.

The Alpha couple exchanged a look before turning back at her. "We need to ask something of you," Rhea said.

"Okay."

"Prima will be going with him to New Orleans, but we would like you to go as well," she continued.

"Why?"

"Simply put, I trust you," Conall said. "Something about his awakening bothers me and I don't know what it is." He cleared his throat once, looking slightly uncomfortable. "There's more to the reason I'm asking you to go. You're a calming influence on others. Always have been. And the way he looks at you... I would bet my life that male won't hurt you. And I want to know if he is up to something. I've been hearing from other Alphas across the globe that more ancients are awakening and I don't know if this is a good or bad thing. If it's a sign of something more to come. If it is, I need to know. We all do."

Sighing, she moved to one of the cushy chairs near his desk and sank down into it. "I have heard from other healers the same thing, that the older dragons are awakening, all within the last month." She wasn't sure if it meant anything at all or if it was just the nature of these things.

"Will you go?" Conall asked.

"Do I have a choice?"

"Yes."

"Damn it," she muttered, half-smiling. "I could've been annoyed if you'd told me I didn't have a choice."

"So this means you'll go?"

"Of course. Clan comes first." Always. Her people mattered to her.

"As I said, Prima will be going as well, and while I love my aunt—and I trust her to an extent—she is still a wild card. But she'll keep you protected."

"I'm over fifteen hundred years old and I'm a healer." Sometimes Greer felt members of her clan forgot that she was highly capable. She might be peaceful by nature, but she could take care of herself.

He nodded once. "I know. But you are one of my own and we all care about you. I'm allowed to worry."

Greer simply nodded, smiling at her kind Alpha. His heart was so big, all he wanted to do was take care of his people. She felt the protective waves roll off him all the time and today was no different. She took a moment to gather her thoughts as she circled back to something he'd said before. "When you said the way Reaper looks at me…" She didn't finish because she wasn't sure she wanted to know exactly what he meant. Okay, she did, but felt strange asking Conall to clarify. Especially since she was certain she knew what he meant. Maybe her haughty dragon half simply wanted it spelled out.

"That dragon wants to bang your brains out," Rhea said before Conall could answer, laughter in her voice.

"He's been in Hibernation a long time and you are the *only* thing he wants. He would cut off his own arm before seeing harm come to you. He might be obnoxious, but he's an honorable dragon according to Prima."

Conall shot his mate a sideways glance. "Multiple females from the clan have offered him sex and he's turned every one of them down."

Greer straightened slightly. The past two days she'd stayed close to home and had made it a point to ignore all gossip so this was definitely news to her. And it annoyed her that some of her clanmates had gone to him for sex. Even though she shouldn't care at all. He meant nothing to her.

Instead of touching on *that* subject, Greer shook their words off. "When do we leave?"

"Tonight."

* * *

"Thank you for driving me to the airport," Greer said to Arya. She could have easily flown, but she didn't feel like carrying her bags in dragon form.

"No problem. I like testing my driving skills. I believe I am getting better." As if to reiterate, she floored it, making the SUV jerk forward.

Greer snorted softly. Prima and Reaper had gone to the airport slightly ahead of her since she'd ended up getting a call from one of her clanmates.

"We'll miss you when you're gone."

"Thank you," she said softly.

"Don't sound so surprised. You are very loved here."

"I know that." And she did. "I'm just surprised that *you* are going to miss me."

Arya grinned as they pulled into the parking lot of the private airport where the clan's jet was waiting. "My son told me you're being sent to keep an eye on the male, but keep an eye on Prima too. She's not always levelheaded."

Greer resisted the urge to laugh aloud. The fact that Arya was saying that felt oh so ironic. "I will." After giving hugs she grabbed her bags and headed to the jet—Arya's tires squealing in her wake as she tore out of the lot.

The pilot was waiting at the bottom of the stairs and immediately grabbed her bags even though she didn't need any help. But she'd learned long ago that some of her clanmates were simply wired to help so she let him take her bags.

When she stepped into the plush interior of the plane, her breath froze for a moment. Reaper sat in one of the leather seats, his long legs stretched out in front of him and…

"You cut your hair," she blurted, then inwardly chastised herself for stating the obvious.

He ran a hand over the now buzz-cut dark hair, standing as she entered the plane. Prima was in the back stretched out, her eyes closed as she slept.

"I will grow it out if you prefer," he said in that deep rumble she felt all the way to her core.

"I don't care what you do with your hair one way or another." Which was a big fat lie because now that he'd cut most of his hair off, it showed off those insane cheekbones even more. And she had the ridiculous urge to run her fingertips over his head to see how soft his hair was. Then she wanted to run her fingers over his cheeks, down to his soft-looking lips... *Nope.*

Turning away from him, she sat in one of the seats closest to the front. To her surprise, Reaper got up and sat right across from her, looking good enough to eat. Someone had given him clothes that fit properly and he wore a fitted long-sleeved T-shirt, cargo pants and boots.

"I'm sorry for what I said about humans when we first met," he said even as the pilot's voice came across the intercom and started going over the takeoff instructions. Not that it really mattered. If anything happened, they could just jump out and shift to their dragon forms. Reaper didn't seem at all concerned about flying in a plane for the first time so she guessed Prima must have given him the rundown on it earlier.

"Have you changed your mind about humans, then?" Somehow she didn't believe that.

"No. I am still better—or stronger—than them. But I *am* sorry I offended you. It was not my intention."

She wasn't sure how to respond to that. He was being honest at least. So she tried for civility. "What do you think of this new world? It's a lot to wake up to, I'm sure."

He shrugged. "Prima has been showing me some of your technology. It is interesting enough but more or less humans still seem the same. The world seems the same. Wars waged and lost. People live and die. Humans keep the weakest, greediest in power. It is very much the same as before. I had thought they might learn from their mistakes."

Okay, then. She pulled her earbuds out of her purse but she didn't put them in just yet because it really would have been too rude. But she wasn't sure how to talk to him. When he didn't say anything more, just stared at her, she felt her cheeks heat up. "What?"

"You are the most beautiful female I have ever seen." He seemed surprised by his admission as he shifted uncomfortably in his seat.

Oh… "Ah, thank you."

"I didn't mean to make you feel uncomfortable. I'm… Not used to…" He cleared his throat, stopping.

She should let it go, she really, really should. But… "Not used to what?"

"You are not the type of female I am usually attracted to," he blurted. "I have always preferred warriors, but I find myself drawn to you."

She blinked at his words and then felt a lot less rude as she plugged her earbuds in. "Okay then, I'm done with this conversation." She thought she heard Prima snicker from the back of the plane but couldn't be sure.

Closing her eyes, she tried to tune him out and listen to her audiobook. It was going to be a long plane ride.

* * *

"This is you." Prima held out her phone as she popped a grape in her mouth.

The airplane was stocked full of food and drinks and quite comfortable—though Reaper would have preferred to fly the entire way in dragon form to this place called New Orleans. Humans had come far in their progress. On some things at least. "Why are you showing me an image of a crying bear?"

"It is a panda. And that's you. A sad panda. I've never seen someone strike out so badly."

He didn't know what a strike was, but he could guess. "It was not that bad." No, it had been worse. He had basically insulted Greer again when that was the last thing he'd wanted to do. He wanted to compliment her, to court her, to somehow put into words what her scent was doing to him. Instead he spoke like a fool around her.

"It was pathetic. You have no game."

He frowned. "What is game?"

"I'm honestly not sure. Not completely anyway. Some of the younger clanmates talk about it. But it means that you are not good with getting women to have sex with you."

He growled low in his throat. For some reason he did not want just sex from Greer. Though he wasn't sure *what* he wanted. Not for her to hate him, that was certain.

He should keep his mouth shut. He was good at killing things, at waging war. But speaking to the sweet healer with the copper-colored hair and most perfect ass in the world was another matter entirely.

And now he had other things to consider—like what would happen to Greer and her clan if the world did succumb to war and fire.

CHAPTER FIVE

G reer smiled as they descended the stairs onto the tarmac of the private airport. Justus was waiting for them as Conall had said he would be. She simply adored the older vampire and hoped he'd finally convinced Cynara to settle down with him. Because she adored Cynara too, and whenever she was around the vampire-demon hybrid she sensed that the female desperately wanted to mate with Justus. If only Cynara would let the male in.

"Greer!" Justus quickly closed the distance between them as she reached the bottom of the stairs. He pulled her into a tight hug that she returned.

Lean and muscular with skin just a bit paler than typical, he stood tall and strong and it was easy to imagine him as the Roman Empire general he'd once been.

She was vaguely aware of Reaper growling not so subtly at the top of the stairs but she ignored him.

"It is so good to see you. Where's Cynara?"

He let out a growl of his own as he stepped back. "Not something I want to talk about right now."

Uh oh. "Fair enough. I hope I get to see her while I'm in town though."

"Even if she is angry at me, I know she would love to see you."

"Good. Justus," she said, stepping back as the other two joined them on the tarmac, "you know Prima, but this is Reaper. He is an ancient as well, and newly awoken. Reaper, Justus leads his own coven. He served as a general in the Imperial Roman Army before being turned." In a situation like this it was standard to introduce people by who they were and where they came from. It gave other supernaturals a way to gauge what level of formality to use. Though she wasn't sure that Reaper would even know what the Roman Army was, he could still understand that Justus had been a general.

Justus nodded respectfully and held out a hand to both of them. Then he surprised her by speaking directly to Reaper. "I read about you in some ancient texts. I read of how you destroyed an army of Akkadian demons. Very impressive." There was complete sincerity and respect in his words.

Reaper straightened and nodded back politely. "Thank you. We will speak of battles fought later. Conall says that you know where Cynbel of Patmos is?"

"Well, I did have a bead on him, but he's not easy to pin down. My...friend owns a new bar not far from here and she's heard that he might be stopping by tonight. The female he has an on-again, off-again thing with is there."

"Is this Cynara's new bar?" Greer had heard through the supernatural grapevine that Cynara and Bo, her brother, had expanded and bought another bar in New Orleans. Cynara had once told Greer that real estate and bars were how they made their money.

"It is."

"Then we go there," Reaper said. He turned to Greer. "What is on-again, off-again?"

It surprised her that he'd asked her and not Prima. For some reason she liked it. "Ah, it means they sleep together occasionally."

He frowned. "Sleep?"

"They fuck occasionally," Prima said.

Reaper nodded once, then swiveled to look at Greer again. He opened that perfect mouth of his as if he wanted to say something to her, but then turned away. "How far is this place?"

"Ten minutes, give or take," Justus said.

"We can fly there, then."

"Ah…" Justus looked around cautiously. "There are enough cameras here that it might just be easier to drive. I've got an SUV ready to go."

"I call shotgun," Prima said, grinning at both Reaper and Greer.

"I have learned about some human weapons but I do not understand why you need a shotgun."

Greer laughed lightly, despite her intention to keep her distance from Reaper. "It's a silly expression one of our younger clanmates must have taught her. It means that she will be sitting in the front seat with Justus."

"The statement makes no sense," he said as they started following Justus to a waiting vehicle.

"I agree. There are many odd colloquialisms you'll hear. It's best not to take everything literally. If you have questions about things, you can ask me." She shouldn't have made the offer, but she couldn't help it. Even if he was kind of obnoxious, he was an ancient and he'd just woken up in an entirely new world. Greer normally would have been the first to offer to help someone adjust and she was ashamed she hadn't so far. She blamed it on her weird reaction to him.

"Thank you," he said as they slid into the back seat. Even with how spacious the vehicle was, it felt cramped considering how close they were next to each other. She hadn't prepared for it and felt off-kilter as she strapped in. His masculine scent reminded her of a place she sometimes escaped to deep in the mountains—clean and fresh. Right now it was going straight to her head and making her want to lean closer and inhale deeply.

"Have you been here before?" he asked her as Prima and Justus started talking in the front.

"New Orleans? Yes. My clan is allied with a wolf pack not far from here, so I've been in this city for various events and just to see friends. Our Alpha female is actually from the wolf pack. And our clan owns a couple homes in New Orleans. Can I ask you something?"

He watched her closely, only slightly unnerving her. "You may ask anything."

"You said that you didn't have a clan. Or...you weren't looking for them?" The concept was foreign to her. Even if dragons weren't like wolves, it was so hard to imagine waking up and not wanting to find her family.

"I've been a warrior for as long as I can remember. I found clan politics tiresome—my clan specifically. They could be petty. So I'm certain I do have relatives out in the world. I just don't care to find them."

"Oh." Well, maybe she wouldn't ask him about Ian, then. Not until she'd talked to Ian anyway. And she'd been texting with Fiona—Ian's mate—to let her know she was going to be in town. But she hadn't mentioned Reaper and his dragon's coloring. It was so similar to Ian's that they had to be related somehow.

"Have clan politics changed in the recent centuries?"

"Some have, I'm sure. My clan has always been progressive. And now many clans, packs and covens are allies. For many years dragons kept their existence secret, even to other shifters. Which Prima might have already told you?"

He nodded, truly listening even if there was a raw sexual hunger in his gaze.

It was unnerving to be on the end of that kind of attention. She was her clan's healer; people came to her when they needed something. And yes, she felt loved and respected, but the way he watched her was different than any other person she'd ever experienced. He wanted her for her. "With so many supernaturals interacting and allied, it gives me hope for a better future for us. I…I can't imagine we stay hidden to humans forever. Technology prevents it. So it's good that most of us are, if not allied, at least connected."

He nodded once, his expression thoughtful. "Supernaturals are already strong. If we're united, we'll be an unconquerable force."

She started to respond, then Justus spoke from the front, asking Reaper something. Sitting back, she let the others talk as she tried not to stare at Reaper's profile, a nearly impossible task with the male sitting barely a foot from her.

She just had to get through this trip. Then she'd be able to get some distance from him. At least that was what she tried to tell herself.

* * *

"This place is interesting." Reaper glanced around the three-level building Justus had told him was a combination bar and club. Neither of those words made sense for this establishment. It was loud, crowded and there were too many smells.

Greer made a sort of humming sound as she scanned the floor where people were gyrating against each other. There were also pillars raised up high where women and men danced, sometimes solo, others with a partner. It appeared as if they were simulating sex.

Arousal pounded through his blood, directed at the female beside him.

"We should probably split up if we want to find your friend," Greer said softly, but he heard her over the din of voices and music.

He wasn't sure what this music was called but it was enjoyable. That was one thing he could concede—humans by far made much better music than any supernatural he had ever known. And in the couple days he had been awake he had gotten quite an education on how much music was out there now and the different ways to listen to it. Prima had given him a crash course on everything she deemed interesting or important. The topics were many.

He didn't like the idea of being separated from Greer, especially after she had thawed toward him a bit during the ride over here, but since he didn't want to risk insulting her again, he simply nodded at the others. "If you see him, let me know. If he doesn't know you, I don't know that he will speak to you." He had tried to retrieve Cynbel's phone number but Prima's clan had been unable to find it. They'd simply found out that he was in New Orleans and had a picture of him.

After agreeing, they all dispersed, with Greer heading straight for the dance floor. He watched the soft sway of her ass as she moved among people wearing little scraps of clothing. Though she was fully clothed in formfitting pants and a long-sleeved sweater, she was by far the greatest prize in here. The female glowed with energy and vitality and didn't need to walk around practically naked for that to be clear. Though he would not mind if she did.

Looking away from her, because otherwise he would stare at her all night, he started in the opposite direction of Prima. Justus was currently talking to a purple-haired female and seemed occupied. That must be Cynara, the female who Greer had asked the former general about earlier. So maybe Justus would not be as big of a help tonight as he'd hoped.

As he made his way through a cluster of tables, he ignored some of the welcoming smiles from males and females. And in one instance, he flashed his teeth at a female who sidled up next to him and wouldn't take the hint when he said, "No, thank you." Unfortunately that seemed to turn her on, if the scent that filled the air was any indication.

He turned away, sliding in between two tables and making a quick exit of the area. Even as he moved, he was constantly aware of where Greer was, while scanning for the familiar face of Cynbel. There were many individuals here tonight of every supernatural race. Or damn close to it if the scents were anything to go by.

According to Justus, New Orleans was more or less neutral territory, though the last couple years, one Alpha had started carving out this area as his own. It was not completely recognized as the male's own yet, but Justus was convinced that soon enough that would happen.

So as it was, Reaper did not have to announce his presence to anyone while here. And this establishment was thankfully supernatural only, so he did not have to hide what he was. That thought alone rankled him.

He shouldn't have to hide what he was. Ever. He was an apex predator and the strongest warrior of his day.

As he reached a set of stairs, he quickly jogged up them, surprised when a male at the top simply lifted a rope for him to pass. He had thought he would have to seek permission but it seemed as if he was allowed into this area. There was much to learn about this new world.

Upstairs was more of the same. More tables, more people dancing, many mixed scents, but he should have a dragon's eye view from up here. So he went to the railing and scanned the dance floor below.

What he saw had fire surging through him, wild and hot and stripping away any sense of civility. Greer was on top of one of the pillars, dancing, her hips swaying with the steady beat of music. She'd taken her long hair down and it flowed around her in soft waves that appeared multicolored under the strobing lights.

Every part of him tightened in anticipation as he watched her. Staring at her like this felt somehow forbidden because she was completely oblivious to his gaze.

He'd thought he only was attracted to warrior females, but as he stared at this strong, kind healer who had stolen his breath time and again, he realized he had been a fool. She was the only one he wanted.

It was clear she was scanning the floor just as he was, using the platform for better viewing, but as if she sensed him watching her, her gaze flicked in his direction.

For a moment she froze, her eyes flickering so that her dragon peered back at him. Then she surprised him as she continued dancing, keeping her gaze pinned to his, her movements sensual and all for him.

Maybe the last part wasn't true, but he could pretend that it was, and it made his mouth go dry.

Right now he imagined what she would look like taking her clothes off to the sound of music, stripping off one piece after the other until she was naked in front of him. Then he would kneel in front of her and taste what was between her legs.

He groaned aloud, the sound muted by the music thumping in time with the pulse between his thighs, but he swore she could hear him if the way she shuddered was any indication. No, he was not alone in this attraction. Even if she was frustrated by him, she still found him appealing.

A surge of arousal raced through him. So maybe his "game" wasn't as bad as he had assumed. Though nothing about what he felt for Greer was a game.

"Got him." Prima's voice nearby snapped him out of his trance.

He forced his gaze away from Greer and realized Prima was right next to him. She should not have been able to approach him without his knowledge, but he'd been too preoccupied by the female he wanted more than his next breath. "Where?"

"He just ducked out one of the back exits. Looked a whole lot like your guy and he didn't like me approaching him."

"Let's go." When he looked back at Greer, she had already jumped down from the platform and was making her way in the direction Prima pointed. Reaper hurried after her. Less than a minute later they were in a back alley.

"I smell him," Reaper said. Once a shifter had a scent, it was for life. Some people could suppress theirs or even hide it temporarily, but not always. And not forever.

"Does anyone else think it's weird that he's running from you?" Greer asked as they hurried down the cobbled alleyway. It spilled out onto a street teeming with people. Lots of humans but many, many supernaturals. The area was filled with similar-looking bars, all stacked next to each other, crammed in as close as possible. And the scents were almost overwhelming—food, humans, supernaturals, perfumes, alcohol, sex, unwashed bodies...all mingled together.

He found the presence of so many supernaturals interesting. Many vampires, shifters, and other beings were just going about their business, mostly talking, and many intoxicated humans stumbled from establishment to establishment.

"I am not sure why he would flee from me." He looked at Prima. "Did you ever have an issue with him?"

"Not that I recall. But it has been thousands upon thousands of years. Perhaps so?" But she shook her head even as she spoke. "I cannot imagine what though. I usually killed all my enemies. Makes things much easier."

Greer made an exasperated sound as she followed after them. He did not like the fact that she was coming
with them.

If Cynbel was fleeing from Reaper or Prima for
some reason and decided to attack, he didn't like the
thought of Greer being anywhere near that violence.
Healers were sacred and off-limits but he still worried
that Cynbel would not respect that law. One thing
Reaper knew, however: he would kill anything or anyone that posed a threat to her.

"I wish we could just fly after him," he muttered.

"There is no reason we can't," Prima said. "Come
on." Then she took off, racing down the sidewalk at a
fast clip, Reaper and Greer hurrying after her. Even in
human form, they were all fast. Humans for the most
part dodged out of the way and only the supernaturals
managed to move without getting jostled. He noticed
that Greer apologized, but he did not bother.

Minutes later they reached a three-story brick building that was falling down, and there were no inhabit-
ants inside from what he could scent.

"What is this place?"

"I have no idea," Prima said. "But it's high enough
and I don't scent anyone inside. We should be able to
shift and camouflage ourselves and track Cynbel easier
from the sky."

Good point.

Soon enough they were on the roof of the building
and it was in just as bad shape as the exterior. Many soft

spots where something had clearly done damage. Water perhaps. But from here he could see for miles and miles in each direction. The night was hazy, with the moon and stars covered by clouds. It would be good for hunting down his former comrade.

He wanted to know why the male had run. Had Cynbel seen him and fled? No. It made no sense. They had fought together. Maybe he had simply left, not having seen Reaper at all.

"You will not come with us," he said to Greer.

She blinked. "Excuse me?"

"Prima and I will hunt him down. We will find you afterward. You will not help with hunting him down." He did not want her anywhere near the other male. Not if there was a possibility of danger.

Prima looked between the two of them, and her expression told him that he had just said something wrong but he couldn't imagine what.

"You are a healer," he said to Greer, which should explain everything. She had no business coming with them. No, she should be somewhere safe, protected.

Greer's jaw simply clenched and she turned away from the two of them, stalking back toward the door.

"Soon you and I are going to talk about what a dumbass you are." Shaking her head, Prima started stripping off her clothes.

"I did nothing wrong." Still, Reaper had the insane urge to call after Greer, to apologize for something. Though he wasn't certain what. How could she think he wanted her to come with them? He would not be able to focus if she was in danger. He would barely be able to think straight.

Even now, his dragon snarled at the mere thought of something happening to her. If it were to happen in reality? There was no telling what his beast would be capable of.

CHAPTER SIX

Greer half-smiled as she reached the exit door of the dilapidated building because she scented Justus. There was a big sign outside saying the place would soon be undergoing construction. Given how close it was to the edge of the Quarter, she imagined it would fetch quite a lot in rent if this turned into a residential building. Not that any of that mattered to her—she was just trying to keep her mind off Reaper and the rude way he'd dismissed her. As if she was nothing.

"You guys ran out of there so fast," Justus said as he pushed off the outside of the building, clearly waiting for her.

"You didn't have to come."

He lifted a shoulder. "I'm always looking for a fight or adventure."

She lifted an eyebrow and fell in step with him as they moved toward the nearby sidewalk. "*You* are always looking for a fight?"

He rolled his shoulders once. "Not always. Just lately."

"Give her time," Greer said, knowing exactly what his problem was. "Supernaturals are all complex creatures. She's no different. But I have faith that she will make the right choice." Greer hoped anyway.

"I've given her everything I can possibly think of. I've offered to leave my coven, but she thinks that's ridiculous. I don't understand why she thinks there is such a divide between us. Even her brothers approve of me now, an impossible feat."

"All her brothers?" Cynara had four.

"Yep. We battled after Christmas and they know how much I care for her. I've shown them I'm physically capable of defending her if necessary and I'm willing to give her the world."

Greer kept her mouth shut because she didn't think he was looking for an answer, and while it might not be clear to *him*, it was clear that Cynara didn't think she was good enough for the older vampire. She was a half-demon, and while it shouldn't matter, some supernaturals had issues with half-demons. Things like that went deep into your psyche, all the way back to childhood, and could be hard to shake. Especially for supernaturals who were very long-lived. "How long are you in New Orleans?"

"As long as it takes to convince Cynara to mate with me."

"Why don't the two of you join me back at our place tonight? I haven't even dropped my bags off yet and I could use some company." She was used to being surrounded by her clanmates. After being dismissed so abruptly by Reaper, she could admit she felt stung, hurt. And she didn't want to think about him anymore.

"We can stop by the bar and grab her. She's supervising tonight but she has plenty of capable people she can leave in charge. And she was disappointed when you guys ran out of there so I know she will love to spend time with you."

"Perfect. I know Nyx is in town as well," Greer added. "She texted me earlier in the week. Could we ask her and Bo as well?" Since Bo was Cynara's brother, Greer already knew the answer but asked anyway.

"Of course."

She'd seen a lot of the supernaturals who lived in New Orleans and Biloxi over Christmas, but she still loved spending time with them. In the last couple years her circle of friends had grown and she adored all of them. Right now she didn't want to be alone with her thoughts at the big mansion in the Garden District that her clan had procured.

After Reaper had refused to let her go with them—as if she was an incapable dragonling— she'd fought her own embarrassment. Because she'd definitely been dancing for him back at the club, and she wasn't sure what had come over her. But she'd wanted him to like what he saw.

Clearly he had, if the way he'd been watching her was any indication. And clearly he didn't see her as an equal. If he had, she would be in the skies right now with him and Prima searching for his friend. But she wasn't an ancient so apparently that made her less. For some reason that hurt a lot more than she could have imagined.

She had no time for a rude male. Even one as sexy as Reaper.

* * *

Reaper glanced at Prima as they stepped into the three-story house in a place Prima had told him was called the Garden District. Homes seemed to be stacked close to each other here but the exterior of this home was lush with trees and other foliage. Her clan either owned this house or was renting it. He'd heard laughter and voices from the street thanks to his supernatural hearing, but now that he was inside it sounded like a full-blown party. He hadn't realized anyone else would be here other than Greer.

Was she entertaining males?

His dragon snarled, his claws releasing so swiftly that Prima's eyes widened. After losing Cynbel's scent, he was even more anxious to get back to her, and now she had other males here? His dragon was close to breaking his threadbare leash.

"This is what a party sounds like, not a battle. Control yourself." She stared at him as if he had lost his mind.

Rolling his shoulders, he forced his claws to recede as they followed the sound of the laughter.

In a spacious kitchen there were a dozen supernatural beings of various species, if their scents were any indication. Vampires, hybrids, and some scents he could not decipher at all.

Greer was speaking to a brown-skinned male with electric blue hair and laughing at something he said.

His dragon eyed the unknown male, annoyed at the sight of her giving her smiles to someone else. Not that she'd actually bestowed any smiles on him, but a dragon could dream.

She flicked a quick look at him and Prima and just as quickly she looked away, but not before he saw something he couldn't quite define in her gaze.

He needed to speak to her in private. Now. Prima had explained to him that he might have been too brusque with her and he needed to remedy that. The only females he had experience with were other warriors and...he was used to giving orders and not being questioned. Perhaps he needed to rethink some things. Okay, there was no perhaps. He did.

As he approached Greer and the unknown male, a petite female with long, dark hair—who was half fae for certain—wrapped her arms around the male next to Greer, and that strange sensation surging through Reaper stilled. The male was taken and not a threat for Greer's attentions.

"May I speak to you in private?" he asked her, ignoring the others completely.

Little lines formed in between her eyebrows as she turned to him. But she nodded, giving him her back.

He couldn't help it—his gaze trailed over that beautiful ass as she headed for a door that led outside to a colorful patio and quite a large backyard, given what he'd seen of the city so far. The yard was completely walled in and truly private from its neighbors, no doubt the reason they were staying here in the first place. Shifters liked their privacy.

When she turned to face him, those green eyes sparked with fire and heat—and he had a feeling he was only getting a small picture of the passion she had inside her. "Yes?"

"I am sorry if I offended you earlier." Apologizing felt strange but he would do anything for her. "Prima pointed out to me that my words were likely misconstrued. I didn't want you coming with us because you are a healer. You are special and to be taken care of. I thought that was clear, but obviously by your anger at me, I was not clear."

To his surprise, her arms dropped, the tenseness in her shoulders loosening. "You didn't tell me to stay put because you thought I was incapable?"

"No. I simply wanted you to stay safe. I thought healers were supposed to be protected, completely revered. Has that changed in this time period?" he asked, even though he knew the answer already. But he wanted to make obvious the truth of his words and actions.

"No, that hasn't changed." Her cheeks flushed slightly. "I'm sorry I got angry. It felt as if you were dismissing me because I'm not an ancient. I jumped to conclusions."

He let out a short laugh with no amusement. "It would be impossible to dismiss someone as incredible as you." Her cheeks flushed even brighter, something he found he liked very much. She was so different from any female he had ever been attracted to—and everything about her eclipsed all past memories. It was as if no one existed for him except Greer. "Why does this statement surprise you?"

Her cheeks remained pink even as she cleared her throat. "I guess I'm just not sure what to say."

"I liked it when you danced," he said bluntly. Now that he had her off-balance, he wanted to make it clear that he was very much attracted to her. Something she must already know, but he felt as if he had better standing to speak boldly to her now. Now that he wasn't making a complete ass of himself.

"Thank you," she whispered, seeming nervous.

Of him? "Were you dancing for me in that club?" His heart rate kicked up as he watched her, waiting for a response. The memory of her dancing was forever seared into his brain.

She made a sort of strangled sound and shook her head. He noticed that she didn't answer aloud, however, and understood why immediately. He would scent her lie if she did.

"You are lying," he murmured, taking another step closer to her, crowding her.

"You think highly of yourself." Her words were raspy and uneven.

"Maybe I do. But I still know that you are lying. Why do you deny the attraction between us?"

She sighed, and pressed a gentle hand to his chest. That simple touch sent pleasure surging out to all his nerve endings. He wanted to lean into her, to feel her entire body pressed up against his. Not just her hand.

"Look, I *am* attracted to you, and it's messed with my head and perhaps my reactions to you as well." It seemed to take a lot for her to admit this. "But you have just woken from a long Hibernation. I was the first female you saw, so it's natural that you would be attracted to me—"

"I'm not attracted to you because you're the first female I saw. I have had many females in the past." None compared to her though. No one could.

Her eyes narrowed slightly.

"Not many, just some," he rushed out. He certainly did not wish to hear of her sexual past. "My awakening has nothing to do with my desire for you. I want you because you are you."

"Even though I'm a healer?" she asked, her words sharp.

"I apologize for what I said before. I seem to blurt out whatever is in my head around you. It is disconcerting. I want you because you are Greer."

"You barely know me."

"I know enough. And I want to know more. Everything." He wanted to learn everything about her, what she liked and disliked, what turned her on.

"We need to stop this discussion right now," she said quickly.

"Why? I like the color of your cheeks right now." He wondered how flushed she would become if he tasted between her legs, and just barely resisted asking her if she would like him to pleasure her. He wondered a lot of things. Like what color her nipples would be.

He should be focused on finding Cynbel and locating the other ancients he needed to speak to, but instead he simply wondered what Greer would sound like as he thrust inside her. What she would feel like. How loud she would be as she came.

"Look, even if we're attracted to each other, it doesn't matter."

"Why not?"

"You said yourself I'm not the type of female you are used to."

"Well I am a fool. You are the perfect female."

She seemed to struggle to find words for a long moment, then she took a small step back. "We are far too different. I heal people, and you..."

"I what? I kill?" It was true enough. He didn't randomly kill; he was not a psychopath. But his life involved killing. It was the way it was.

Before she could respond, the door flew open and the purple-haired hybrid—Cynara—stuck her head out, smiling widely at the two of them. She had imbibed much alcohol, he thought. Or enough that she felt the effects of it, he was certain. "I think we're going to play strip poker. You guys in?"

Greer made another strangled sound as she looked at Reaper with far too many emotions, then back at the female. "Ah...I don't know."

"What is this strip poker?" He had so many questions about this time period. So much of the language was inane.

"It's a game you play with cards. You get naked when you lose different hands."

He looked back at Greer. He didn't like the thought of her naked in front of anyone else, which was ridiculous. They were shifters after all. But he did not care for the thought. Still, he would like to show off for her so he reached for the hem of his shirt and started to pull it off. "How does this work? Surely we don't lose our actual hands?"

Greer made a sort of squeaking sound and grasped his wrists, stilling him. He savored the feel of her gentle touch on him, wishing she would keep holding him. So he remained still, not pulling away. "No. You don't get naked to play. Poker is a card game and hands refer to different rounds you play with the cards. Strip poker is a made-up thing that's all very silly and childish," she said, shooting Cynara a sharp look.

"Justus thinks it's beneath him as well but *I* will be playing." There was more than a spark of challenge in Cynara's words, and Reaper was certain they were meant for the vampire in the kitchen.

"With your brother here?"

"Eww, gross. No way. Bo and Nyx are about to leave soon. They need to get back to my sweet niece."

He sensed a bit of disappointment rolling off Greer and realized she must really like the other couple. "I will play if Greer plays," he said.

Greer glanced at him, surprise etched into her fine features. "Okay, I'll play." Her luscious lips curved up ever so slightly. "Even though I think the concept of this is beyond ridiculous for supernaturals our age."

"Age doesn't matter. Fun is fun." Cynara winked before she ducked back inside.

CHAPTER SEVEN

"You are cheating." Cynara narrowed her gaze at Justus, who was sitting across the table from Greer and Cynara—wearing only boxers.

For some reason the boxers surprised Greer. Not that she had ever thought of Justus in any sort of stages of undress but she'd kind of assumed he would be a commando type of guy. Instead he wore boxers with little fangs and hearts on them. A gift from Cynara if she had to guess.

"How am I cheating? I'm almost completely naked. I'm losing." He lifted a challenging eyebrow, staring right back at Cynara.

"I don't care. You are cheating."

Greer stifled a laugh as she met the gaze of Reaper, who was also sitting across the huge oak table in the dining room. She had a feeling that both Reaper and Justus were cheating but for different reasons.

Because the two males were the only ones who were pretty much naked by this point. She was certain that Reaper was losing intentionally so he could get naked—to take off his clothes slowly, methodically, as he tried to turn her into a puddle of hormones. It was hard to concentrate while he just sat there all sexy and confident.

And she was also certain that Justus was losing intentionally so that Cynara wouldn't have to take off any of her own clothes. All other supernaturals had long since gone and just the four of them continued to play this absolutely silly game of strip poker. Greer had only lost her shoes so far.

Even if the game was ridiculous, she could admit that she was having a good time. Her clan came to her for advice, for therapy basically, and she was always happy to help out. But right now she liked just being Greer. Free to have fun and do what she wanted.

And after Reaper had admitted to her why he hadn't wanted her coming along for that flight earlier, it was impossible to be mad at him.

Prima strode into the room, a plate of food in her hands. She'd disappeared an hour ago but it seemed she was finally back. She picked up a chicken wing and popped the whole thing in her mouth. Then she shook her head. "This is a sad display."

"Oh, I don't know about that." Cynara's tone was light and teasing as she eyed Justus and Reaper—but mainly Justus. "There's nothing sad about these two guys."

"Eyes only on me." Justus's voice was a low growl, making everyone go still as he stared at Cynara, his eyes starting to glow amber.

Uh oh.

Clearing her throat, Greer dropped her cards onto the table. "I'm done for the night. Reaper, so are you."

He didn't argue, simply stood—still wearing boxer briefs, thank the stars—and followed after her.

Whatever was going on between Justus and Cynara was about to come to a head, and Greer didn't want to stick around for it. They were either going to kill each other or screw each other on the dining room table. She was betting on the latter. "You too, Prima!" she called out when the ancient female stood there watching the other two as if they were entertainment. No wonder Conall had wanted her here.

"Let's head to the third floor," Prima said, joining both her and Reaper on the stairs, grabbing two bottles of wine in her free hand on the way out. "There's a balcony in one of the rooms. We'll give them some privacy."

"Did you want to grab some clothes first?" Greer asked Reaper.

He simply grinned and shook his head.

Okay, then. They were just going to hang out and he was going to be mostly naked. *Awesome.*

On the balcony there was a rectangular mosaic table with four chairs already set up—as well as a tray of wineglasses. If she didn't know better, she'd say that Prima had set this up.

Greer had snagged a bedroom on the second floor when she'd arrived earlier and it seemed as if no one had taken the attached bedroom to this balcony. She was curious where Reaper and Prima would be sleeping but she definitely wasn't going to ask. The bags that she and Justus had left in the downstairs living room had been moved, so clearly someone—Prima, she was guessing, since Reaper hadn't been far from Greer all night—had put them up in bedrooms.

"Hey, I'll be back," Prima said as she sat the wine bottles and opener on the table. Then with no more explanation she simply disappeared with her plate of chicken wings.

Greer sat at one of the chairs, feeling inexplicably nervous around Reaper now that it was just the two of them—and he was half dressed. She wasn't a young dragon; she was over a thousand years old. But Reaper made her feel as if she was experiencing her first infatuation again.

Though it was far more than that because her dragon half was involved. That alone made her cautious being around him. Not that she really had a choice. She'd promised to keep an eye on him and Prima. "So what happened with the male you hunted down?" Obviously they hadn't found him. Or she assumed since he hadn't said anything.

"We lost his scent. But after a few hours of sleep I plan to go after him again."

"Why do you think he ran?"

"I do not know that he did. Prima and Mira had a long list of enemies—as did I—before their Hibernation. It is possible that Cynbel saw Prima and left. Or...I simply do not know."

"Why is it important for you to find him?" He'd been scarce on the details, at least with her. And she could admit she was curious to know more about him. If the information was important, she would tell her Alpha.

He paused for a moment, searching her face with those bright amber and green eyes she found intoxicating. She could easily lose herself under Reaper's watchful gaze. "He is someone from my past I wish to connect with."

Oh wow, that wasn't vague or anything. "Have you ever thought of settling down with a clan? Not your former one but…a different one. The world is different now for shifters. There aren't wars like there used to be. Well, there are human wars but things are different for our kind." And it would be helpful for him to have clanmates, friends. She was just asking to be polite—at least that was what she told herself. It wasn't as if she cared where he went after this.

Liar, liar, her dragon half sneered.

He made a sort of noncommittal sound as he reached for the bottle and opened it. "Would you like some?"

"Sure, thanks. So you're just going to ignore my question?"

He gave her one of those wicked grins as he poured. "I don't have an answer to that right now. I have not been awake long enough to have solid plans. But the offer from your house still stands."

"Offer?"

"To pleasure you with my tongue." He sat back, looking pleased with himself.

She nearly dropped the glass she'd just picked up. "Reaper!"

"I enjoy it when you say my name."

She set the glass down, feeling her cheeks warm up. "You can't say things like that."

"Why not? It is true."

"Because...you just can't." She cleared her throat, unnerved by the way he watched her. Like a hunter watching prey. "What are your plans for tomorrow?"

He paused, still watching her intently, but answered. "To look for Cynbel and the other ancients I would like to speak to."

"Do you want company?" Whatever he felt regarding her being a healer, she was still able to hold her own.

"I would. But at the first sign of danger, I will protect you at all costs."

Oh. *Oh, hell.* The way he made that promise was so incredibly hot. "I'm quite capable of taking care of myself."

He lifted a shoulder—his bare shoulder, drawing her gaze across his chest and down to those cut abs. Why the hell was he out here like this? To drive her crazy, for certain. "Regardless, it is what I will do."

She took a sip of her wine, finding herself flustered once again. How the heck did she respond to that? "I might head to bed." She needed distance from him, and the longer she stayed out here with him, the more likely she was to do something stupid.

"Would you like me to join you?"

She stared at him for a moment. "Ah...no." She was such a liar.

"If you change your mind, I chose the bedroom right next to yours." He spoke so calmly, though his eyes sparked with heat. "Come get me at any time."

"I'll keep that in mind." She held her wineglass as she stood, and almost snagged the whole bottle. She needed something to take the edge off tonight. And since she'd decided to retain *some* control, she wouldn't be taking off the edge with him. Unfortunately.

"Please do. I promise not to rest until you have found release multiple times."

She opened her mouth once but couldn't find any words. Nope, heat pooled low in her belly and she was so very tempted to take him up on the offer. Because she was almost positive he wouldn't be disappointing. Oh no, he had that confidence for a reason. But the possessive glint in his eyes told her that would be a mistake. He wasn't offering simple sex, he was offering *more*.

And the thought terrified her. Because dragons mated for life.

Making nonsensical sounds, she hurried from the balcony, desperate to escape from him as more heat surged through her. Her nipples were tight little beads against her bra as she imagined him going down on her, stroking her over and over until she came against his face. Oh, he must scent her need for him too, which was even more embarrassing. She couldn't even attempt to hide it now.

Why had he given her such a bold offer? He must have known she'd say no. Gah, he was determined to make her crazy. Now she was going to have to get herself off tonight.

Because she was turned on with no one to turn to. Well, that wasn't true. There was only one male she wanted, but he was the exact opposite of what she needed. And she wasn't going to cross that line.

Something told her that if she did, there would be no going back.

CHAPTER EIGHT

"What is the matter with you?" Cynara pushed up from her chair once she heard the others moving up the stairs and farther away from her and Justus.

"You shouldn't be looking at anyone else but me." There wasn't a hint of apology in his words for the way he'd just growled at her in front of everyone.

"I wasn't! And it wasn't like I was flirting with him. I just made a comment, complimenting both of you!"

"I only ever want your eyes on me." He rounded the table so fast she barely saw him move. Yep, Justus was a powerful vamp—and the sexy male was driving her crazy. Right now his normally brown eyes were flaring a wild amber.

"Where is this jealousy coming from?"

He stepped into her personal space and had to look down, given that she wasn't wearing heels and was half a foot shorter than him. "I think you know exactly where this is coming from." His words were a rough whisper. "You just keep pushing my buttons."

"What buttons are those?" She put her hands on her hips and knew her violet eyes were likely sparking right now too—for multiple reasons. Being this close to him when he was practically naked, wearing boxers she'd given him as a joke, had electricity humming through her body. She was also annoyed at him, but she was more turned on than anything. She was *always* turned on because of Justus, damn him.

"Strip poker? Really? You think I'm going to let other people see you naked?"

"It was just a game." She'd never seen him so angry before. She wasn't afraid he would hurt her. He would never, ever do that. Not physically anyway. And not intentionally. But this male held her heart in his hands, and for some reason he wouldn't leave New Orleans until she agreed to his ridiculous request to mate. He'd followed her here from Biloxi when he should be back in upstate New York dealing with his coven.

"I don't think it was." He leaned down a fraction until his nose was nearly touching hers, his scent making her dizzy. "I think you knew exactly what you were doing. And for the record, I *was* cheating—I lost because you're not taking off clothes in front of anyone but me." He was full-on growling now.

And she liked it. "When did you become so puritanical?"

"What the hell does that mean?"

"It means I know all about your exploits!" Damn it, she hadn't meant to say anything.

He frowned, moving back to give her a little space. But not much. "What are you talking about?"

"Nothing." Embarrassment rolled through her.

"Tell me."

"Or what?"

"Or nothing. Just tell me." He leaned against the table as he crossed his arms over his chest. Unlike shifters, he wasn't so massive, but lean and corded with muscle. She loved that look. Loved him. Not that she'd tell him the latter.

"It's nothing," she muttered, feeling stupid. He had the ability to make her feel stupid without trying. Worse, she knew he'd feel awful if she told him that. "Aurelia stopped by the club earlier, when you were out looking for Greer and the others."

"She did?" Confusion rolled off him.

"She said you've been away from the coven too long, that I'm keeping you away." Cynara couldn't stand Aurelia and the way the bloodborn vamp looked down on her.

"I've made a choice to stay away. They're fine without me. Paris is in charge and he's reported nothing out of the ordinary. What else did she say? Because that can't be what's bothering you."

"She started talking about the two of you and how there had never been anything you wouldn't try with her—and others. How you used to be absolutely hedonistic and that you'd turned into a pussy since meeting me."

He blinked again before laughing. "I've never fucked her."

Cynara's anger cooled. "You haven't?"

"No! I have better taste than that. And the only reason she's still part of the coven is because she hasn't given me a legal reason to kick her out."

"I didn't scent any lies coming off her." And given the combination of her demon and vamp side, Cynara would have.

"She's a fucking sociopath, of course you couldn't scent a lie coming off her. I knew she was in town on holiday but she was very clearly baiting you." He scrubbed a hand over his face, suddenly looking exhausted. "Why didn't you just tell me what she'd said?"

"I didn't want you to know it bothered me," she muttered.

"Why not?"

"I...didn't know if it would matter. If you'd care. And honestly, I was scared she was right. That you'd changed for me."

He covered the short distance between them. "I care about anything you do. I never want you hurt. And I have changed, I'm in lov—"

She grabbed him by the back of the head and crushed her mouth to his. He'd told her before that he loved her but she couldn't let him finish. Every time he said the words to her, she came a little closer to caving and giving him what he wanted.

What she desperately wanted.

But she wasn't a fool. Cynara was a half-demon and he was Alpha of his own coven. He was over two thousand years old and respected by everyone. Why the hell he'd want to settle for a hybrid nobody was insane to her. She pushed the thought away as he wrapped his fingers possessively around one hip and shoved her against the nearest wall.

"Should we go back to my place?" she asked after managing to tear her mouth from his.

His fangs had descended as he stared at her. Letting out another one of those sexy growls she felt all the way to her core, he shook his head and glanced around. "Later. After this." Moving with supernatural speed, he carried her to what turned out to be a powder room with gray and blue wallpaper covered in fleurs-de-lis. "You. Naked. Now."

When he got to the point where he could barely get words out, Cynara knew she was going to love what came next. Namely, him inside her. "We have to be quiet," she whispered, turned on and practically panting for him.

In response he growled again. Seriously, it shouldn't be so hot, but everything he did was. She just wished things could be different between them. That she wasn't who she was. *Ugh.* She knew she had baggage but it was impossible to shake it off. Especially since his coven would never accept her as an Alpha's mate. That much she knew.

As he pinned her up against the wall, he peeled off her sparkly purple top. She'd also worn a black and pur-ple plaid skirt and boots tonight—though she'd lost the boots during poker. Apparently he wanted her to keep her skirt on because he didn't make a move to take it off. And with Justus, he always did what he wanted. Something she found insanely hot.

He reached between their bodies, cupping her mound even as he raked his fangs along her neck. Right now she desperately wanted him to sink his fangs into her, to mark her. But if he did, she would want to do the same to him. And that was dangerous. If they bit each other at the same time during sex it would bond them, mate them.

"I miss your taste," he murmured, biting her ear gently.

A shudder slid through her. "Take a wrist," she whispered, even as she arched against him, heat pooling low in her belly.

"I want your neck."

"Bite me," she rasped out. Her own fangs descended as he sank his fangs into her neck, but she refrained from attacking him. Barely.

As he pulled on her, dragging blood from her vein, he slid two fingers inside her folds. She was already slick with need, something he would have scented long before they'd ended up in here. It was impossible to not be turned on around him. Her inner walls tightened around his fingers, desperate for more.

"God," he murmured, pulling back and licking where he'd bitten her. She was already healing but that would make her heal even faster. "I can't get enough of you."

Then his mouth was on hers, hungry and dominating. She was vaguely aware of when he ditched his boxers. His cock was thick between them, making her ache to feel him. When he pushed inside her she cried out, barely able to handle all the possessive, love-infused emotions she felt rolling off him.

The sensation of being filled up by him was familiar, yet every time they ended up like this, he took her breath away in more ways than one.

Because every time they had sex, it was as if he couldn't get enough of her, as if he was starving for her.

So what happened if they mated and then he grew to resent her later on? She wasn't from a pure bloodline. She wasn't what he deserved. She was a hybrid who had a demon king father who'd raped her mother. She came from monsters—both of whom were thankfully dead. Justus, however, had led actual armies and he helped keep the peace among their people. She was a small business owner with a hybrid family of misfits. He was everything she wasn't.

Fuck. She shoved those thoughts away as he sucked a nipple between his lips.

"Justus," she moaned as he thrust hard once before stilling inside her.

Her inner walls tightened around him as he stayed deep inside her, oh so slowly teasing one nipple, then the next. She dug her fingers into his shoulders as she rolled her hips, silently begging him to do more. But he knew exactly what he was doing. How much he was teasing her. This was pure Justus right here.

Surprising her, he suddenly pulled back, his amber eyes intent. "I love you, Cynara. Nothing's going to change that. Accept it." His final two words were an order and a desperate plea, mixed in one.

He took her breath away with his confession but she couldn't find her voice so she did what she always did.

She kissed him hard, teasing her tongue against his and trying to tell him exactly how she felt. That she loved him too, even if she felt selfish for doing so. But she'd never expected to fall for someone like him—someone so giving and wonderful that he surprised her with every kind thing he did.

He began thrusting again even as he cupped her breasts, teasing her exactly the way he knew she liked. And just when she was about to climax, he stilled again, a wicked laugh rumbling through him as he slowly pulled out. *What the hell?*

Before she could protest, he turned her around and bent her over the little pedestal sink.

"Look at me," he said. A bronze-framed oval mirror hung above the sink.

She stared at him as he shoved her little skirt up and thrust into her again.

She pushed back into him, keeping her gaze on his as long as she could and savoring the sensation of him filling her up. She gripped onto the edge of the sink, ignoring the cracking sound as he thrust harder and harder. When he reached around her and barely grazed her clit, it was enough to send her over the edge.

She surged into climax, pleasure punching through her as he added more pressure, making her completely crazy. Her eyes flared as bright as his, twin beacons reflecting back at them as she came hard. Just as quickly, he followed, burying his face against her neck, just grazing her with his fangs as he came inside her in long, hard strokes.

His climax was raw and loud, leaving no doubt to anyone what they were doing. Not that she cared. She wanted the whole world to know that Justus was hers. If only for now.

As he pulled out of her, he immediately gathered her into his arms, holding her close. "I'm pretty sure we owe them a new sink," Cynara rasped out, laying her forehead against his chest.

He laughed lightly as he held her close. She felt secure in his hold and there was nowhere else she'd rather be than in his arms. "Let's head back to my place," he said. "I'm not done with you."

She wasn't done with him either. Ever. That had barely taken the edge off.

She kept telling herself to end things. Over the holidays she'd broken up with him. Sort of. She'd tried but she couldn't seem to walk away. Not when he was always there, showing her that he wasn't going anywhere. That he was perfect and had her back.

But they were supernaturals and mating was forever. Once they crossed that line there was no going back. And it carved her up thinking that he could one day regret her. That she wouldn't be good enough.

Her own mother had been miserable, had taken it out on Cynara every day until she'd run away. She'd made it clear that Cynara was unwanted, that her blood was tainted, that she was a mistake.

She locked those thoughts up. They had no place in her mind right now. Not when she was in Justus's arms.

So she pasted on a smile and took the shirt Justus handed her.

"I'm not even embarrassed we did that." Cynara laughed as they opened the bathroom door. Maybe she should be but they were supernatural after all. She was too old to care about someone overhearing them having sex.

To her surprise, Justus's cheeks tinged red. "Speak for yourself."

She blinked once before laughing even harder. He seriously never stopped surprising her. The big bad general was embarrassed about what they'd done.

For some reason she liked him just a little bit more because of it.

CHAPTER NINE

Reaper strode into the kitchen to find Greer and Prima already there, both drinking coffee—something new to him that he found he enjoyed. The house smelled faintly of sex, no doubt from Justus and Cynara's escapade last night. And the smell of sex made him think of taking Greer right on the countertop.

Though to be fair, most anything made him think of her and sex.

But he shoved all of that back down for now. Instead, he nodded politely at Prima and smiled at Greer.

To his delight, her cheeks flushed pink. He'd surprised her last night with his offer to please her, and he'd realized that she wanted him more than he originally thought. She must have been suppressing her desire for him. And if she was hiding her scent, she was fighting her need for him. He wasn't certain why.

So he was going to be careful with how he courted her. He was a strategist by nature and he simply had to figure out a way to win her heart. With a female like Greer, he couldn't simply claim her body—though he planned to. He must claim both her body and heart.

He was going to start now by being as honest as possible. But he would not tell her about the reason he believed he had woken up, about the fire and war he sensed on the horizon. He did not want to ever bring her any sort of pain.

Walking around to her side of the center island, he pulled out his cell phone, even though he did not care for the thing. Then he handed it to Greer. "Cynbel texted me just now. He said he got my information from someone at Cynara's club." It sounded true enough as he had left his contact information there in case Cynbel decided to reach out to him. He wanted to make it as easy as possible for the other ancient to make contact.

Greer seemed surprised that he was offering the phone even as she took it from his hand. An electric arc sparked between them as their fingers brushed and he knew he did not imagine the slight shudder that passed through her.

She looked at the text, then handed it to Prima, who simply frowned at the screen.

"This could be a trap," Greer said.

"I do not like his message either." Cynbel had told him that he'd seen Prima with Reaper at the club last night and decided to reach out to him later without the female around. "And I am obviously not familiar with this meeting point."

Greer was already on her phone doing...something. "The location he gave you appears to be near an alligator farm out in the bayou. It will be quite hard for humans to get there unless they're using a boat, but it's easy for dragons." She turned her screen around and pointed to a spot on the map. The maps of today were

DARKNESS RISING | 101

different than the ones from his time but he could figure out easily enough what he was looking at.

"I don't remember making enemies with this dragon," Prima said. "Though I don't know why he would lie."

"I do not know either but I have been asleep for a very long time." None of this sat right with him, however.

"We should have Camden do a deeper search on him," Prima said.

"He's already on it," Greer said, glancing between the two of them. There was something in her eyes that he couldn't quite define—as if she wasn't sure she should have told them that.

"Who is Camden?"

"He's a member of my clan and he's very good at finding people and digging up dirt on them. He's currently gathering info on Cynbel and any of his known associates from before he went into Hibernation and since he has awakened. He has done the same with the other ancients you wish to find."

Reaper nodded. "I am going to meet him at this place he indicated, but I want you two to act as my sentries." Truthfully he hated the thought of bringing Greer with them even though she was a dragon, which meant she was completely capable. And he had felt the effects of her healer's fire when it hit him.

For some reason his body had seemed to absorb it and he wasn't certain why, but it was potent and would hurt another dragon, he was certain. At least if there was enough anger behind it. Not to mention he would protect her to the death if any danger arose. But the main reason he was bringing her today was to show her that he did indeed think she was capable. He had inadvertently insulted her before, even though he wanted to do the opposite. He would simply have to be on the highest alert, which was normal enough for him.

Greer looked surprised at his request, as did Prima.

"Both of us?" Prima asked, her words carefully spoken. A wise answer.

Greer glanced at her and raised an eyebrow. "You have a problem with me coming?"

Prima simply shook her head, her lips twitching as if she was fighting a smile. "Nope." A wise answer.

"Given what my GPS says, we can fly there easily in twenty minutes," Greer said, looking back at him. "I'm ready when you are. Since he doesn't want to meet for another hour it might not hurt to arrive early and do some recon."

"Agreed."

"Then let's go." Prima pushed off the chair, looking ready for battle as always.

"We can simply take flight from the yard, I suppose?" Greer said.

This particular house was surrounded by a very high wall, keeping prying human eyes out. Apparently the clan owned it, and when they first purchased it they'd increased the height by two feet. It was unlikely humans would be able to spot them. Not unless they used something Prima had called a drone. If they did, they did. He would not worry about such things. Unlike Greer and her clan, he cared little if humans knew about him. Though he could understand why the clan wanted to keep their existence a secret, the thought of war did not bother him.

It never had.

In the backyard, the sun was in the east, barely up, illuminating everything in a soft glow. Bright red and purple flowers created a soft background behind Greer's body. Prima immediately started stripping off her clothes but Greer gave him a pointed look. "Turn around."

He desperately wanted to see her naked again—he had only gotten a quick glimpse before—but he would respect her. Before he turned around, however, he stripped off his shirt and took pleasure in the way her eyes roved over him. Hungry and needy.

Oh yes, she liked what she saw. Then he turned and stripped his pants off, giving her a shot of his ass. Which was nowhere near as perfect as her own, but he figured she liked what she saw if the little inhalation of breath he heard was any indication.

By the time he was undressed and had shifted, Greer had shifted as well. A pity. Though her dragon was just as gorgeous as her.

He'd seen her before but the sight was no less awe-inspiring. Her dragon scales glittered a pale green and silver, like the finest jewels carved from deep in the earth, but her eyes were the same striking green. Before he had time to enjoy the full sight of her dragon, she called on her camouflage.

So he did the same. Despite the fact that humans wouldn't be able to see them, it was easy enough to follow the shimmering images of Prima and Greer. And because he was attuned to Greer's scent, he could follow her anywhere.

* * *

Reaper stretched his wings wide as he swooped down over the plethora of greenery below. He'd never been in a place like this before. Despite the cooler weather, the foliage was green, lush and grew everywhere, with no encumbrances as he'd seen in the city. The trees, plants and animals ruled this place called the bayou.

The scent of various animals filled the air—and he spotted more than a few from his dragon's eye view as he flew over the interconnected rivers. As he glided right over the water, his wings caused it to ripple outward, sending an explosion of birds flying into the air. Which was probably a good thing considering the alligator that had been lurking nearby looking for a snack. Hmm, maybe he'd eat the gator later.

He pushed back up into the air, careful not to run into Greer or Prima. Though they were all camouflaged, he could still see the outline of their dragon bodies shimmering against the sunlight. Greer's image was embedded into his brain now, even her camouflaged one.

As the wind shifted, a charcoal-ish scent filled the air though he could not see anything burning. But he could scent for miles if the wind and atmosphere were right. And something told him they were heading straight to where the burning originated from. He was not sure what that meant.

He didn't like this entire setup, nor the meeting out in the middle of nowhere. Cynbel might have been afraid of Prima but he had been a warrior. No, Reaper wasn't certain he bought the fear angle at all. It did not make sense.

He continued onward, surpassing the females, his annoyance building by the time they reached a giant, charred area that had incinerated trees and other animal habitat right along the shoreline of one of the rivers. He scanned the immediate area, looking and scenting for predators. He did not scent any other shifters nearby, though with the recent fire, that could be the reason.

His senses were acute, but fire had many uses.

When he was certain the place was uninhabited by other shifters, he descended to the outskirts of where the fire had been and shifted to his human form.

"This was dragon fire." Prima appeared next to him moments later.

Greer did the same and he had to force himself not to stare at her strong, lithe and naked form as she eyed the destruction. "I smell more than one dragon."

"Same," Prima said even as Reaper nodded.

"Stay here," he ordered both of them, not caring about his tone as he stalked across the ashes of trees and anything else that had been unfortunate enough to be here when this had been started. He recognized the scent of dragon fire, though he could not decipher who it belonged to. And from the air he'd easily seen that the pattern of burn circles had been created from a being in the sky—a dragon.

"There's something else under the dragon fire." Greer's voice was soft as she came up next to him. "Not just the destroyed land and animals."

"It's a dragon." His words were blunt. "It smells like Cynbel. And there's too much ash piled around here." He indicated the scorched earth they walked across and frowned at the sight of Greer's feet and ankles covered in the filth.

"You think he was the dragon who ashed another dragon, or do you think he's dead?" Now Prima spoke, both females clearly having ignored his order to stay put.

"I do not know." He scanned the skies now, looking for a threat, but saw nothing aside from little white clouds and birds far in the distance. "I want to scan the area for a few miles in all directions, but then we should head back." He did not think they would find anything but he would still look. None of this felt right. "His scent is strong here." He motioned to the ashes. "I believe...this might be him."

To his surprise, Greer put her soft hand on his upper arm. "I'm sorry about your friend."

"He...was not a friend." Not exactly. "But thank you." When he felt his gaze begin to dip lower, he forced himself to turn away from her. He would not disrespect her and ogle her while she was here with him acting as backup.

"Let's go," Prima said abruptly. "I don't like this place."

Yes, Reaper did not like something about it either. Even though he couldn't see or scent anyone, he felt eyes on him. And he did not like that at all.

He reached out and placed his own hand on Greer's back, urging her toward the shoreline and out of all this death and destruction. "Come."

One way or another, Reaper would find out what was going on.

* * *

They made it to the mansion in record time, something Reaper was glad for. He'd sensed someone watching them and he couldn't think of a good reason for someone not to reveal themselves. If he hadn't been with Greer, he would have taken to the skies and shot his fire around, aiming for whoever had been spying on them. Because if Cynbel was dead, whoever was watching them was a prime suspect in his killing.

Now he and Prima were in the kitchen, discussing their next move, while Greer contacted her Alpha.

She'd been vague about why she was calling him, and it wasn't Reaper's place to question her, even though he wanted to.

"I've reached out to some of my contacts," Prima said, looking down at her phone and doing...something on it. "And I think you'll be happy to learn that Cale is in New Orleans as well. He's with his half-brother, Damari."

He stilled at her words. "Truly?"

"Truly."

The males were brothers, though they had different fathers. They were ancients like he and Prima. "They contacted you?"

"Actually, they left word at Cynara's club for you. They apparently tried to text you?"

"Oh, my phone is in the bedroom." He did not carry the thing around everywhere like Prima and the others seemed to do. It was not second nature to him.

"Well, when they didn't hear back, they contacted me. Cale did anyway. They would like to see us."

"Good." While he did not like to leave Greer, he wasn't certain he wanted to bring her to this meeting either.

Thankfully Prima had the same thought because she said, "We are not bringing Greer. Not after this morning."

"Agreed. I do not like the fact that they are contacting us so soon after finding those ashes." His instinct told him Cynbel was dead, but he would not claim it was so until he knew for certain.

"We are on the same page, then. And since I know you don't want to be the bad guy, I'll tell Greer that just the two of us are going."

"Thank you." He had done enough to annoy the female and he felt like he was finally making progress with her. Very small, dragonling steps, but he would take what he could get. One battle at a time was how wars were won. "Do you know if she likes anything in particular?"

Prima's head tilted to the side ever so slightly, her inky black braid spilling over her shoulder. "What do you mean?"

"I would like to buy her a gift—with money that I do not have." Something that bothered him very much. He needed to get to his hoard, which was far, far north of all civilization.

"I have plenty of funds. You may have what you wish. I know you will eventually pay me back. And if you don't, I don't care."

"I will pay you back. And you have not answered my question."

She lifted a shoulder. "I do not know what she would like. But I can ask some clanmates and see if they have any ideas."

"Thank you."

Prima paused for a long moment, watching him closely, even ignoring the little ping of her phone. "Do you think she is your mate?" Her words were spoken so quietly, there was no way Greer could overhear them upstairs if she was eavesdropping.

Something told Reaper that Greer was so civil and polite she would never do such a thing, regardless. Still, he did not answer audibly, but simply nodded. He felt the mating call in his bones, all the way to his core, that they were connected. Considering how different they were, it did not make sense. But the attraction and connection between he and Greer was electric, something he never even imagined before. He'd heard of the mating pull, but this…it defied logic.

To his surprise, he cared little about the lack of logic. He only cared about claiming her, possessing her. Making her happy for the rest of her life.

"Ah," was all Prima said.

"Did the brothers say anything about their cousins?" He needed to change the subject. Reaper had fought alongside Cale and Damari many times, and unlike him, they had loved their clanmates. They'd been warriors, yes, but they hadn't forsaken their clan as he had. They should still be in contact with their clan.

"No. The message was brief. And the meeting place is a home. I looked up the address. It's not the bayou at least."

"Okay, then. Go tell Greer we have to leave." He wanted to see her before they left but decided against it. He might be weak and ask her to come along. His dragon craved being close to her, but right now that was not the smart move. He needed her to stay put for her safety, and his sanity. And if she pushed back and asked if she could come, he was fairly certain he could not tell her no.

This was a revelation about himself and he was not sure how he felt about it.

She had changed everything.

CHAPTER TEN

"I scent more than simply two dragons," Reaper murmured to Prima as they approached the house from the east. On a sidewalk that badly needed fixing, they kept their strides casual. Beaded necklaces and other sparkly things littered the tree branches above them. Such a strange custom.

She simply nodded. "I recognize only two."

It was the same for him. He recognized Cale and Damari, but with the various scents, he wasn't certain if this was a trap or not. "New plan." Instead of turning onto the stone path through the open gate toward the walled-in home not far from where they were staying, he continued walking and Prima did the same.

It would take some maneuvering but they were going to infiltrate the house instead of directly approaching the front door.

They found a place to hide, strip their clothes and call on their camouflage. Leaving their clothing bundled up and hidden in some bushes was the only option.

"Human or dragon?" Prima asked as they stepped out from behind a tree, naked but invisible to humans.

"Human." Less damage that way. If they weren't being set up by Cale and Damari, they wouldn't want to go into full-on battle mode as dragons.

Though the gate was open, they decided to scale the wall from opposite sides of the yard. Then, using their natural gift of speed, they approached the house. He took the west side while she took the east.

The purple-colored house rose three stories with balconies on each level, making it easy for him to scale to the third floor. The set of two glass doors was locked, but he did not see any other mechanism set up as a trap. Manipulating the lock with his mind, he turned it until it opened. In the past he had mainly used it to move stone—as a weapon. In this new world, he figured he would have many chances to use this particular gift.

Once inside, he quickly scanned the bedroom. It held the faint scent of Damari, but no one was inside. His feet were quiet against the wood floors as he approached the already open doorway. As he stepped into the hallway, he heard voices from down below.

All male.

Soon enough he would be scented, and so would Prima. Soundlessly he released his claws, and using his supernatural speed, he raced down the stairs, his feet barely touching the steps.

"There's no way he's involved in any of this." Reaper recognized Cale's voice. What was he speaking of? And involved in what?

"We can't take the risk." Another familiar voice. Damari.

He had once considered these dragons his brothers-in-arms. He hoped it was still the same. So much had changed in this new world.

Suddenly it went silent and he knew they were aware of his presence. He'd masked his scent as much as possible, but these were ancients like himself.

"Show yourself," Cale called out.

Reaper let his camouflage fall as he stepped around the corner into what turned out to be a large kitchen. Both males were standing at the ready, claws extended, their dragons in their eyes.

"What the fuck? Why are you naked?" Damari growled at him.

"Why the fuck do you think? Who else is here?"

Another male stepped inside the kitchen, followed by two more. Reaper vaguely recognized them but only because of the familial resemblance to Cale and Damari. They all had the same sun-kissed bronze skin, pale green eyes and dark hair.

"You thought to attack us?" Damari's eyes sparked with rage.

"No. I scented more than the two of you—I wasn't sure if I could trust you."

"You're not alone." Cale shifted slightly, scenting the air.

Reaper didn't respond, just watched them, waiting, all his muscles tight as he prepared to take them on. If that happened, this house would be destroyed and humans would surely know of their existence. There would be no way around it then—and he wasn't certain if that mattered to these dragons. He was not certain it mattered to him.

"That's right." Prima let her camouflage drop as she strode up next to him, equally naked, her own claws out.

He noted that the three males behind his friends eyed her with interest. God, males were so fucking typical. And he was no different, except that he had eyes only for a certain beautiful healer.

"Prima." Damari gave her a wide, flirty smile. "When we heard you and your sister had risen, we knew the world was right again."

"How long have you two been awake?" she asked, not returning his flirty, obnoxious grin.

"A year."

"Did you kill Cynbel?" Cale asked abruptly, looking between the two of them.

"No," they both said. Then Reaper continued, "I was supposed to meet him this morning and found a pile of ash instead. I don't know that it was him."

"It's him."

"How do you know?"

"Because someone delivered his head in a box an hour ago. Your scent was on it."

He blinked. "Mine was?"

"Yes. But such things can be manufactured, especially if you were near the site of his murder. Which is why we're not killing you now," Cale said.

He snorted. They could try to kill him. There might be a lot about this world that he was adjusting to, but killing to defend himself? He had not forgotten how to do that.

"I had no reason to kill Cynbel. I was in fact looking for him since rising. And you," he said, nodding at Cale.

"Did either of you kill Enaes?" Damari spoke this time, his question as abrupt as his brother's had been.

Reaper blinked in surprise but shook his head. "No. I have no reason to kill anyone and I have just woken from Hibernation in the last week."

The tension in both men's shoulders eased, their claws retracting. No doubt they scented the truth in his words. "Where are your clothes?"

"Hidden in a cache not far away from here."

Damari turned and looked at one of the males. "Grab both of them clothing."

The male nodded and disappeared from the room.

"Your cousin is dead?" Reaper asked, referring to Enaes.

Expression grim, Damari leaned against the center island. "Yes. And not just him. At least a dozen ancients were killed upon their awakening."

Next to him Prima straightened. "This is the first I've heard of this."

Damari nodded. "This news has not spread far. The murdered dragons were slaughtered before they could fully arise. They must have trusted the wrong people with the location of their Hibernation."

"Not necessarily," Prima said. "Someone could have been working with a witch to find their locations."

"Ah," Cale said, even as Damari nodded slowly.

"Fucking witches," Prima muttered.

"Fucking witches indeed." There were not many beings that Reaper loathed. But witches were one of them. He knew there were a few good ones out there, but none of the ones he had ever met were. The ones he'd known had embraced the darkness, using what should be a gift for their own gain, to hurt others. It was disgraceful.

The male who had disappeared to find clothing returned, carrying two bundles in his hands.

"It seems a shame to cover all that up," the male said, handing a bundle directly to Prima.

"It does, doesn't it," she said even as she slipped the very tight T-shirt over her head.

Yeah, something told Reaper that this young male had picked that shirt intentionally.

Ignoring the unknowns for now, he looked back at his friends as he pulled on a pair of pants. "What do you know about who is killing ancients? And why was Cynbel killed?"

"For the first question—not enough, unfortunately," Cale said. "We haven't been awake for long and we are still adapting to this new world. We only found out about a few of the kills by accident. After, we started digging on our own. As far as Cynbel, he asked us to come to New Orleans after we recently discovered another murdered ancient. And we do not know if the things are connected."

Reaper was silent for a long moment. "There are a lot of reasons to kill ancients, but so many at one time? It is organized, with purpose. I do not like this."

"I can talk to my clan," Prima said. "Because if they'd known about this, we all would have known. They have what they call a hacker who is great at researching people and things. And we have a healer who is also skilled at research."

Reaper frowned, looking at Prima.

"Not *her*," she said, clearly reading his mind even though he hadn't said Greer's name aloud. "I'm talking about Drake's mate."

"Wait…you have two healers in your clan?" Damari asked, his interest clear.

She nodded once. "Yes. We are very blessed."

"Best sex I ever had was with a healer," Damari said, causing all heads to turn his way. "What? The female used me then disappeared. Best. Sex. Ever."

"Your mind is always on your dick," Cale muttered, rolling his eyes.

An unexpected laugh bubbled up inside Reaper. "I am glad that some things have not changed despite all the time that has passed."

"We should contact my clan, let them know what you've told us," Prima interjected. "They'll want the names of the dead and any other details." She turned to Reaper. "And we need to inform Greer as well. She should be kept up to date since she was with us when we found Cynbel."

"Who is Greer?" Damari asked.

"Mine." The word tore from Reaper's throat, his tone possessive and murderous.

Both males raised their eyebrows but did not push any further.

Reaper's beast had risen to the surface so quickly, he was barely holding on to his dragon, keeping him in check. And the male—his friend—had simply asked who she was.

Reaper needed to stay in control.

CHAPTER ELEVEN

Greer was surprised to run into Reaper and Prima as she reached the bottom of the stairs. They must have just gotten back.

Almost immediately upon returning from the bayou that morning, the two ancients had disappeared from the house to meet up with "someone" and hadn't offered her any more info than that. She wanted to be annoyed—and she kind of was since Prima had been the one to deliver the news. Reaper had been conspicuously absent.

"Where are you going looking so sexy?" Prima asked, hanging her coat on the hook by the door.

Reaper simply growled at Greer as he drank her in with his eyes.

Greer blinked, wondering at his reaction. Since she liked the sound of that growl way too much, she ignored him. "I'm meeting up with an old friend for dinner." She'd had to wait until after sunset since her particular friend was a vampire.

Prima's smile turned pure wicked. "Is this friend of the male variety?" She flicked a quick glance at Reaper, clearly watching for his reaction with glee.

What the heck was wrong with Prima? Was she trying to bait Reaper? Yes, maybe her outfit was sexy, but it wasn't obscene. She wore tight black pants, knee-high, heeled boots that gave her another couple inches, and her silky green top with flutter sleeves did have a deep vee. And she wasn't ashamed of it. "Not that it matters, but yes." She glanced down at her phone and saw that her Uber had arrived. "How did your meeting go?"

"Fine. I'll tell you about it when you return," Prima said. "Go enjoy yourself."

Reaper stared at her as if he wanted to say something but didn't.

Greer figured that if it was urgent, Prima would have told her so she simply smiled. "Okay. I've got my phone if you need me."

When she got into the car, she found she could breathe again, not being so close to Reaper. That male. Maybe she should have stayed and pushed them more about their meeting, but since an old vampire friend had contacted her to get together, she didn't want to ditch him now. Besides, he might be able to tell her more about what had happened to Reaper's friend, Cynbel.

Reaper.

Even thinking his name got her worked up. Just being in his presence again for mere minutes had stirred things deep inside her she wasn't ready to acknowledge. Maybe she would never be ready. He was simply not the type of male she'd ever envisioned being with. Her lovers had all been gentle and kind.

And Reaper?

The male was a fierce warrior who clearly gave orders and expected them to be followed. He would never join her clan. Never be part of a clan, period. That much was clear. And she needed her clan, her family. Healing and taking care of others was part of who she was at her core.

Sighing, she tried to table thoughts of the ancient, sexy-as-sin male, but it was difficult. Especially when she kept remembering the way he'd strode across that ash in the bayou like a determined god, uncaring about any danger and secure in who he was. The confidence thing? Yeah, that was sexy. He was just so damn arrogant.

Thankfully the drive didn't take long, and soon her driver pulled right up to the curb of the little hole-in-the-wall restaurant surrounded by homes. She imagined it did well in the mostly residential area.

She smiled as she approached her very old vampire friend, Christian, sitting at a little mosaic table outside. The cold wouldn't bother him just as it didn't bother her. Christian was one of her oldest friends and they'd kept in touch over the centuries—something that didn't always happen with supernaturals. "I'm surprised these tables are even open," she said, kissing him on both cheeks as he stood to greet her.

"I used a little persuasion and they opened the patio for me. I wanted a little bit of privacy." He'd grown his pale blond hair out to his shoulders since she'd last seen him and had pulled it back with a little tie at the nape of his neck.

"Humans usually don't listen to anything that doesn't concern them anyway," she murmured as she sat down, glad to see that he had already ordered a bottle of wine. "Will it bother you if I order food?"

"Of course not, but thank you for asking."

Their server stepped outside before she could even look at the menu, but she'd been here before so she ordered two appetizers as her meal.

"Pretty light on the food for a dragon," Christian said once they were alone again.

She lifted a shoulder, though it was true. Dragons tended to eat as much as wolf shifters, and that was saying something. "I have a lot on my mind."

One of his eyebrows lifted. "Is that right?"

"Yes that is right. Don't push." She wasn't in the mood to talk about Reaper.

He laughed lightly. "What's his name?"

"I really don't want to talk about it."

"It, or him?"

She paused for a beat before grinning. "Him."

"Fine, be that way." He gave a mock pout, making him look even more adorable than usual. He'd been turned in his early twenties many, many centuries ago and he still retained a sort of boyish charm. "So how long are you in town this time? And why did I have to hear through the supernatural grapevine that you were?" Now that boyish charm disappeared to be replaced by the faintest hint of hurt. Which was fair, since they were friends—who emailed, texted and even talked on the phone.

"This trip happened so last minute even I was not prepared for it. I planned to contact you, I promise. I only just arrived. And how did you hear about me being here?"

"I heard from a friend of a friend that you were at Cynara's new club."

Ah, that made sense. Supernaturals were such gossips. "I promise to make it up to you for not calling the moment I arrived but I do have a question. Have you noticed or heard of any strange happenings around here lately?"

"Honey, it's New Orleans. Strange things happen every second of every day."

"Yeah, I know. I just meant in general, I guess." She wasn't certain how much she wanted to share with Christian. He was one of the few beings she'd been friends with when dragons hadn't been out to other supernaturals—the majority of supernaturals had assumed that dragons were extinct until recently. But he came from a different time and had dealt with different prejudices before he'd been turned. She'd always felt safe with him knowing of her kind's existence.

"I have been hearing some interesting rumblings lately, since you ask. And one in particular is that King is going to make an official play for claiming New Orleans's territory."

"That isn't exactly surprising." King was a wolf shifter, and though New Orleans was considered neutral territory, the shifters who made this city their home often looked to him for guidance. "How do vampires feel about this?"

"If he takes a vampire mate, I think everything will be fine."

She nodded once. "Where is he, anyway? I asked around and he's not in town. I couldn't get a solid answer about where he's gotten off to." And as far as she knew, that wolf rarely left the city. This was his domain.

"I think he might be hunting himself down a vampire mate." Christian grinned now. "And in case you are not aware, we are not alone."

Frowning, she glanced around, subtly inhaling—and she scented *him*. She gritted her teeth.

"Is this that male you didn't want to talk about?" He reached across the table and took her hand in his.

Oh no—she knew what he was doing, and this was a dangerous game. He brought her hand to his mouth and had begun to brush his lips over her knuckles when Reaper appeared out of nowhere, with supernatural speed, looking as if he was ready to take off Christian's head.

He looked like an avenging warrior, his green-amber eyes bright with a promise that blood was about to be shed. *Holy. Shit.* There was no civilization in his eyes right now.

Greer stood abruptly, jerking her hand back. Moving between Christian and Reaper, she placed a hand in the middle of Reaper's chest. "I'm not sure what you're doing here, but you will sit down and remain civil. You will have a glass of wine with us and be nice to my friend." She certainly wasn't asking, but she was surprised that he acquiesced so quickly and sank into the seat closest to hers.

"Touch her again and I'll take off your head." Reaper's tone was casual as he rudely plucked the wineglass from her friend.

Of course, Christian threw his head back and laughed uproariously—that male had always loved living on the edge. It was how he'd been turned. He'd been an obnoxious little shit when human and had robbed the wrong human—and been killed for it. But a vampire had liked his arrogance and had changed him simply for that alone.

Then he looked at Greer, amusement dancing in his baby blues. "Honey, I don't blame you. This one is gorgeous."

Reaper looked confused for a moment, then seemed to completely relax, his shoulders settling as he realized that Christian was no threat to him. Not for her attentions anyway. And…probably not against him regardless. Power rolled off Reaper in waves. "Where I'm from, we don't touch what is not ours," he added, still watching Christian.

Christian simply grinned wider as Greer shook her head. She was so not going to touch on what he'd just said. "Why did you follow me?"

He gave her a look that said the answer should be obvious. And maybe it was, but she couldn't believe he'd actually followed her here.

"I take it you were eavesdropping?"

He gave an unapologetic shrug. "Of course."

"Good, then. Why don't you tell Christian what we discovered today? Maybe he can offer some insight." Christian had lived in the city for centuries and knew everyone and everything. Unlike most vamps, he didn't live in a coven, but stuck to himself mainly. His mate had died centuries ago and Christian had never gotten over the loss. Not truly.

She always thought it was better for dragons that if their mate died, they perished with them. Because a dragon in mourning? No. They would go mad and burn the world.

Reaper lifted a shoulder again and told the vampire about the dead ancient from the bayou. Then he asked, "Did you know him?"

Greer noted that he specifically said Cynbel was dead, and this morning he hadn't been certain. Something had happened at his meeting. Damn it, she should have pressed him and Prima for more information.

Christian nodded once. "I've met Cynbel. He hasn't been here long, maybe a year. I don't care for him. I know who he hangs out with and the places he frequents, however. And I find it hard to believe he's dead."

"So do I. But he must have been killed by one of my kind." It was said with a sort of arrogance.

"You're very certain of that," Christian murmured.

"I scented another dragon there. More than one. But even if I hadn't, it is very hard to kill my kind. Who does—or did—he associate with that you know of?"

"You're not even going to try to butter me up before asking all these questions?" Christian lifted an eyebrow.

Reaper glanced at Greer, his expression horrified. "He wants me to put butter on him?"

Greer couldn't help herself as a giggle escaped. Reaching out, she squeezed his forearm. "No, he doesn't. I promise. He just means that you're not bothering with polite small talk before jumping straight into what you want."

"Oh." His gaze flicked down to where her fingers were gently clasping his arm and he let out a low growl when he looked back up at her.

She told herself to let go, but found her gaze hooked with his, unable to turn away from those sparking eyes.

"Should I give y'all some privacy?" Christian murmured.

"Yes," Reaper said as Greer said, "No."

She dropped her hand and looked away, ignoring the amusement in Christian's expression.

"Cynbel associated with a male named Brennus. They frequented a club called Red Devils that is exclusive to supernaturals. Much like Cynara's. Unlike Cynara's, there don't seem to be any rules there. No protection for the weaker." There was disgust in his voice. "I don't care for the owner either. But that's not what you wanted to know. Brennus is—"

"I know the male," Reaper said.

"Is he friend or foe?" Greer asked.

He paused a moment before answering. "Neither. We fought with and against each other over a few centuries. He was a killer for hire, I believe would be the right phrase. His clan was large, spanning various continents. They were very…ah, they did not believe in interspecies matings. I don't imagine they'll have changed much."

"From what I know of Brennus, he doesn't like anyone who isn't a dragon. To him, humans are basically bugs. I don't know anything about his family, however. They could be here, for all I know. I've avoided that male as well as Cynbel. They've got nasty streaks."

"What does King think of them?" Greer asked. She didn't know the Alpha wolf, not in the sense that they were friends. But she'd met him and she respected the way he unofficially ran New Orleans.

"I would never deign to answer for King. But if those dragons left town, I don't think he'd lose any sleep over it."

That was answer enough. Since Reaper didn't ask who King was, she figured he might know. And because the energy rolling off him right now felt almost electrified, she knew it was time to leave. He was keyed up and that was never a good thing when a dragon was involved.

Pulling out cash, she set some on the table and smiled apologetically at Christian. "I think I need to go, but I'll be in town a while. We'll definitely get together again."

Smiling, he stood and pushed her money back at her. "I would kiss your cheek but I like my head where it is."

Reaper simply grunted in approval as Greer shot him a dark look. She kissed Christian on the cheek anyway and left her money where it was. "I'll call you."

She and Reaper strolled out onto the uneven sidewalk.

"Did you walk here?" she asked him.

"No."

Okay, then. "Would you like to walk back?"

"Yes... Soon I will find my hoard and retrieve my treasure."

She blinked at the odd, abrupt change in topic. "Oh, ah, okay. That's great for you."

Two human females holding hands as they walked their dog strolled by so she and Reaper moved out of the way, stepping onto the street to avoid them.

"I'm telling you so you know that soon I will have funds with which to take care of myself. Of you."

Wait...what? It took her all of a second to understand what he meant. "Look, Reaper—"

"I know you desire me," he said confidently as they stepped back onto the sidewalk.

Thankfully there weren't many people walking right now to overhear this bizarre conversation. "Reaper—"

"I definitely enjoy when you say my name." He gently took her elbow as they stepped over a broken sidewalk square.

She'd be a liar if she said she didn't like the feel of his hand on her. "I might be attracted to you, but that means nothing."

"I told you, I will have funds—"

Sighing, she stopped and moved to stand in front of him on the sidewalk. "I don't care about money. I don't need you to 'take care of' me. We're far too different to do...anything."

He frowned, watching her for a long moment before his gaze dipped to her mouth. Heat and hunger burned bright, as if he'd completely ignored everything she'd just said. She had the insane urge to lean in and nip that delicious bottom lip. "Do you like ice cream?" he abruptly asked.

"Ah...yes. Chocolate is my favorite. Why?"

"Prima gave me some and I enjoy this chocolate as well. See, we do have some things in common."

She laughed lightly and had started to respond when he straightened subtly and started moving again, wrapping his arm around her shoulders.

It didn't feel possessive, however. It was more protective than anything. And he was hurrying her along.

"What's wrong?" she murmured.

"We are not alone."

That could mean any number of things, but for him to want to move her away from here, he must sense another supernatural. She did too, but...there were supernatural scents everywhere. That in itself was not strange.

"What is this place?" he asked as they passed a large wall and two oversized gates.

"A graveyard. It's where humans bury their dead. This one is closed at night, hence the locked gate."

"No one is inside?"

"I doubt it."

"Good." He looked around, then broke the lock with one hand. "We need to shift and fly."

She wanted to question him, but on this she would trust him. Reaper didn't seem afraid, just concerned. And she would trust his concern—especially since she scented at least half a dozen dragon shifters nearby.

None that she knew either. Which didn't mean anything, but Reaper had her best interests at heart.

That, she would bet her life on.

* * *

Brennus cursed internally as he watched Reaper and the attractive female he had recently learned was part of the Petronilla clan enter the graveyard. This would be the perfect place to attack Reaper but he wasn't certain he could overtake the male. He was certainly strong enough, but he wasn't ready to play his hand just yet. He didn't know enough about the female with him, other than her clan.

He'd thought that Cale of the Cearrach clan would kill Reaper once he scented Reaper on Cynbel's head. But instead, Reaper had met with them and then left. Fucking Cale and Damari should have eliminated him.

Instead of following after Reaper and the female, he called out, using his clanmates' signal, indicating they should return to base.

Changing directions, he soared over the city, his camouflage still firmly in place. Brennus hated that he lived in secret, that all supernaturals did. They were fucking kings. Gods. They should not be living in the shadows, worried that humans might see them. Right now he should be flying over the city in all his glory, with humans watching in fear and awe. Soon they wouldn't hide.

Soon humans would bow to them.

It was the way it had once been, so long ago that the humans of today did not remember. It had not been recorded in their history. Instead dragons were the things of myth, legends.

Soon they would all rise up and his clan would rule *everyone*. For half a century they had been putting their plans into place. His own clan was working with others around the globe.

Technology had expanded far faster than they'd been prepared for. So they had to strike before they were revealed inadvertently, unintentionally. It was a wonder that humans hadn't discovered them already—and it was why there were those stupid bigfoot legends. Some stupid fucking werewolf or bear shifter revealed himself to humans.

Fuck the humans and their pettiness. Their weakness.

The time was upon them. Now that Reaper, the twins and many other ancients had risen, it was time for war. Before he made any decisions, he needed to converse with the rest of his clan—specifically his father. They were spread across the world, working together for the greater good. He did not see the point in waiting any longer. They were ready for the future.

Soon humans would bow before them, would cower in fear at their majesty.

CHAPTER TWELVE

"What's going on?" Greer asked as she returned downstairs, fully dressed yet again. She was getting tired of having to get naked in public because of random situations. Back home this didn't happen often.

Both Prima and Reaper were in the kitchen waiting for her, thankfully. And she wanted her questions answered.

"Ancients are dying," Prima said, pushing up from the center island and crossing her arms over her chest. Her long, inky black hair was wrapped in a tight coil at her neck, and per usual, she had on slim-fitting pants, boots, and a skin-hugging long-sleeved T-shirt.

Reaper was also dressed again and now leaning against the island. He'd clearly dressed much faster than her. He looked almost as good clothed as he did naked. Almost.

"What are you talking about?" Greer asked.

"Earlier we met with two other ancients like us. There were others there," Reaper added. "But only two dragons that Prima and I used to battle alongside."

She listened as they outlined what they'd talked about but for some reason she felt as if they were holding back. Though she couldn't imagine what, considering everything.

"So who do you think was watching us, then?" she asked once he finished.

Reaper glanced at Prima and lifted a shoulder before looking back at Greer. "I honestly do not know. I haven't been awake long enough."

Greer pulled her cell phone out, annoyance bubbling up inside her. "We're calling my Alpha now. And you're going to relay everything to him," she said pointedly, looking directly at Prima. "You should have told him before now."

Prima seemed to sulk for a moment but nodded. "I guess."

"There are certain rules you have to follow," she snapped, because it seemed as if Prima wasn't fully appreciating the situation. "You should know better. And you should have told me the moment you walked back in the house."

"I'd planned to."

"Why didn't you?"

"I…had something else to do. I wanted to go searching for someone and did not feel like getting trapped in a long conversation." Prima sniffed haughtily.

Which made Greer grit her teeth. Ancient or not, Prima was still part of a clan and she had to act like it. Prima and Mira were different in that they had been hatched, not live-born. They were two of the most unique dragons she had ever met but that didn't matter. Clan had to mean something if the two females were going to be a part of it. "That is not a good enough answer."

"You are right, I apologize," she said as Greer scrolled to Conall's name.

"Don't apologize to me. Apologize to Conall."

"I've never seen her get this feisty before. I kinda like it," Prima murmured to Reaper, who was silent.

"I can hear you, Prima." Her phone was ringing already and her Alpha picked up on the second ring. "I'm putting you on speaker. Something happened today that I feel you need to know about, and Reaper and your aunt are going to tell you *everything*."

There was steel in her words and she didn't care. She might be a natural-born nurturer, but she was seriously annoyed that these two had waited so long to tell her and her Alpha these facts. A bunch of ancients dying was serious business. She wasn't going to hold any of this against Reaper. He wasn't part of their clan and didn't really owe them anything. But Prima? Oh, the ancient female was going to drive her mad.

Conall was silent as they outlined their meeting from earlier.

Finally he spoke. "I've recently heard the same thing about ancients dying. We're compiling a list of all known murders. Not only that, a few of our sentinels just spotted a couple unknown dragons around our territory today. I'm hearing from other contacts that there is movement around the globe with dragons. It's subtle, but something has shifted. I'm currently in communication with different packs, clans, and covens around the world. Keep me up to date on anything you find out. And Prima?"

"Yes?"

"I can't get ahold of Mira. Have you spoken to her recently?"

"No, but our psychic link is open. What would you like me to do?"

"Nothing for now. I know she went on a mission and said she might go dark. If you can still feel her, then we're okay."

"What about Vega?" Greer asked, thinking of the young hybrid. Vega was on the same mission in South America that Mira had basically tagged along on.

"I've spoken to her mother and their psychic link is open as well."

"Good." That meant Vega was still alive too.

"I don't care how inconsequential you think something might be, I want to be kept in constant contact if anything changes in New Orleans. Finn and Lyra are nearby if you need anything," he said, referring to Vega's parents who lived only an hour and a half away.

"Have you spoken to King?" Greer asked.

"No. I can't get ahold of him. If that changes, I'll let you know."

"What are you guys holding back?" Greer asked once she'd ended the call.

Both of them looked at her for a long moment and she couldn't tell if they were confused or what.

"What do you mean?" Prima asked while Reaper remained silent.

"I feel like you guys are lying. Or, maybe not lying, but…is there something you didn't tell Conall about the meeting?"

"We have not lied to you," Reaper said. "Your Alpha is now privy to what we discussed with Cale and Damari."

She didn't scent a lie rolling off him. Before she could respond, there was a sharp knock on the front door. They weren't expecting any company. Frowning, she turned to go answer it but Reaper moved so dang fast, sweeping past her in long, sexy strides.

"Stay here." His order was softly spoken.

Of course she ignored him. Moments later in the foyer, she found a very attractive, dark-haired male with Reaper. He was dressed in the same style as Reaper and Prima and it was clear the male was a warrior as well.

When he spotted her, he gave a flirty grin, and stepped forward. He extended a hand as Reaper shut the door behind him. "I'm Damari," he said.

To her surprise, Reaper smacked his hand like one might a misbehaving dog. "You don't touch her."

Greer's eyes widened. "Reaper!"

He didn't look at her, but simply stared at the male, who was definitely a dragon, given his scent.

"Why are you here?" Reaper demanded.

"I asked him to come over and spar with me," Prima said, moving into the foyer as well. She grabbed the other male's wrist and dragged him away from Reaper and Greer.

"You've really got to stop this whole possessive act," Greer snapped out, even though part of her *really* liked it.

He moved in close, using his big body to crowd her back until she was flush up against the closed front door. Suddenly her shirt felt too tight as she tried to drag in breaths.

"I am not acting," he murmured, leaning down and deeply inhaling her scent.

He placed his hands on either side of her head, not touching, but not giving her room to move. Once again he was invading all of her personal space—and it was hard to care. She couldn't think straight as he oh so gently nipped her earlobe between his teeth.

Heat flooded between her legs because this was simply too hot. Too much. Too Reaper.

He was crossing all sorts of boundaries and she should most definitely care but her brain had short-circuited as sensation shot straight to her core, building and building until she wanted to wrap her body around his and ride him until they were both exhausted.

She placed both hands on his chest—his very muscular, defined chest. His muscles tensed under her feather-light touch.

"You smell like heaven," he whispered, his words wrapping around her like a sensual, silky embrace. The low, gravelly quality of his voice sent spirals of heat through her, making thought or words impossible.

She should shove him back, but she really, really didn't want to. Against her better judgment, she slid her hands up his chest and clasped her fingers behind his neck. "Reaper," she whispered, not quite sure where she was going with this. She wanted to tell him to carry her upstairs and to hell with the consequences.

He groaned slightly, rolling his hips against her once.

That was when she felt his very real, very huge reaction to her.

Oh, God. Heat was everywhere now, her nipples tightening into little points as she arched into him. They hadn't even kissed yet and she felt as if she might come apart at the seams.

Or just jump him, getting naked again for very different reasons than earlier today.

Bam! Bam!

She nearly jumped as she felt the front door rumble against her back.

"Greer, it's me!" She recognized Cynara's voice even as she scented Justus and two others. "We've gotta talk."

Reaper let out a rumble, nipping at her neck this time. Oh...God. This was too much and not enough. "I will get rid of them," he growled.

"Um...we can hear you." Cynara sounded confused. "What's going on?"

"Hold on." She pushed at Reaper's chest, fighting the heat flooding her cheeks and knowing it was pointless to try and cover up the scent of her desire. So she was just going to deal with it and move on.

Reaper growled but stepped back. Before she could open the door, he shoved her behind him and opened it himself. Really, the protective thing was sweet, but come on.

She was still a dragon, and these were her friends.

Greer gently nudged Reaper out of the way as Cynara, Justus, Fiona and Ian strode into the foyer. She hadn't realized Fiona and Ian would be here and joy filled her at the sight of them. They were two wonderful supernaturals who had found their way back to each other after being separated for far too long by Fiona's insane family. And Greer's romantic heart simply loved it.

"King is on his way here," Justus said, not bothering with any type of greeting. "We came by to give you a heads-up in person and to hang out for the meeting. Someone has been talking shit about Prima and you." He looked between Reaper and Greer.

"I am not familiar with the phrase 'talking shit' but I understand what this means," Reaper said.

Greer ignored what Justus had said for one moment and pulled Fiona into a hug. "My friend, it is so good to see you." Fiona and Ian were long-distance members of the Petronilla clan, Ian having been basically adopted by Arya as "one of her own," and Greer simply adored both of them.

"I'm so sorry I haven't returned your recent texts. We've had a lot going on." She clasped Greer's hands in her own. "It's why I insisted on coming tonight when Cynara told me they were coming here. I'm pregnant."

Greer realized that fact even as Fiona told her. As a healer, sometimes she simply sensed other life and she could very clearly sense strong life within Fiona. "With twins," she said, smiling.

Fiona blinked, then her smile grew even wider. "Okay, that's crazy that you can do that."

"What the hell are you looking at?" Ian snapped, pulling Greer out of her conversation with Fiona. Both she and Fiona turned to stare at him in shock at his harsh tone. Ian was staring hard at Reaper, his dragon lurking in his gaze.

Reaper frowned at the male. "I was looking at you."

Ian rolled his eyes. "Yeah, no kidding. Cut it out. And step away from my female."

Fiona let out an exasperated sigh and placed a hand on Ian's forearm. "We've talked about this."

"I know we talked about it, but I don't care. I don't know this guy and I don't like the way he's watching me. And he's too close to you."

Greer looked at Reaper, who simply lifted his shoulders, clearly confused by Ian's reaction.

"His mate is pregnant," Greer murmured, though he must have overheard her and Fiona speaking. And males could go absolutely crazy when their mates became pregnant. The normally relaxed Ian was a perfect example of that. She'd never heard him speak to anyone the way he was speaking to Reaper.

"I respect your need to protect your female." Reaper stepped back a few feet. "I will keep ten feet from her at all times."

"Oh my God," Fiona muttered even as Cynara snickered.

But Justus and Ian simply nodded, as if this was totally normal. Someone save her from mated males.

Ian seemed to relax after that, the tension in his shoulders easing as he wrapped an arm around Fiona's shoulders and pulled her close.

"Let's get back to the whole reason we're here," Justus said. "Where's Prima?"

"She's in the backyard sparring with another dragon."

"Fine, let's grab her. I only want to have this conversation once."

It only took a few minutes to gather everyone in the kitchen, and Greer noticed that Reaper did sneak a few glances at Ian, watching him curiously.

She wanted to tell Reaper about Ian's dragon coloring when he was in shifted form, but now definitely wasn't the time. Not after the weird way Ian had snapped at Reaper. If she had to bet money, however, she would almost guarantee these two were somehow related. But she didn't know enough about Reaper's clan, and Ian wasn't connected to his original one.

Justus eyed Damari curiously as everyone gathered around. "Who are you?" Introductions were quickly made, but Justus continued. "Do you trust him?"

Prima shrugged and Reaper nodded even as he ordered Damari to stand away from both Fiona and Greer.

"That will have to do, then. Someone is spreading rumors about Reaper and Prima, stating that they are in New Orleans to carve out some territory. That they are recently woken ancients who have decided this is the territory they will claim for their own."

Prima simply snorted and Reaper kept his expression neutral.

"Who's starting these rumors?" Greer asked. Because that was all that really mattered.

"I'm not sure," Cynara said. "But I heard whispers about it at the club earlier tonight. Then I heard people talking about King heading this way to see who Prima and Reaper are. Apparently he's putting some credence in the rumor."

Reaper looked completely unconcerned but Greer knew exactly how things could get out of hand if a bunch of Alphas got together in one room and someone said the wrong thing.

It would be chaos.

"We will simply talk to him once he arrives." Reaper's tone was as unconcerned as his expression. He stood next to Greer, barely giving her a couple inches of space.

She'd tried to move over a couple times, but he was liquid smooth, moving with her so subtly she barely noticed it.

Justus nodded. "I figured as much. But we're still going to be here as backup because he will definitely bring his packmates."

It didn't surprise her when Prima snorted as if highly amused. "Thank you for staying as backup," she said, though it was more like she was talking to a child than a trained general. She might as well have patted him on the head.

Justus tightened his jaw, but instead of responding let out a breath, as if restraining himself.

"I'm a half-demon," Ian snapped, surprising everyone in the room, his Irish accent sharp and deadly.

Greer turned to look at him in surprise, unsure what was going on with the normally cool-headed male.

"You keep staring at me, and I know you're trying to figure out what I am," Ian said, directing his annoyance at Reaper.

"I was not trying to figure out what you are. I already know—you are a hybrid with demon and dragon capabilities. But your scent smells somehow familiar to me. I was trying to figure out why."

"Honey," Fiona said, placing a hand on the middle of Ian's chest. "We need level heads tonight."

When the giant male looked down at her, his expression softened completely. And Greer's heart ached, wishing she had that for herself.

At the sound of the front door opening, they all stilled.

It seemed as if King would not be knocking and acting civil. Tonight was off to a great start.

Just freaking great.

CHAPTER THIRTEEN

Reaper immediately went to stand in front of Greer as the Alpha named King, with brown skin and a sharp buzz cut, strode in. Behind him, half a dozen of his wolves followed into the kitchen as if they owned the place. His dragon immediately pushed to the surface, the scent of all these unknown threats in the room near Greer shoving at his control.

"Everyone listen up," Greer snapped out, making the room go quiet in surprise. She pointed at herself. "I am a healer and part of the Petronilla clan. She," she said, pointing at Fiona, "is pregnant. You guys know clan and pack rules. You will not act like jackasses and put anyone in danger." Next she pointed at Reaper, Prima and then King. "Everyone except you three will leave this room. Go to the living room or the backyard or just leave altogether and go get ice cream. I don't care. But you rude wolves will not just march into our home and expect to be accommodated."

King paused for a moment, then nodded at his wolves, who silently strode out of the kitchen and toward the backyard. The others did the same so they clearly weren't going far.

But just like that, the tension in the room eased a fraction. Reaper looked at Greer with a new respect. Her steel spine was impressive. He wondered if she

149

would order him around in the bedroom, order him to taste between her legs. *No.* He must not think of such things. Not now anyway. But later he would.

"I apologize for barging into your clan's home like this," King said, his faint accent one Reaper couldn't place, his tone and expression casual. Wearing a black leather jacket, black pants and boots, there wasn't an ounce of apology in his scent. He was arrogant, if anything.

"You are definitely not sorry," Greer said, exasperation in her words. But just as quickly she smiled. And the most possessive part of Reaper did *not* like that she was smiling at this wolf who might be considered handsome. "It's nice to see you again, however."

The Alpha smiled back at her, all charm and arrogance. "Likewise."

Oh, Reaper did not like this male. His dragon wanted to claw his face off for smiling at Greer. Claw it off, then rip his heart from his chest. Yes, his dragon thought, he would make a nice snack.

"King, this is Reaper and Prima." She added a bit more to the introductions then ordered everybody to sit in that haughty little tone of hers that Reaper liked far more than he should.

Reaper wanted to pull her into his lap, to keep her as close to him as possible. But he knew she wouldn't like that at all, so he simply sat but made sure it was close to her.

"I've been hearing fairly substantial rumors that you two are looking to carve out some territory here."

King's words were neutral enough but his wolf was in his eyes as he looked between the two of them.

"The territory isn't taken," Prima said simply because she liked to bait others.

Under normal circumstances, Reaper might have enjoyed watching this play out, but not with Greer in the room. And a pregnant female nearby. No, this would not do. "Prima." Reaper gave her a hard look. "Is this necessary?"

She lifted a shoulder, grinning. "No, but it is fun." Sighing, she looked back at the Alpha. "I have a clan, and while this city is pleasant enough to visit, I'm not looking to take any of this territory—unclaimed as it is."

King looked at Reaper then, eyebrows raised.

"Nor am I," Reaper said. "I have been awake for only a week. I have no desire to take any of the land here." Then he looked at Greer, thinking that he would only live where she lived. Since this was not her home, it would not be his either.

She looked at him, but quickly glanced away, her cheeks turning pink. Oh yes, he liked that very much.

The Alpha was silent for a long moment. "So why is someone spreading rumors about you? Because normally I can brush them off, but these came from decent sources."

"As I said, I have not been awake long. So I do not know. Perhaps someone seeks to sow dissent in your city? Perhaps the rumors are for your benefit only."

"Perhaps." Reaper noticed that King did not deny it was his city. "Do you have any enemies I should know about?"

"I'm sure I have a lot of enemies." Something Prima was not concerned about.

Reaper simply shrugged because he wasn't going to repeat himself that he hadn't been awake long. He did not like being questioned in general and he did not know this wolf. His tolerance would only go so far.

King looked exasperated as he glanced between the two of them. "If you're not looking to carve out territory, we have no problem." Adjusting his jacket, he stood from his chair. "But things are changing, and soon enough this territory won't be neutral anymore. So you can tell your Alpha that." He looked to Greer then, his expression sharp.

Moving quickly, Reaper was off his seat and standing in front of her. It might be forbidden for shifters to hurt healers but assholes did not always follow the rules. And Reaper would bring this house down around King's head if he looked at Greer like that again.

To his surprise, King simply grinned at the two of them. "That's what I thought."

Reaper didn't care if the male knew how he felt about Greer. It wasn't a secret and he wasn't going to hide it.

"Clearly you two have enemies," King said. "If you have trouble with someone, let me know. Cynara will know how to contact me." Then he turned away from them, not afraid to give them his back.

Considering the substantial power Reaper felt rolling off the wolf, he could understand the arrogance. Hopefully he would be a good Alpha for this region. Reaper did not believe in having neutral territories anyway. All territories needed to have a leader or they eventually devolved into chaos.

Within seconds, the Alpha's wolves strode through the kitchen, following after him.

Greer let out a long breath as the door shut behind them.

"Well that could have gone differently," Cynara said, striding back into the room with the others.

"I could have ripped his head off for speaking to you like that," Reaper said to Greer. He was still tempted to go after the wolf, even if the male had simply been baiting Reaper.

Greer patted him once on the chest. "Simmer down."

He liked the feel of her touching him so he did not respond. Just stayed still, hoping she would keep her hand on him. And maybe move it a bit lower.

As if she sensed his thoughts, she turned to look at him, her eyes narrowing.

He simply grinned until she dropped her hand.

* * *

Greer's heart was still racing even though King and his wolves were gone. She had no doubt that her clanmates and friends here could have taken on the wolves.

154 | KATIE REUS

But everyone would have been injured and some potentially killed. And that kind of bloodshed in the middle of the city? No one wanted that. It was such a balance for supernaturals, maintaining the peace. Especially when they had to keep their existence hidden from humans. "Fiona, Ian? I would like to talk to both of you alone."

Reaper frowned at her but she ignored him. Something she had to force herself to do, because ignoring such a sexy, enigmatic male was damn near impossible. The way he'd jumped in front of her when King had been acting like an ass was sweet.

Once she was outside on the back patio with the mated couple, she sat at the large, rectangular table with them. "You guys are part of our clan even though you don't live with us," she said, stating the obvious because she wanted to set the tone for this conversation. "With your news today, I realized I haven't checked in with you nearly enough, especially considering the way you've been acting tonight." She arched a brow at Ian. "It seems I need to."

Fiona let out a sigh of relief, reaching out to squeeze Ian's hand. "He's been stressed out because of the pregnancy."

Ian simply gave her a strained nod. His espresso-colored hair had grown a little bit longer since the last time she'd seen him and he had scruff on his face. His amber eyes glowed with far too many emotions right now.

"Talk to me. Tell me what's going on."

"I'm fine." But when his eyes shifted to his demon side, then dragon, then human, flickering out of control, she knew he was lying.

Greer reached across the table and took one of his hands in hers. She could feel the tension rolling off him. "You're not fine, so let's not pretend otherwise. I'm not going to force you to talk to me right now, but the door is open. And if you're willing, I can inject some of my healing gift to calm you. Sort of like human drugs but no weird aftereffects. I won't do anything you don't want, but I don't like what I'm seeing from you, Ian. You've got to be a rock for Fiona right now."

He was silent for a long moment as she withdrew her hands. Finally he spoke. "I lost Fiona for so long and I'm terrified that something is going to happen to her and the babies." His Irish accent, normally faint, was thick now as emotions choked him. "I'm afraid that they'll be taken from me somehow. I've…been having nightmares."

"Oh, honey." Fiona leaned into him and wrapped her arms around him in a big hug. "We're not going anywhere."

Sighing, he returned her hug as he laid his chin on top of her head, inhaling deeply. "Knowing that doesn't make the nightmares any better."

Greer stood and smiled at both of them. "You two need to talk more." Clearly. "Don't keep things bottled up inside, Ian. Talk to your mate. You're a team and you support each other. And don't forget that I'm here. Even though you live hundreds of miles away, I am still your healer. Please come to me for anything. I can't force you, but I'd like to do a phone conference once a week to check in right now."

Ian paused, then nodded. "I'm okay with that. And...I'm sorry I was a dick to your friend."

Greer brushed it off. "He's a big boy. It's fine." She still wanted to tell Ian about her suspicions but now wasn't the time. Ian and Fiona needed some privacy. "If you feel like it, come share a drink with us before you guys leave."

"Thank you," Ian murmured.

Once inside the living room, Greer found Reaper waiting. For her, she guessed. She'd assumed he'd be in the kitchen with the others talking about King's visit and trying to narrow down who was talking trash about him and Prima.

Nope, he was waiting in front of the massive fireplace instead, his arm stretched out on the mantel, looking all sexy and good enough to eat. He surprised her by staying where he was, just watching her.

Dang it. "I assumed you'd be trying to figure out who was making false claims about you." She needed to keep the conversation on anything other than the way he was staring at her with unbridled hunger.

He blinked once, his dragon eyes disappearing to be replaced by bright green-amber eyes she wanted to drown in. "Prima has decided to go find out who the liars are. By her own admission she plans to 'bash some heads in and make people scream in agony as I set them on fire.'"

Greer wanted to be surprised, she really did. But that sounded about right. "And you didn't want to partake in the fun?"

"The only fun I want to have is between your legs."

"Reaper!" Once again, he seemed to just say what was in his head. And it was all about her.

He shoved away from the mantel, covering the distance between them in seconds. "You would have let me take you up against the door earlier. Or at least demanded I carry you upstairs. Deny it."

She shook her head, because she couldn't. Because she'd wanted just that. To find privacy with him and completely lose herself with Reaper.

When he took another step toward her, she held up a hand, needing distance. "Look, I…like you. A lot." Far more than she should. "But we have things we need to deal with right now. Your former friend is dead and someone is going around spreading rumors about you. Tonight could have ended very differently if King had been less levelheaded."

"Yes, he could be dead right now." He was all arrogant confidence.

"I don't think we need to…explore anything between us right now."

"Explore?"

"You understand exactly what I'm saying. We need to…not…" *Ugh.* She couldn't even think, let alone make complete sentences around him right now. She sounded like an idiot. "We're not having sex," she finally rushed out.

He lifted an eyebrow. "Right now."

She wanted to say *ever*, but couldn't find the word. Because she wasn't sure she believed it herself. Getting involved with this dragon would only bring her heartache, however.

"How are your friends? The ones outside?" he finally asked, breaking the tension.

She blinked, surprised by his question. But she liked that he'd asked because she could tell the question was sincere. "Oh…they're fine. But thank you for asking. What you said back there in the kitchen, about Ian's scent being familiar. How so?"

He shrugged. "I cannot explain it, he just has a familiar scent. It is pleasing to my dragon."

Hmm. "Okay. Let me say goodbye to Cynara and Justus. I'm sure they're ready to get out of here." Greer could hear them talking in the kitchen in undertones. "Did your friend Damari leave already?"

"He left before Prima." Reaper watched her closely, not backing up or giving her any personal space.

God, it was impossible to breathe around him. She simply nodded and left the room.

"So are you going to jump that fine dragon?" Cynara asked as Greer walked her to the main gate at the end of the driveway.

"Are you going to mate with Justus?"

"Ouch, okay." Cynara grinned and gave her a hug. "I guess I deserved that."

Greer glanced back up the driveway to see Reaper and Justus talking by the front door, their words too low to overhear even with her supernatural hearing. She kept her own voice low as she turned back to Cynara. "He loves you and he wants to spend forever with you. This is the only advice I'll give. Don't wait too long or someone else will snap him up." Greer wasn't sure that was true because Justus had eyes for no one but Cynara. But she didn't want her friend to lose out on mating because of her fears. Of course, Greer should probably listen to her own advice, but things were far different where Reaper and her were concerned. There had been no hint of the mating manifestation, so what she was feeling was raw lust, nothing more. It wouldn't be smart to pursue anything with him.

Cynara simply made a humming sound and shrugged.

Okay, she didn't want to talk about it. Greer respected that. She just wanted her friend to be happy.

By the time she said goodbye to Justus, Cynara, then Ian and Fiona, who followed after them, and returned to the house, Reaper wasn't waiting for her.

She fought the disappointment coursing through her and sent her own Alpha a message about what had happened with King and the others.

Because Conall was right—no matter how small something seemed, he needed to be kept in the loop. Something was going on right now and she hated that they couldn't figure out what it was.

No matter that Reaper was so nonchalant about everything, she didn't like that ancients were dying across the globe and that someone was now trying to start trouble for him and Prima. She wasn't sure the two things were connected, but either way she didn't like them.

She didn't want anything bad to happen to Reaper. The male was definitely growing on her.

Okay, more than growing on her. He was under her skin and all she could think about. Even as she stripped off her clothes and got in the shower, the hot jets of water pulsing everywhere, all she could think about was what it would feel like to have his hands on her, his cock inside her as his mouth devoured her own.

Oh, she was in trouble. So. Much. Trouble.

Once she'd dried off and slipped under the covers of the huge bed, there was a knock on her door. Even without calling out, she knew who it was. "Yes?"

"Go on a date with me tomorrow?" Reaper asked.

"Date?"

"I am told that is what it is called. I would like to take you out and get to know you better away from interruptions and other supernaturals." His voice was seductive, luring her in.

But...ancients had been murdered and someone was spreading rumors about him and Prima. She should say no, but...there was always going to be something going wrong, and her dragon had released her claws and was threatening a revolt if she said no. "Okay." The response was out before she could stop herself. And really, she didn't want to. At this point, she had to stop trying to fool herself because her dragon was having none of it. They'd go on a date and if something happened, well, it happened. She was a grown woman.

And he was trouble.

CHAPTER FOURTEEN

Standing, Brennus looked at the six men seated around the long, rectangular table. Behind him, four screens were on as they waited for his fellow clan-mates to join them for this conference call.

Humans and their technology did have a purpose after all.

A moment later, the first image blinked on-screen, then the next, then all of the individuals on the screen looked back at him and his people.

His father was on the top left screen, his expression formidable. "Let's get right to this. Ancients are waking up faster than we predicted and we can't kill them all. So we need to make our move now. We need to establish dominance in our chosen territories."

"How soon?" he asked, nodding once in respect at his father. This was the moment he'd been waiting for. Hell would soon rain down on humans. It was time to take their rightful place.

"Two days. Max. Perhaps sooner. Too many clans have spotted our sentries scouting their land, and if they communicate regularly, this won't end well for us. We must strike now that we are all aligned and ready.

"Is everything in place?"

His father paused. "More or less. Our numbers are many and we are *dragons*. The humans and other shifters will bow to us. Once we create chaos and disable all nuclear sites, the world is ours for the taking."

As it should be. "What about Abana?" he asked, referring to an ancient who had recently risen in Africa. The female had been friends with the twins—the only known dragon twins hatched into existence. Abana was still a wild card as far as Brennus was concerned. Reaper, the twins, and certain dragons around the globe they already knew would never work alongside them so his clan had dismissed them as possible allies. But Abana? They were undecided on her.

"She will be a strong ally or a dead foe. She gets to decide."

That didn't exactly answer Brennus's question, which pissed him off, but he held his temper. His father was Alpha after all.

His father continued. "Also, Mira will be taken care of soon."

He knew that Mira was in South America...for some reason. She was there with a male they did not trust. August McGuire. The male had too many ties to the US human government. He had far too many allies, with humans and supernaturals alike—all over the globe. He was part bear and part something else. Brennus didn't trust hybrids to begin with, but he really didn't trust August—it was impossible to truly trust the male without knowing his other nature. "Good. I take it the plan is the same as always?"

They were to wreak havoc on supernatural-run territories, creating death and destruction at a maximum capacity and ensure as many humans died as possible. At the same time they would neutralize all nuclear sites and take over as many news outlets as possible. They would also be taking down satellites, creating even more chaos. At first.

Then they would rule. They wouldn't take down *all* satellites or communications. No, they wanted to live in a civilized society. Just one where humans knew their place.

His own part in this would be simple enough: unleash Hell in New Orleans. Then they would strike down those who sought to help humans, eliminating his clan's main problem. Humans were nothing but weak, ineffectual creatures. But all supernaturals wouldn't fall in line—they would want to help the weak humans. So his clan had to eliminate as many of them as possible right out of the gate. Establish dominance. Then rule with an iron fist.

"Yes. I will confirm the exact time and date, but plan on two days from now." His father started barking out orders to everyone, making it clear they'd better handle their own territories. Then he disconnected and the other members on video did the same.

Brennus turned to face the room, looking at the males and females before him. "We need to take care of our territory. That means targeting King and Cynara."

"Why the hybrid?" asked the male closest to him.

"Because the hybrid has four powerful brothers. She needs to die. Or we capture her and use her later. Yes…capture the hybrid instead. She may be valuable. But if necessary, kill her." Cynara, a vampire-demon hybrid, was strong in her own right. Born of a demon king, she had power in her for certain.

But so did he. So did his clan. They. Were. Dragons.

"We need to take out Prima and Reaper," another of his clanmates said.

"Not Reaper yet." No, definitely not yet.

"Why not?" the same clanmate asked.

"Because my intel says he's close to mating with a female. A *healer*." He spat the word. "Once they're mated, we will simply go after her. Kill her, then he's dead too." And it would easily eliminate one of his problems. Prima was another issue altogether, but her twin wasn't with her. She would go down eventually.

They would simply have to attack her when she was isolated. Attack as a team until there was nothing left.

The battle here wouldn't be easy, but they would prevail.

He had no doubt. They'd been planning this for half a century. Everything was in place to take over.

Soon they would be recognized as the gods they were.

CHAPTER FIFTEEN

Greer rolled over at the sound of her phone buzz-
ing. It was only four in the morning. She snagged
it, worried because she'd never heard Prima come in.
But it was Camden. "Yeah?"

"Hey, sorry to call so early."

"It's fine. I know you keep weird hours. What's up?"

"I found something interesting on Cynbel. I've seen
some movement on his cell phone so even if the guy is
dead, his cell phone isn't. You'll be able to track the
phone from your own with what I'm going to send you.
Just download the app."

She shoved the covers off and sat up fully. "Thank
you, that's great news." Maybe whoever had killed him
had taken it. Though that seemed like such a stupid
move for someone strong enough to kill a dragon. Not
that strength equaled brains, so maybe.

"So how is it down in New Orleans? Is Prima behaving herself?"

She laughed lightly as she stretched. "Define behaving herself."

"Oh?"

"I'm kidding. She's fine. She's…Prima. She probably
cracked some skulls early this morning. Her words, not
mine."

168 | KATIE REUS

Camden let out a loud laugh. "I would expect nothing less... We miss you."

Though she needed to go find Reaper and tell him what Camden had told her, she leaned back against her pillow for a second. Moonlight filtered in through the drapes, giving the huge canopy bed an ethereal feel. "I miss you guys too. How is everyone? I haven't got much gossip, since I've been here."

"You know how it is. Everybody's trying to basically stay healthy and not bother Victoria."

She smiled at that. Of course they were because they were a good clan. "Staying healthy" basically meant not getting injured during sparring sessions so Victoria wouldn't have to use any of her healer's energy. Victoria had recently had a baby, and though she'd healed quickly—something she deserved after having one of the longest pregnancies in shifter history—she needed some down time.

"So what's up with you and the ancient?" Camden asked slyly.

"What are you talking about?"

"Come on. You know supernaturals better than that, and I've heard little tendrils of gossip that something might be happening with you guys. Are you two hooking up?"

"I'm not answering any questions about this at four in the morning. Good night." She ended the call. Because that was the only way to shut something like this down. Of course she'd probably only stoked the fires of gossip now. She was finding it hard to care, however.

Even with her own baggage, with what had happened all those years ago, it was so hard to deny the attraction between her and Reaper. Not just hard—impossible.

Shaking off remnants of the past, of a warrior male who'd wanted to control her, she quickly dressed, brushed her teeth and pulled her hair into a ponytail before going to find the sexy ancient consuming her thoughts.

She didn't even get a chance to knock on his door before it swung open. Looking far too good, he leaned against the doorframe, completely shirtless as he crossed his arms over his massive chest.

It took her a long moment to find her voice. "I take it I didn't wake you?"

He simply shook his head, his gaze raking over her face, down the length of her and back up in a slow, hungry crawl. Heat infused her entire body as she tried to find her voice again. "I just got a call from Camden—"

He started growling.

She blinked. "Camden is my clan's hacker. Ring a bell?"

The growl stopped.

"As I was saying, Camden called and said there's movement on Cynbel's cell phone." At his confused expression, she shook her head. "I'll explain it in a minute. Just grab a shirt and let's get out of here." Even though covering up all that sexiness seemed like a crime.

It didn't take long for him to dress before they got on the road.

"Can you explain how we're finding his cell phone?" Reaper asked from the passenger seat of the SUV.

Even though this vehicle was huge, somehow it seemed tiny with him inside. It was like he simply sucked up all the space with his presence.

She glanced over from the driver's seat. Since it was after four in the morning and sunrise was still a short ways off, the streets seemed extra-quiet right now. Even for a city like New Orleans. "Honestly, I'm not entirely certain. Camden is from a much younger generation than mine. He's barely fifty years old and he has a knack for technology. He can do things most people of his generation cannot. He tried to explain it to me once but I swear my brain shut down listening to him. I can use my computer and do basic things but what he does is on another level."

"You sound impressed."

"I am. And from what I gather, he has used some sort of location device or application or something to ping where the phone is."

"Ping?"

She grinned and shrugged. "His word, not mine."

"Did Prima ever contact you?" He looked out the side window, glancing out over the street.

A few tree branches draped with gauzy Spanish moss swayed with the breeze, the little beads and trinkets caught in the branches moving as well. "No. I texted her but she told me she was busy and left it at that."

"I am certain she is fine," he said.

She snorted. "Oh I'm sure she's fine. It's the entire city I'm worried about. So did you and Prima ever…" She let the question hang in the air, her intent clear.

He frowned at her. "Did we what?"

"Have sex?"

He blinked, clearly taken off guard. Then his mouth curved up into a slow, seductive grin. "Would you care if we had?"

"Yes. No. I'm not certain how to answer that." There was no sense in lying.

"No. We have never. Both she and Mira were always good friends. We have very similar outlooks on the world."

"Can I ask you something else personal?"

He nodded as they pulled up to a stop sign. She glanced at her cell phone to see they were getting closer on the map to the app's GPS location. "I know that they were hatched as opposed to born. Were you?"

He nodded once. "I was."

She took that information in, realizing how very different he was even from someone like her. It didn't matter that they were both dragon shifters, he was much more in touch with his animal side than her. She wasn't really surprised though, not when it came down to it. He hadn't made a secret of who he was. No, he was the Dragon of War.

"May I ask you something personal now?" he asked.

"Of course," she said, making a left onto a narrow side street lined with shotgun-style houses. There were bars on some of the windows but others were freshly painted and their small front yards—if they could even be called that, given the limited space—were well-maintained. It was interesting to see how much of the city was being restored one neighborhood at a time.

"Why do you fight the attraction between us? It can't be simply because I annoyed you when we first met."

Her fingers flexed around the steering wheel once as she made another turn. "It's not that. I was in a serious relationship many years ago. Many hundreds of years ago in fact. He was a warrior, like you."

He growled low in his throat in that way that sent tingles of awareness spiraling throughout her. Why did she like it so much?

"Okay, I don't mean he was like *you*, I just mean he was a warrior. But he was very arrogant, like you. And he tried to order me around, tried to make me into something I wasn't. He thought because I'm a healer that I would be subservient, sort of a beta, I guess. It was borderline abusive and some part of me thought that I could change him. The grown-up Greer knows how impossibly stupid and wrong that is, but I was young at the time and thought I was in love."

"Is he dead?" Reaper's words were more animal than man, his dragon prowling just beneath the surface.

Surprised, she slowed the vehicle as they came to a stop sign. "I have no idea. It was so long ago. The last I heard he had gone into Hibernation. He could be alive or dead." And the truth was, she didn't care one way or another.

"You never cared enough to do research on him." It was a smug statement, not a question, and he seemed supremely satisfied by this knowledge.

Even though he hadn't asked her, she answered anyway. "That is correct. I haven't thought about him for a long time. And it wasn't love. It was infatuation more than anything. But being with him made me realize that there is a certain type of male out there for me."

"Yes, there is. Me."

The laugh escaped at his confidence. "You really are arrogant."

"That is true. But I would never try to change you. I like you just the way you are. And I do not think there is a subservient bone in your body. I liked the way you spoke to the wolf Alpha. You sounded like a general giving orders. It was one of the sexiest things I have ever seen."

Her cheeks flushed and she was grateful for the darkness of the interior of the vehicle. Ignoring his statement, she turned down another side street to find a huge construction site. Two townhomes sitting side by side had been gutted and there was a big dumpster in front of the houses. Her stomach sank, as she realized where this was going. Someone had likely tossed the phone here.

"I think this is a dead-end but we'll check it out anyway. It's likely in that dumpster." She pointed toward it, frustrated. "We know Cynbel is dead regardless."

"Will you stay put while I search?" he asked, and something told her it took all of his self-control to ask and *not* order her.

She nodded as he got out of the vehicle and did a quick search of the area. He might not be familiar with everything in this period, but he knew what a phone looked like. It didn't take long until he came back with the smartphone. "Can your hacker friend do anything with this?"

"I don't know. That's a good question." She quickly dialed Camden who answered on the first ring. He told her to courier him the phone just in case he could scrape information from it.

"Would you like to go get food?" Reaper asked after she finished her call with Camden.

"I could eat." She only needed a few hours of sleep anyway and being with him had her all keyed up. "Plus I need coffee."

"This does not count as our date. I am still taking you out tonight."

She lifted an eyebrow at his tone. "Oh yeah?"

"I mean...I would still like to take you out tonight." Still not a question.

"You could decide after breakfast that you don't want to go out on a date with me."

He shot her a look that said she'd lost her mind. Which made more warmth spread through her. Damn hormones.

"Are your parents in Hibernation, or still in Montana?" he asked as she plugged in the address for a nearby diner.

She loved the way he stretched out the syllables of Montana. "My mother was killed in a cross-dragon battle. It was long ago. So they both died." Which of course he would know, as he was a dragon.

"Ah. It was the same with mine. My father was struck down in battle and my mother went down at the same time. I avenged them, however."

Of course he had. "It's been so long but I miss my parents still," she said quietly. Something she hadn't admitted even to herself in a long time. It had been centuries; she should be less connected to them. But...that wasn't how life worked.

"I miss mine too." He seemed surprised by his own admission. "Their death is part of the reason I left my clan. There were too many reminders of them there."

She glanced at him as she pulled up to a stoplight. "There's something I need to tell you."

"What?"

She turned left as the GPS ordered. "I think you and Ian might be related somehow. I have seen him in his dragon form and his colors are similar to yours. Very similar. They are so unique and beautiful, so it was hard to miss."

Reaper stilled. "You think my dragon is beautiful?"

"I do." No need to deny it.

"That is interesting about Ian," he continued. "He does not live with his clan?"

176 | KATIE REUS

"No, he does not. He's officially part of my clan, though he lives not far from here. His mate rejected her own clan for so many reasons and now she's considered part of ours as well. But her work keeps her where she is. She's been established for a long time."

"It explains why his scent was familiar to me." He nodded slowly as if digesting this information. "Have you told him?"

"No. They seem to have a lot on their plate with the pregnancy. But I felt weird keeping the information to myself."

"Thank you for telling me."

She smiled as they pulled into the diner parking lot, her stomach rumbling, making her cheeks flushed. She was very clearly hungry.

Though she was definitely hungry for more than just food. Something she would not think about right now.

Greer enjoyed breakfast with Reaper. He was amusing and seemed oblivious to how insanely sexy he was. The diner hadn't been full but there had been enough people inside who'd given him a few second and third glances. Which was understandable. He was huge by human standards—and dragon standards. He looked like he could be one of those football players. She couldn't stop staring at him either, and breakfast was over far too soon.

The drive back was short and uneventful, the streets still quiet. As they strode up to the front door of the mansion, they nearly ran into Prima, who must have just shifted to her human form because she was naked and carrying a bundle of clothing.

She smiled when she saw them, unconcerned about her nudity or anything else. "Where are you two getting in from?"

"I think the question is where are *you* getting in from?" Greer asked, the scent of sex filling the air. Oh sweet dragons, the scent was wild and everywhere.

Prima grinned widely. "I think you know the answer to that. And now I am hungry and exhausted. So I will see you two later. Do not bother me unless something is on fire."

As she hurried past them, the wild scents lingered in the air. For some reason, the scents went to Greer's head.

And it very definitely affected Reaper. But if she was going to see if there was anything between them, she wasn't going to base a relationship solely on sex. She'd done that before and it had gotten nowhere. Of course she'd never felt for anyone like she did for him. She and her dragon were completely aligned right now, which was sort of frustrating. He was so damn unexpected.

He was...

Mine, her dragon snapped.

Mine, mine, mine.

They both stared at each other for a long moment, then Reaper moved so quickly she barely tracked him.

Growling low in his throat, his green-amber eyes bright, he wrapped his arms around her, pulling her

178 | KATIE REUS

close—possessively, protectively. "If you tell me to walk away, I will," he murmured.

She slid her hands up his chest, swallowing hard. It had been so long and she'd never felt like this before. She shook her head.

"Say the words." A demanding order.

Heat flooded her core. "Stay. Kiss me." How was that for telling him what she wanted?

He crushed his mouth to hers, his tongue invading like a conquering warrior. She'd thought he might build up to it, but he simply took what he wanted. And she loved every second of it.

She wrapped her arms and legs around him as he hoisted her up. She couldn't seem to get close enough. Suddenly they were moving to...somewhere.

Seconds later she found herself flat on her back on a giant rug in front of a long unused fireplace. She let out a delighted laugh as he covered her body with his, his expression purely wicked.

She wasn't sure what she was ready for but she liked this position, liked the weight of him on top of her. And she loved the way he stared at her as if she'd hung the moon.

She reached for him, wrapping her fingers around the back of his neck even as he slanted his mouth over hers once again.

In the back of her head she thought that they should probably find a bedroom or somewhere more private, but screw it.

They were supernaturals. Prima had told them not to disturb her. And she would be able to hear them and stay away because nothing could drag Greer away from this moment.

From Reaper.

She questioned her sanity as he slid his hands under her sweater, quickly and expertly pulling it off. His fingers stroked over her skin, sending shivers spiraling everywhere.

He might have been in Hibernation for a long damn time but he clearly knew what he wanted. Her.

Well, she wanted him undressed too, wanted to feel all that strength against her fingertips. She nipped at his bottom lip as his hands slid over her breasts, her bra. Teasing, hungry, determined.

"What the hell is this thing?" he growled out against her mouth as he lifted his head, staring down at her bra. Before she could answer, one of his claws slipped out and he sliced it through the middle without touching her skin.

She let out a little gasp as her breasts spilled free.

"Mine," he growled.

Her gasp turned into a moan as he bent his head and sucked one of her nipples into his mouth. No buildup, just pure wicked Reaper taking what he wanted. God, why was that so hot?

Heat surrounded her, the energy inside her waking up, little arcs of electricity flickering against her skin. This was all strange and new, this wild sensation, and she wasn't sure if it was just that she hadn't had sex in ages, or something else. Something…more. Something she didn't want to think about right now.

He lifted his head once, his eyes sparking with heat before he kissed her again, harder this time.

As their mouths mated, she wondered why the hell she'd been fighting this so hard. Then he cupped her breasts, teasing her nipples into hard little points as he rolled his hips against hers.

Slam!

She jerked at the sound of… Something breaking apart.

Before she had processed what was going on, Reaper was on his feet, his claws out. Covering her breasts, she jumped up next to him and stared into the entryway where their front door was in tatters.

Before she could say anything, a large bearded male with red hair strode into the foyer, actually breathing fire. He was in human form, but little wisps of fire came out of his mouth as he turned to face them. *Holy cats.*

The male let out a loud growl until he saw Reaper. His claws retracted and the fire turned to smoke. "Reaper?" The male had a thick Celtic accent and similar coloring to Reaper. "What are you doing here?"

Reaper still had his claws out as he eyed the male, strategically placing his body in front of Greer's half-naked one. "Me? What the fuck are you doing!" Reaper roared, his beast clearly riding close to the surface.

Greer scrambled to grab her sweater for cover, though she had to shrug out of her ruined bra before putting it on.

By the time she'd stood back up, Prima was at the bottom of the stairs, her own eyes full dragon.

She raised an eyebrow as she looked at the mess. "Arthur, what is this?"

"You leave my bed and steal my watch?" he snarled, taking a menacing step toward her.

She lifted up her wrist, the sparkly gold watch glinting under the light from the foyer. "I like this timepiece. It's shiny—and it's now mine."

"Why did you leave my bed?" the male demanded.

She lifted a shoulder, her eyes glinting mischievously. "I got what I wanted. And so did you for that matter. Why are you here? Did you follow me?"

"I wasn't done," he snarled. "And you're *not* keeping my watch."

She sniffed, all haughty dragon. "We'll see about that."

"Fine. Keep the watch, but you're coming with me."

She stepped down the rest of the stairs until she was at the bottom and nearly eye to eye with him, given that she was almost as tall as the giant dragon shifter. "You don't give me orders."

"You like it when I give orders." The male's words were softly spoken, but loud enough for Greer to hear.

Prima snarled once. "You are going to fix this door. Now. Then I'll see about joining you in bed again."

The male snarled once more, more fire coming out of his mouth. "Fine. It will be fixed within the hour. When it's done, you'd better be back at my place. Naked."

182 | KATIE REUS

Prima simply sniffed and turned back toward the stairs but not before shooting a curious glance at Greer and Reaper.

Oh, she was curious about *them*? Seriously? Greer stared at the mess in the foyer, wondering who the hell this male was and why Prima had stolen from him.

"Prima? Really? That seems like a bold move," Reaper said to the male he clearly knew.

"I've always wanted that female. She is fucking crazy. But so am I." Arthur looked once at Greer, then back at Reaper. "This is your female, then?"

"I belong to nobody, dumbass," Greer snapped. This fool had interrupted what would no doubt have been amazing sex and she was more than cranky about it. "And you'd better fix that door quickly before she comes back down." Greer's tone was tart, making the big, bearded male throw back his head and laugh as if she'd said the funniest thing in the world. "Can you deal with him and this mess?" she asked Reaper, exasperated.

"Of course." He didn't reach for her, but something told her that he wanted to.

"Thank you. I'll be...somewhere else." She had no patience for the jerk who'd just destroyed her clan's front door and she didn't care to be introduced to him. No, what she wanted was to be naked with Reaper right now and it was taking all of her patience to keep her cool. She'd started to leave the room when he called out to her.

"Greer..."

She turned with what little dignity she could muster—which was hard since she had her shredded bra in her hand. "Yes?"

His eyes were full dragon now, amber and fire. "I'll come find you when I'm done with him."

Something about the glint in his eyes had her blushing and feeling like a young dragon, so she simply nodded and hurried past the male who eyed her curiously—but smartly kept a good distance from her.

She heard Reaper tell the male that he was going to "Rip your fucking head off for interrupting," as she hurried up the stairs, and for some reason that eased the tension inside her. But she suppressed a giggle.

Yeah, she wouldn't mind ripping that male's head off too. Or maybe nothing quite that violent, but she was simultaneously annoyed and relieved at the interruption.

She and Reaper had definitely crossed a line and she wasn't sure they could come back from it.

She wasn't sure that she wanted to. He was nothing she thought she'd ever wanted but now... Maybe he was exactly what she needed.

CHAPTER SIXTEEN

"I don't like this." Reaper scanned the third floor of the outdoor bar area they had been "summoned" to. As if he answered to anyone. The only reason he had come was because Greer had told him she was going.

"You don't like anything right now because you're a horny bastard." Prima leaned against the edge of the rooftop wall, looking over at the people partying below on the street.

"True enough." Reaper's gaze strayed over to where Greer was talking with some shifters she knew from a wolf pack who lived not far from here. They were here on "holiday" or some other nonsense. There were people from the other night here as well, including the half-demon and his demigod mate. He found he liked those two. Apparently the demigod could transport anywhere within seconds so it was easy enough for them to visit the male's sister.

"So what's up with you and Greer?" Prima asked, turning back to him.

Streaks of purple raced across the sky as the sun descended. Right now he wished he was flying. Flying with Greer. He had never had a partner to take to the skies with before. Bed partners, yes. Anything else? No. But he wanted to share in everything with the female. Especially now that he had gotten a taste of her. But ever since this morning, he swore that the cosmos had conspired to interfere with them.

"I'm not talking about that with you." He shot her a sideways glance. "Unless you want to tell me what possessed you to sleep with Arthur?"

She grinned, her dragon flickering wild and free in her gaze. "I did it because I felt like it. And I liked his timepiece."

He snorted softly, his gaze moving back to Greer. She wore tight black pants that hugged her long, lean legs and perfect ass. She'd worn similar pants before and he found he liked them very much. Anything that showed off her ass, he liked. The bright red top she had on wrapped around her like a second skin, showing off enough of her breasts that all he could think about was ripping it off and seeing her fully naked once again. But that clearly was not happening anytime soon. And that made him cranky. He'd gotten a mere taste and now he had to be patient. Something he was not good at when it came to Greer. "You did not fuck him because you liked his timepiece," he muttered. That much he knew.

"True enough. He is from our time. He is easygoing and creative in the bedroom. There was no harm in fucking."

Reaper simply lifted a shoulder. Dragons could be very possessive, and though Arthur *was* easygoing as she'd said, Reaper had seen the way he looked at Prima. Not to mention he had broken down the door to see her. Though...that was more or less just a dragon being a dragon. "I'm surprised he is even in town. Did you ask him why he found himself in New Orleans?" Reaper found it interesting that Arthur, Damari and Cale were all here since they had all been on his list of dragons to find.

"I asked him why he came to New Orleans of all places and he said it was because he had heard I was here. Can you believe that nonsense? Ridiculous male." She shook her head and looked back over the ledge down to the streets. Music and laughter filled the air, humans and supernaturals alike enjoying themselves.

"I do believe him." Reaper's eyes narrowed as Greer approached a male wolf he did not know and hugged him.

Without another word to Prima, he shoved off the wall and crossed the distance, shoving a couple supernaturals out of the way as he moved. He ignored their grunts of annoyance. Then he was standing next to her, staring hard at the other male who was most definitely Alpha in nature.

The guy lifted an eyebrow at Reaper's sudden appearance, and that was when Reaper saw the petite female next to him, her arm wrapped around his middle. She looked to be in her early twenties, but he could sense that she was a few hundred years older. And there was something else about her. She had that same calming energy as Greer emanating off her. Rich waves of energy that soothed everything—she was a healer.

Greer smiled up at him. "Reaper, this is Ophelia. She's a healer like me and part of the Stavros wolf pack. And this is her mate, Gray. He's a talented artist. We actually have one of his sculptures in the house. It's the one of the dragon that you commented on in the living room."

Some of the tension in Reaper eased as he realized the male was mated and not a threat. The male was less than a century old, if Reaper had to guess. But he was still annoyed in general that he couldn't be alone with Greer right now. Annoyed that he had listened to the summons of a wolf who hadn't bothered to show up yet. He didn't follow orders. He led armies. But Greer had said she was coming tonight since King asked, so here he was. Somehow he managed to tug on a cloak of civility and nodded politely at the two of them.

"So I hear that you basically just woke up from a long Hibernation," Ophelia said. "Like really long. How are you adjusting to things?"

Reaper shifted a step closer to Greer, erasing the small distance between them. He smoothly slid his arm around her shoulders. For some reason he needed to touch her. Okay, not for some reason—he understood exactly why. They were surrounded by far too many supernaturals and he didn't like it. He needed to be touching her.

He was thankful when she wrapped her arm around him and smiled up at him, her cheeks flushing pink. Gods, that pink. He wanted to see her turn that shade all over when he got her naked next time.

He caught the flicker of surprise in Ophelia's eyes as he answered. "It is an adjustment. But I find I like this time period. Very much." He looked down at Greer as he said it, his intention clear. His only regret was that he'd been asleep for so very long while she had been topside.

She blushed again. They definitely needed to get out of here. He wanted to finish what they had started earlier in the day. Arthur was lucky he was walking around right now. Bastard. Or "cock block," as he'd heard Prima call him, laughing her head off as she had said the words. Apparently that was slang from the current generation. And appropriate for what Arthur was. A stupid cock block. Maybe one day Reaper would return the favor. Yes, he liked that idea very much.

Before Reaper could gently suggest that they leave, King finally came through the entrance to the third story.

Reaper found himself irrationally annoyed with the male. "Let's see what he wants and get out of here," he muttered.

Greer lightly pinched his side. "You look a little like you want to take his head off. Calm yourself."

"I will be polite."

She gave him a look that said she did not believe him, which was fine. He wasn't certain he believed himself. Right now he was on a rooftop bar and not naked with Greer. His face was not buried between her legs and she was not coming on his tongue. Someone needed to pay for that.

"If you'll excuse us," Greer said, "we need to take care of something."

Prima joined them at the same time King and a couple of his wolves strode up to Reaper and Greer.

"Thank you for meeting me here. I figured a neutral place like Cynara's bar was good for everyone. And I apologize for being late," King said.

"It's no problem," Greer said quickly, as if she was worried that Reaper would say something obnoxious.

She was not wrong.

"Why are we here?" Reaper asked. "You are not my Alpha." *Translation: I am doing you a favor by being here.*

King's wolf flickered in his eyes as a wave of power rolled off him.

Reaper unleashed some of his own power, letting the reins slip free and pushing back against the male's show of strength. He'd been gentle as a fucking kitten since waking. But if this male pushed him, that was over.

King lifted an eyebrow. "I am well aware you are not one of my people. But we've been digging since Cynbel's death—which is why I'm here. So you're fucking welcome. I think a male named Brennus might be involved in his death. One of my hackers found him on a few cameras somewhere he was not supposed to be. Without going into all the details, he was with Cynbel before his death. And it appeared as if they were arguing. Which might mean nothing, but Brennus has gone to ground. My wolves can't find him but I know he's been in the city for a while. And he tried to recruit some dragons I'm friends with."

"Recruit for what?"

"Some bullshit about dragons being the best and how they should all stick together, blah blah blah. He didn't get very far in his spiel before they shut him down. But he's a powerful dragon so I've been keeping an eye on him. With him in hiding now...I don't like it."

"Thank you for this information," Reaper said, meaning it.

The wolf nodded. "How long are you planning on staying in town?" The question was neutral enough and Reaper wasn't sure of the meaning behind it.

He had already told the male he did not want his territory. "As long as I want." He did not feel like playing nice tonight. He had far too much energy pent up inside him, desperate to get out—desperate to claim Greer.

Greer elbowed him once. And not subtly.

King simply grunted in annoyance and walked away without another word but he didn't leave the bar area. Instead he approached Ophelia and Gray, greeting the other healer with respect.

"Would you like to leave now?" Reaper asked as he turned to Greer. "I am ready."

To his surprise she laughed, the sound infectious and intoxicating. And those cheeks were pink again. Would she be pink all over when he brought her pleasure?

"Why do you want to leave?"

Prima laughed aloud. "Because he wants to—"

"Do not finish that sentence," Reaper ordered Prima. He could only imagine what obnoxious thing would come out of her mouth.

Greer surprised him by tugging his shirt and pulling him closer, her mouth brushing against his ear. "I hope you want to get out of here so we can finally be alone." Her words were laced with sensual hunger and a little nervousness. But no fear.

Good. He could admit he was nervous too. Something he had never experienced with a woman. He wanted to be gentle with her, but every time he thought of burying himself between her thighs—

A scream ripped through the air, causing them both to step back.

"What the hell?" someone muttered.

There was another scream. Then another. And another. Somewhere in the distance. He focused on that direction as more cries of terror lifted in the air, louder than the raucous party on the street below.

"Oh my God," Greer breathed out even as he spotted the hulking gray form in the distance, fire arcing through the air, the bright red flames a horrific backdrop to the setting sun.

It was a dragon. Not a shifter dragon but a full-blooded dragon—evident by the dull gray coloring and the slightly smaller size. Long ago, dragon shifters had been forced to eliminate them—or so he had thought. They caused far too much destruction to everyone and everything, uncaring and unfeeling about what they hurt. They were not mindless creatures, but they were predators. And anything was fair game to them. This dragon should not be here. Should not be alive at all.

Fuck.

"How far can you shoot your healer's energy?" he snapped out as he started stripping off his clothes. Prima was doing the same. Around him, other supernaturals were starting to prepare for battle but he ignored them all. He would kill this beast.

"A few hundred yards, I guess."

"Good. If it gets too close, shoot it. But I will take this out. Back me up," he ordered Prima. He knew he wasn't her general but he was going to take the lead on this. "This is my kill." Some primal part of him needed to do this, needed to show Greer that he was a worthy mate. It was woven into his DNA.

To his surprise, Prima nodded as she tossed her clothes onto the ground next to his.

It looked as if humans were about to discover dragons really existed.

Reaper dove over the edge of the rooftop, already calling on the shift. Pain and pleasure punched through him simultaneously, immediately, as his wings and tail unfolded. His tail hit the side of a building but he ignored it as he pushed higher, higher into the sky. He also ignored the screams far below.

The only thing that mattered was killing this dragon before it hurt any humans.

Because he knew humans well enough, and they would lump dragons in with dragon shifters—and then all supernaturals together—unless they took care of this now. He might not have learned much in the last few days but humans were still the same. And he had to protect his own kind.

He had to protect Greer.

So many thoughts tumbled through his mind but as he focused on the beast shooting fire in wild arcs, everything narrowed down to this point.

Hunt and kill.

He released a stream of fire in an upward arc, screaming out a battle cry.

The gray-scaled beast changed course and flew straight at Reaper. It might be smaller than dragon shifters, but it made up for it in other ways—like a venom-filled, spiked tail.

Now that he had its attention, Reaper shot up into the air, wanting to have this battle as far away from humans as possible. Damage had been done but he could still save people.

Something he'd never cared about before. But Greer cared. And he found that he did too. He was vaguely aware of Prima—who had donned camouflage—close by, but she was keeping her distance.

He flapped his wings hard, shooting upward in a powerful, sweeping path.

The dragon followed, fire licking at Reaper's tail.

Quickly, he twisted in midair and released a burning streak of fire. His attack rolled over the dragon's gray scales, the beast shaking them off as he'd known it would.

But he would take this dragon down. He'd killed them before and he would again. Like dragon shifters, regular dragons were only fire-resistant. Not fireproof.

The dragon returned fire, blasting Reaper in the face.

He tossed it off, his scales rock-hard and damn near impenetrable as he spiraled in a sharp dive, straight at the beast. When he was a few dragon lengths away, he blasted the dragon back in the face. He needed it distracted and annoyed before he attacked with claws.

The beast roared, tossing his head back and forth in a pathetic attempt to avoid the fire. Which was what Reaper wanted. As he flew past it, Reaper twisted midair and reached out with his claws, slicing down the dragon's wing.

A cry of agony filled the air as the beast started screaming and struggled to fly.

Reaper blasted him again with fire, red-hot orange flames engulfing it even though the beast didn't burn. But he was breaking down its scales little by little. Weakening its armor.

The dragon screamed again as Reaper dove onto it, wrapping his jaws around the beast's other wing. Tendons tore and bones broke.

The beast struggled against him, thrashing his last weapon—his venomous tail.

Reaper felt the sharp spikes of the dragon's tail slam into his back. But it didn't pierce his scales. If it had hit his underbelly in the right spot, it could have poisoned him.

But this dragon wasn't thinking clearly now, not when it had been brutally attacked.

Reaper released another stream of fire over the broken, slashed wing as he held on to the dragon's back with his talons. Using all his strength, he wrapped his jaws around the thrashing dragon's neck.

A wild volcano of blood and fire erupted everywhere as he ripped the head free. Though his instinct was to simply toss the head and body away, he didn't want to risk hurting anyone.

Holding on to the dead dragon, he flew downward, spotting Greer and the others still on the rooftop. He landed in the middle of the deserted street. He could see humans hiding in doorways and behind windows in bars but no one was left on the street. He let the body and head fall to the ground before burning them to ash.

As the gray dust scattered in the wind, he let his human form take over, his dragon half revved up from the fight. Ignoring the fearful faces he spotted inside the bars, he looked up at Greer, who was watching him intently.

"Are you okay?" she called out.

Something strange shifted in his chest. No female had ever asked that of him before. He nodded once. Right now he was in uncharted territory. He wasn't sure what the hell they were supposed to do at this point. Humans here now knew about his kind. There was no hiding it, especially since he'd spotted more than one human filming him. *Fools.*

Another scream tore through the air, farther away in the city but the sound was over-pronounced, given how eerily quiet the street here had become.

Greer turned away from him, and though three stories separated them he heard her gasp of surprise.

And just like that, Prima—still naked—jumped over the ledge and shifted once more.

Shit. The threat wasn't over. Reaper called on his own shift again. Rising into the air, he spotted five more beasts coming their way.

It seemed the threat was just beginning—and he would do whatever it took to keep Greer safe.

CHAPTER SEVENTEEN

Greer couldn't stand by and do nothing as these beasts descended on the city. This was absolute terror and destruction.

Dragons were supposed to be extinct. Long killed and forgotten about just as dragon shifters had been forgotten about by humans.

Had someone released them intentionally?

Reaper had killed one in a savage, incredible display for all the city to see. But he couldn't fight off five dragons by himself. Following Prima's lead, she ignored everyone around her even as she saw King and his wolves mobilizing for battle, the same as Justus, Cynara and the others were doing. Everyone would fight.

She might be a healer but she would defend her friends and the city as well. She would not let Reaper and the others do this alone.

Not bothering to take off her clothes, she called on her dragon and jumped off the ledge, her wings unfurling in a wild swoop as her skin was replaced with dragon scales. Her wingspan was too large to fit between the buildings comfortably so she shot upward and veered east, aiming toward the impending threat.

Where the male she'd come to care about was already battling with two dragons while Prima was flying straight at another.

As she flew, she called on her healer's energy, something she'd never done before in dragon form. Healing was sacred, part of her. She'd only ever used it to help.

She would be helping now as well but in a different way.

Out of the corner of her eye something bright blue and glowing flew past her. She wasn't sure what the hell it was...other than a female with wings of blue fire. *Holy flying cats.*

As the female flew at one dragon, Greer picked the closest to her and called on her energy, digging deep for her power.

Green fire shot out of her mouth, a wild, burning streak across the night sky. It slammed into the dragon's face and, to her surprise, the beast shifted off course and started falling as if it were a puppet with its strings cut.

Oh God, the humans.

She dove after it as it slammed into the cobblestone streets below. Before she could land, King and his wolves were there.

Unfortunately she had just stunned the dragon because it shook its head and blasted out fire at the Alpha wolf.

To her surprise, King strode right through the flames and pulled out a huge fucking sword, slamming it straight into the face of the dragon.

Since King was clearly okay, she shot back into the sky and headed toward Reaper, who had killed one of the beasts but was now battling two more. And another dragon shifter was headed his way. When the shifter released fire at Reaper, rage filled Greer.

She didn't care who this dragon was. The only thing she knew was that he intended to harm

Reaper. For all she knew he had released these dragons.

It didn't matter now.

Helping Reaper was the only thing she cared about. Her beast took over, laser focused as she arrowed straight at the other dragon.

The beast hadn't noticed her yet so she called on her healer's fire again, the bright green flames lighting up the sky and slamming into the body of the unknown male.

The dragon shifter screamed, turning toward her, its huge body whipping around and hurtling straight for her.

She had never been in battle, not truly. But she could do this.

She pulled her wings in tight and spiraled, diving underneath the dragon as it shot at her. She looped back up, flapping her wings quick and fast as she attacked him from behind, slamming another blast of healer's fire at him.

The dragon returned fire, its reddish-orange flames hitting her in the face. She squeezed her eyes shut, felt the heat, but her scales protected her.

Before she could recover, Reaper blasted the brightest blue fire she had ever seen at the dragon's face,

202 | KATIE REUS

down its body, slicing it in half as if he'd physically cleaved it with an ax.

If she hadn't seen it with her eyes, she wasn't sure she would have believed it.

She'd heard of fire like this before but…it only appeared when a male was defending his mate. And they were not mates.

CHAPTER EIGHTEEN

Justus raced from the bar with Cynara and at least fifty other supernaturals, but only Cynara remained by his side as they sprinted down a side street—heading straight for the giant dragons battling in the air. Right now they had to protect the city from fallout.

As they reached Jackson Square in the heart of the French Quarter, screams and fire hurtled through the air above them. He withdrew his sword, ready to take flight now. As an old vampire, he could levitate for short periods of time. Not truly fly, like dragons, but he could get some serious air time.

Two more dragons appeared in the air.

They were everywhere now, clashing in complete savagery. Cars and buildings were on fire, smoke billowing wildly. People randomly screamed in terror, their fear a palpable thing filling the air.

Next to him, Cynara drew a flaming, bright purple sword—the same color as her shocking hair—from thin air, and held it like she knew how to use it.

He blinked once at her.

"You don't know everything about me," she said as she looked up at the sky again. "This is so bad."

When one of the dragons swooped low, Justus used his gift of flight and jumped into the air, sword at the ready. He sliced where the dragon's wing met its body, severing the wing. Then he rolled midair to avoid a burst of flames.

The dragon faltered and started falling, unable to fly with one wing so badly damaged.

Below, he saw Cynara rushing at it, her flaming sword held securely in her hands, looking like a warrior goddess. Her short plaid skirt and combat boots should have looked ridiculous but everything about her was fierce as she jumped straight at the dragon's face.

He nearly lost his immortality as the dragon released flames but... The fire rolled off her because she was half demon. She let out a battle cry as she sliced down its face, drawing blood and cleaving through its scales in a sharp, clean sweep.

From above, he dove onto the beast's back, slamming his sword into its spine and carving upward. He wasn't sure if dragons were like dragon shifters in that you had to take off the head or cut out the heart. So he was just going to slice this thing to ribbons.

Its tail thrashed wildly so he dove to the side to avoid the ball of spikes at the end.

Cynara did the same, but a spike caught her shoulder. She screamed as she flew back, slamming into the concrete.

"Cynara!" Her name tore from his lips. He needed to get to her—but had to kill this thing first. In a quick, practiced move, he raised his sword and sliced the dragon's head clean off. Then he jumped down onto the street, but not before he ducked to narrowly avoid a dragon head that slammed into the ground.

Cynara lay flat on her back against the cobblestones, her sword gone, but she was awake. "Cynara." He knelt beside her as she struggled to sit up.

"Poison," she rasped out. "Think... Poisoned."

"Son of a bitch," he ground out, helping her to her feet as he looked around. He wanted to scoop her up in his arms, but he needed a free hand in case someone tried to attack.

Blood and death were everywhere—wolves, dragon shifters, vampires and other supernaturals battling the gray beasts in the sky. At least it appeared their side was winning.

When he saw a dragon shifter swoop down through the air, his eyes widened. It was going to attack King, who was currently slicing the head off another fallen dragon.

"King!" he shouted.

The male turned at the oncoming attack and lifted his sword, more than capable as he defended himself.

"Come on." Justus lifted Cynara up into his arms and raced toward the entrance of the Catholic church. He needed to get her to relative safety.

"Will you burst into flames if you step inside the church?" he asked in all seriousness.

"Oh my God, no." Despite everything, she actually laughed before wincing in pain. "I'm...okay. Just...need to stand still." Her face was pale and he could see dark streaks along her shoulder where her top had been ripped open from one of the spikes.

He set her on her feet, still outside the church, but under the covering. She grasped onto one of the huge columns. *Shit.* "Cynara—"

"Go. Help them. Those are our friends out there. I'll be okay. I swear." Her fingers dug into the column, the strength of her grip causing the plaster to crumble. Her pupils were dilated but she wasn't bleeding from her shoulder wound.

Random sirens wailed in the distance, adding to the insane melee. For the first time in his life he was torn. Stay or go. He needed to keep her safe. And the only way to keep her truly safe was to end this battle. "I'll come back for you."

She waved her hand and pulled one of those wild, flaming swords out of midair again. "I can take care of myself if anything happens." Her skin was pale, but her words were strong.

He nodded once and crushed his mouth to hers for a millisecond before turning and racing back into the fray. After this he was claiming her forever. Fuck everything else. He'd quit as Alpha of his coven and that was that. Cynara was his and he'd protect her with his life.

A dragon dove at King who easily rolled to the side.

Justus levitated into the air and pulled his sword back, ready to hurl it at the beast when a flaming blue *something* flew through the air and landed on the dragon's back. The female looked like an angel but he knew that couldn't be right. She plunged her hands into the beast, grabbed the dragon's spine, and ripped it out.

All right, then.

Two more dragons appeared in the air right as a group of young human males ran into the streets, actually filming everything with their cell phones.

They were going to get themselves killed.

One of the dragons spotted them. Sensing easy prey, it broke away from the others, diving straight for the stupid humans. Oblivious, the humans didn't seem to notice the giant scaled beast heading right for them.

"Mars save me from stupidity," he muttered, levitating once again into the air. He didn't have time for this shit—his mate had been poisoned. Every second he was away from her was its own wretched eternity. He wanted to leave these fools to their fate, but he simply couldn't do it. Couldn't let them just die.

Thankfully the dragon was so focused on the trio of human males that he didn't notice Justus until the last second. By then it was too late. Flying low, Justus slashed his sword against the underbelly of the beast, driving it straight up where he hoped the heart was.

The dragon screamed in agony, fire arcing wildly against the dark sky.

Justus drew his sword back as he fell back to earth, his boots slamming into the concrete.

He ran at the dragon to finish it off, but one of King's wolves was on it, claws out at the ready, taking its wings off in seconds. The dragon continued to spew fire so Justus raced at the humans, grabbing them up in a tackle with his supernatural strength, and dumped them on the steps of the church.

"Watch these morons," he growled to Cynara who was still holding on to the column.

Cynara nodded, her sword clutched tightly in one hand. She looked paler but she was still standing. He wanted to get her out of here, find out what was wrong and help her. They needed...a healer. They needed Greer!

But then Cynara's eyes rolled back in her head and she fell, her purple sword disappearing. He dove and caught her in his arms—and lost all sense of sanity when he realized he couldn't hear her heartbeat.

CHAPTER NINETEEN

Greer landed on Decatur Street and let the shift come over her. Reaper flew overhead, his brilliant colors highlighted against the flames billowing out of a nearby building. *He is okay.* And she cared about that—a lot.

Sore from battling dragons and in a semi-state of shock, she looked down the length of the street. Cars were on fire, some completely ashed or crushed. The green and white awnings of Café Du Monde were on fire as well. Terrified human faces were plastered against shop windows.

The battle in the air was over for now but today would have far-reaching consequences. The entire world had changed in an instant—because there would be no putting this back into a box. Wolf shifters and vampires strode out of the middle of Jackson Square's grassy park. The giant wrought-iron fence surrounding the park was destroyed in most places, the statue in the middle had toppled over, and dead dragons and other supernaturals were littered everywhere.

She'd seen and done a lot in her very long life, but today… Today never should have happened.

Powerful wings rippled through the air above her as Reaper descended to the street across from her. Even with everything going on around them, he was the most beautiful thing she'd ever seen. Lavender, gold, and dark purple created a shimmering waterfall of brilliant colors. A sharp burst of sparking magic filled the air, then a moment later he was in human form, bruised and bloodied as he strode across the street. His jaw was tight, his eyes sparking amber.

He is okay. For some reason she had to remind herself of that. She'd seen him in the air. Seen the insanely hot fireballs he'd shot at that dragon who'd tried to kill her. The heat from the blue flames had filled the sky, pushing other battling warriors away from the scorching massacre.

"Greer." He said her name like a prayer, desperate and fearful. *For me.*

"I'm okay... Are they all dead?" She was fairly certain they—the dragons and treacherous dragon shifters who'd decided to fight their own kind—were, or she wouldn't have landed. But one of the dragons had bitten her wing, causing her to free fall. She'd needed to change to her human form to heal. And recover. Fighting, she'd expended far more of her healer's energy than she'd wanted. She had no outward wounds now, but her underarm muscles were sore, as if she'd been punched over and over. The shift couldn't heal everything. Only time would do that. Unfortunately she didn't think they had time. Too many people had been injured and she needed to help.

Without responding, he covered the distance between them in seconds and gathered her into his arms, his big hands gently cupping her face as he pulled her close.

Then his mouth was on hers, the timing insanely inappropriate—and she didn't care that humans and other supernaturals could see them. The gentle hold of his hands was in direct contrast to the hungry, needy way he kissed her—as he ate at her mouth as if he might die without her.

She clung to his shoulders, kissing him back, fervent and desperate as everything burned around them. Too soon he pulled back, his expression fierce as he suddenly shoved her behind him.

King and one of his wolves strode up to them, most of their clothing burned off, their expressions as grim as she felt.

"I'm securing the city," King snapped out, as if expecting them to argue.

Reaper simply nodded. Greer tried to step around him, but he kept her firmly behind him. Whether because she was naked or what, she wasn't certain, so she simply peered around his body.

"Look, we need to set up triage centers around the city and find out if the hospitals were affected," she said to King. So many people would have been injured in the fallout and Greer wanted to help. "And we'll need to—"

"I know what to do," King said, his tone much softer as he spoke directly to her. "My pack has had a plan in place for a long time in case anything like this ever happened. Can you set up a hospital at your mansion?"

"Of course," she said. "I'll need some supplies but for the most part I'll use my energy to heal. Do you know other healers in the city?"

"Yes."

"There will be law enforcement to deal with," Reaper said. He had learned a little about the human police since awakening—Prima had given him brief lessons on various things.

Almost on cue, three uniformed, armed men—and one woman—slipped out of the shadows from across the street.

"Hands in the air!" the male on the left shouted.

Reaper frowned at the strange order. Why should they put their hands in the air? What was wrong with these humans?

King turned to look at the humans, unconcerned, his expression dry. "You're going to want to put those things down."

Reaper stared at the humans and their weapons. They would not injure shifters. Not for long anyway. But a stray bullet might hurt a human, or one of these humans might hurt themselves if they tried to attack.

He focused on the small weapons in their hands—he believed they were called pistols—and focused all his energy on the components of the weapons.

As if pulled by a magnet, all the pistols slammed to the ground with great force. Using mental persuasion, he drew them to him so they landed in a pile directly at his feet. Then he crushed the pistols under his heel, turning them to twisted metal.

King's eyes flashed wolf once in clear surprise. "Thank you."

Reaper nodded once, aware of the shocked expressions of the humans and the overwhelming scent of their fear. It popped in the air, sharp and potent. His dragon half craved the scent of fear but only from enemies. Not scared humans who had just had their world ripped apart.

"I am in charge of the city now," King snapped out as he turned back to the humans who seemed to have gotten their expressions under control, if not their fear. "My name is King. And there is a supernatural war going on as you can very well see. If you want to be helpful, step up. If not, go home and lock your doors. I won't tolerate any bullshit in my city. And rest assured, I will do everything in my power to protect it. Weapons don't work against us—though you're welcome to try and end up locked up somewhere. My tolerance is limited right now." His blue eyes were shards of ice, his claws extended as he dared the humans to step out of line.

Out of the corner of his eye, a female wearing a black uniform similar to the others who were standing at the ready—even without their weapons, so they were brave enough for humans, Reaper decided—strode out of the shadows.

She was a shifter, he realized. Young, but definitely a wolf. "I can vouch for King," the female with dark brown braids tight against her head said.

The uniformed officers looked at her in surprise, their stances easing slightly. But just barely.

But she continued. "He is a good male. Right now this is a problem that humans can't deal with alone. Trust me. We need to get the city in order before panic starts. We need law and order and people will need to feel safe. The only way that happens is if King is in charge. You guys remember what happened with Katrina. If we'd been in charge, that wouldn't have happened. And it's *not* happening again. We can't trust that the government will do shit for us. And..."

She looked at her Alpha before looking back at the others, but only after he nodded once.

"I'm a shifter too. And well over half of the force is. Closer to seventy five percent, if you want to get technical. We've been working side by side with you for the last few years. Nothing should change now. Teresa, I'm still the same woman who picks your kid up from school when you get stuck on long shifts. And Marco, I'm still the same woman who eats your overcooked burgers at PD barbeques even though they should be outlawed."

There was a long moment of tense silence but the human woman finally snorted. "All right, I'm in. I saw what you guys did, how you took out those things that wanted to destroy the city. Tell us what to do."

"Dragons. They are called dragons," Reaper said. "Not things. And we are dragon shifters. There is a difference."

The female looked at him once, her expression neutral, though he scented her fear. She was masking it though and he respected that. "Fine. Dragons."

"You fucking serious?" a male with blond hair asked, looking at his female friend. His own emotions were riotous.

"Yep. I'm going to adapt to all this," the human female said. "And I suggest you do too. We're outgunned, and we all want the same thing—to keep the city safe. I'm sure as shit not going home and locking my door. I want to make sure my kid—and all kids—stay safe."

"How is Leesa?" the female wolf asked, true concern in her voice.

"Good. With my mom. They're all safe, thank God," Teresa said.

The male nodded slowly and then so did the other two males, including the one named Marco, who said, "I'm in too."

King pointed at the female wolf. "Cat, round up all the officers you know. Meeting in Jackson Square in fifteen. Captain Santiago is already on the way—"

"Greer!" Justus was racing across the grassy area of Jackson Square toward them, Cynara limp in his hands.

Still in her combat boots, skirt and black top, she was completely still—and she was injured, Reaper saw. On her shoulder. Her shirt had been torn open.

Greer and Reaper both moved toward the vampire.

"She was hit by a dragon tail. One of the spikes barely glanced her shoulder. She said she was fine but then she collapsed. She's been poisoned." Raw fear etched Justus's face.

Reaper could relate. If anything happened to Greer...he would not deal with it well.

"I'll take care of her." Greer turned and looked at Reaper, so much concern in her eyes. "We've got to get that triage center set up at the house, now."

Reaper nodded as he turned back to King. "You heard her, and you have the address. Send as many as will fit into the house. Supernaturals only."

King lifted an eyebrow.

"I only mean because if supernaturals are injured, they can lash out and might hurt humans. We do not want that to happen." Reaper did not like explaining himself, but right now things would be a powder keg around the city. Supernaturals could not do anything to make it worse. He might not know much about this time period, but he knew that much about humans.

"I'll make it happen. In the meantime..." King turned and glanced at one of his guys. "Grab them some clothes."

"No need," Reaper said. "Justus, I will allow you and Cynara to ride on my back this one time. We will make it there quicker." In minutes.

Justus nodded, his expression tense. "I owe you for life."

"No, you do not. Greer, can you shift? I saw your wing is injured." It was taking all of his self-control not to scoop her up and fly far, far away. He'd been battling the need since he'd seen her standing naked on the street, her expression pure shock.

"I'll ride on your back as well," she said. He noted that she didn't directly respond to his question about shifting and he understood that she would not want to show weakness in front of others. "I want to start healing Cynara now," she added.

"Let's go." Before he allowed the shift to overcome him, he looked back at King. "Prima is burning all the dead dragons and dragon shifters to ash. This is necessary to my kind. Tell your wolves not to try to stop her or we are enemies." Reaper would not explain to him why the bodies needed to be burned. The wolf should know, and Reaper would not let humans overhear anything about dragons. In his experience, humans could not be trusted with the secrets of dragons. His kind had been in hiding a long time, their secrets many. And none of the dragon bones could be allowed to get into the wrong hands.

Once King nodded, Reaper let the magic take over, ignoring the gasps of the uniformed humans as his beast took control. Right now he only cared about getting Greer away from here and helping the hybrid female.

Let King take care of the city. Reaper would take care of his own.

CHAPTER TWENTY

Cynara blinked, struggling to open her eyes. Something smelled… *Good.* A muted vanilla scent lingered in the air. And she felt warm all over. Her eyes snapped open.

Fire. Destruction. The dragons.

"You're fine." Greer's soothing voice rolled over her.

She turned and found the beautiful dragon shifter sitting in a rocking chair next to the bed. Her long copper-colored hair was in a braid and she had on the equivalent of hospital scrubs in a pale purple.

Cynara realized she was lying in a bed, that it was nighttime, and the smell she'd liked was the little tea lights flickering on the windowsill. "The dragon attack?" she rasped out, her throat dry.

Greer stood, the chair rocking back with the movement as the healer strode to a serving tray set on a six-drawer dresser. She poured a glass of water as she spoke. "The dragons are dead and the city is safe. We're in lockdown, but safe enough. King and his people have completely taken over and secured the city and surrounding areas. Turns out the majority of the New Orleans PD are shifters of some sort anyway. It's one of the only reasons the city fared so well compared to…" Sighing, Greer brought the glass over as Cynara sat up.

She pulled open the neck of the oversized plain white T-shirt someone had put on her and saw that the wound on her shoulder was completely healed. She still felt exhausted, however. "Compared to what?"

"Compared to the majority of the rest of the world."

"What do you mean?" And how long had she been out?

"Large portions of the world have been completely decimated. I'm talking...razed earth." Greer's voice hitched, but she tightened her jaw before continuing. "Many rural areas weren't touched at all, and basically any supernatural territory is left in decent shape. Rio de Janeiro, Edinburgh, Kyoto...and some others I can't think of right now are all still standing and functioning, as New Orleans is. But this wasn't random. It was a planned and well-coordinated attack. The masterminds behind everything disabled all nuclear centers around the world. Otherwise some humans might have gotten trigger-happy and unleashed them. But that's the only positive thing. And whoever is behind this didn't take out satellites or communications. Not all of them anyway. Not even a majority. They didn't want to destroy everything—just as many humans as possible. But they wanted to keep the world still functioning."

"Holy shit." Cynara took a small sip, then gulped the entire thing down as her brain registered everything that Greer had told her. "Oh God, my brothers!"

"They're fine. After the battle here Nyx transported the Stavros packmates who were here back to Biloxi.

But she brought your brothers back. They're all downstairs. And only because I forced them and Justus to go eat. Justus gave you a lot of his blood to help boost my healing powers, but he needed to feed. It's the only reason he's not by your side."

"He gave me his blood?" She set the glass on the nightstand next to her. Cynara wasn't actually surprised. The male was…everything.

"He did. I had to stop him from giving you too much." A soft smile lifted Greer's lips. "He cares for you deeply."

Yeah, she knew that. And she cared for him. Hell, she loved him. More than anything. "I can't believe…the world…"

"The world will wait." Greer's tone was pragmatic. "Right now I'm so glad that you're awake. But you'll need to rest for at least another twenty-four hours. Dragon poison is potent."

"How long have I been out?"

"About two days."

That was when Cynara realized how exhausted *Greer* looked. "When's the last time you got any sleep?"

Greer gave her a ghost of a smile, her green eyes flashing to her dragon. "I don't remember. We've set up a triage center here in the mansion. You were definitely the worst of the lot so almost everybody has left except a couple wolves who were burned by dragon fire. I've spent the last two days healing shifters who got caught in the fray. It's been…exhausting."

"I've never seen anything so terrifying in my life." Cynara was still trying to wrap her head around this new reality. "Well, at least not in the human realm." Because she had seen some crazy shit in Hell realms. She was a hybrid after all.

"Agreed."

"So King has really claimed this territory?" After Greer's nod, she continued. "What about phones, internet, stuff like that?"

"Like I said, the satellites are still up. So far our phones are still working and all the different packs, clans and covens with alliances across the globe have been working as a team to share communication. Some things are limited but there are various news reports that have managed to make it through to what's left of everyone."

"This is insane."

"It might feel like it, but it's the new reality." Greer said it so simply, reminding Cynara how much older the dragon shifter was than her. She'd been around over a thousand years, Cynara thought. Maybe longer.

"How's your clan? I'm sorry I didn't think to ask."

Greer smiled serenely in that calm healer's way as she sat back down on the rocking chair. "You just woke up after being poisoned by a dragon. It's okay. And my clan is fine. They live in a fairly remote area and there were a few rogue attacks on a nearby ski resort but they ended it *very* quickly. No loss of life there other than the assholes who deserved it. The majority of places hit and decimated were densely populated cities, where our kind tend not to live. New Orleans is just a different type of city in that supernaturals tend to gravitate here. You've woken up to a different world. Also, Washington is completely destroyed."

"The state?"

"Oh, no, I mean Washington, DC. It's gone. The humans' main government structure in the US is destroyed. So are a few states lining the eastern seaboard—they were decimated, with some still burning out of control. Most human government capitals around the world are destroyed as well. You don't need to worry about that right now though. You're safe and eventually things will work themselves out. Let me call Justus and your brothers."

"Just Justus for right now." She desperately needed to see him and since she knew her brothers were alive, she was okay seeing him first.

Greer nodded and quietly left the room with promises of getting her bagged blood. Less than twenty seconds later, Justus strode into the room, his eyes bright. "Cynara," he rasped out, sitting on the bed beside her. "You're awake." He gently took her hands in his and brought them to his mouth reverently. So unlike the lethal warrior she'd seen in action not long ago. Closing his eyes, he kissed her fingertips.

She withdrew her hands only so she could cup his face. She needed to touch him. "I heard you fed me. Thank you."

"I would bleed myself dry for you."

224 | KATIE REUS

To her horror, tears leaked out and she quickly dashed them away. "How do you always say the perfect thing?"

"I'm not trying to. I simply love you." There was so much raw honesty in his words.

And he deserved the same from her. She'd been a damn coward. Well, no more. "I love you too." She'd thought she was going to die, and there was no way she was denying this any longer. She'd almost died before—more than once—but this time had been different. She had something to fight for now, and she'd been a coward for too long where Justus was concerned.

His eyes widened as he shifted closer to her, his eyes vampire amber now. "Did I hear you correctly?"

"You heard me, old man." She half-smiled at the spark in his gaze. "I love you. I love you so much it hurts."

Before she could say any more, he crushed his mouth to hers just as Greer stepped inside the room.

"Justus!" Greer had a tray of various bags of blood, no doubt different types. "I told you she needed her rest." Greer looked at him, all disapproving healer. "I expected more from you." Oh yeah, that was definite disappointment.

To Cynara's surprise, Justus's cheeks flushed ever so slightly. "She loves me."

At that, Greer smiled and set the blood on the dresser top next to the tray of water. "Your brothers and their mates will be up in less than five minutes. It's as long as I can keep them away. Make sure she's fed."

She gave Justus a pointed look before closing the door and leaving them in privacy.

Cynara didn't care if her brothers walked in on them kissing. She grabbed Justus and pulled him to her, kissing him again. The world had apparently changed in an instant.

She was going to claim the vampire she loved—maybe not this instant, but as soon as possible. They were going to face this new world together.

CHAPTER TWENTY-ONE

Greer stepped out of the bedroom where two injured wolf shifters were now sleeping peacefully—basically healed up at this point. Thankfully shifters healed at a rapid rate compared to humans, so even though the wolves had been burned they were almost back to normal. If they'd been human, they wouldn't have survived the dragon fire.

She, however, was beyond the point of exhaustion. Sighing, she leaned against the door, closing her eyes for a long moment. Cynara had visited with her brothers and their mates a couple hours ago, but they'd finally let her be. And of course Justus hadn't left her side. Which was good. His presence alone was positive for Cynara.

Reaper had been in and out of the house, a solid presence whenever she saw him. She'd asked for supplies in the beginning and he'd gotten them. She'd asked to be kept up to date on the city—so he kept her up to date. The male was nothing short of amazing.

"Greer." Reaper's voice made her eyes fly open. He strode down the hall on silent feet, looking every inch the predator he was. It was like he simply appeared out of nowhere whenever she thought about him. "When's the last time you ate?"

The fact that she had to think about her answer said a lot for how busy they'd been. Various shifters had set up triage homes around the city for humans and supernaturals, keeping them separated, as supernaturals could be volatile when injured. Not to mention the human hospitals thankfully were open and operating. But the entire city was in lockdown, with King having taken over all law enforcement. This was a supernatural-run city now and everyone was still adjusting. She'd checked in with some of her friends, including Christian, and everyone was doing as well as could be.

"I had some fruit and yogurt earlier."

His frown deepened as he came to stand directly in front of her, inspecting her closely. "That was this morning. You have been running yourself ragged for forty-eight hours straight. You are getting some food and then sleep."

She shifted slightly under his knowing gaze. "Reaper—"

"This is not up for discussion. Everyone is stable in this house. You are a healer. If you do not take care of yourself, you won't be able to help anyone else. Besides, the two wolves and Cynara are the only ones left. They are going to recover."

He was right. He was absolutely right, and the truth was that she was exhausted. But part of her was afraid to stop for even a moment, because then she would have to *think* about the insanity of what had happened. The fact that humans *knew* about supernaturals now.

The fact that the entire world had changed in a moment. Now supernaturals were out to humans, and half the world—maybe even more—had been decimated. As in, billions were now gone. So much death and destruction. So many lives lost.

She closed her eyes for a moment and tried not to think about that. Not yet anyway. She pushed up from the door and leaned on him when he offered an arm around her shoulders. He was a rock right now and she would take it. He smelled of sunshine and...home. "How bad is it?"

"Things are...interesting. I have not been awake long enough to gauge how bad things are but according to King, he says it could be worse."

She snorted as they reached the top of the stairs. "Things could always be worse."

Downstairs she found a handful of her friends, including Bo and Nyx, sitting at the center island. She smiled tiredly at the two of them.

"Sit," Bo ordered even as he headed for the refrigerator and started pulling out a bunch of food.

"I will feed her," Reaper growled, immediately taking over and starting to put things in the microwave.

Greer was exhausted but still managed to smile at his bossy tone. She really shouldn't like it but she did. Just as she admired his courage and protectiveness. She'd been wrong about him, she realized. She'd jumped to conclusions because she hadn't understood that strange attraction to him. But he'd stepped up to the plate when he hadn't needed to. He'd defended the

city. Defended her. He could be as arrogant and obnoxious as he wanted.

"Bo, I heard you managed to piece back a lot of the
city with your gift." Bo was mated to Nyx, the daughter
of Chaos. And Nyx tended to create actual chaos wherever she went—breaking things on a small and sometimes massive scale. Luckily Bo had the gift of literally
fixing things. If glass broke, he could put it back together. And apparently the entire city.

He nodded. "I've helped mend the city as best I can.
But there was a lot of structural damage and I still have
work to do. I've focused on the necessities and have
been back and forth between here and Biloxi, helping
Finn and his pack. It's too exhausting to do it all at
once. I can't afford to be completely drained right now.
Not when there are far too many unknown threats out
there. Not when I have Nyx and our daughter to worry
about."

"Is there any news on Brennus and his clan?"

"No." Reaper slid a plate of delicious-smelling food
in front of her—a dark green salad, grilled chicken
topped with tomatoes and mozzarella cheese, and a side
of wild rice and mixed vegetables. "Brennus and his clan
have created their havoc and got what they wanted. A
new world and dead humans."

"You think that's what they wanted?" She couldn't
understand why anyone wanted this chaos.

He paused once before nodding. "I believe so, yes. I
also do not think things went as well as they planned.
Many cities are still standing, and while supernaturals

are in charge…it is whoever saved the cities that are now running things. Not his clanmates. We should expect an attack from his clan at some point. They created this havoc for a reason and they are not done yet."

Bo nodded in agreement. "The Stavros pack is on alert for that, as well as Justus's coven and anyone involved in the worldwide alliances of supernaturals."

Greer dug into her food, listening as they continued talking, but not contributing at this point. She wasn't sure how long she sat there eating—because as soon as she finished one plate, Reaper gave her another. She felt as if she'd eaten the contents of the entire fridge. And her energy reserves still weren't completely filled up. The last two days had taken so much from her. That was the real weakness in being a healer—the more she gave, the more exhausted she became, making her more vulnerable in general. But she'd been willing to take the risk of being weak to help so many people.

As she pushed her final plate away from her, Ian and Fiona stepped into the room along with Rory, Liberty and Javier, who all looked in much better spirits now that they'd gotten to see Cynara earlier. From what she'd gathered from Bo, they'd been out patrolling the grounds and neighborhood, making sure everything was secure.

To her surprise, Ian stepped up to Reaper and they did a sort of fist-bump-then-hug type of thing. Wait…what was that all about?

"Hey, so what did you think?" Fiona asked as she grabbed a bottle of wine from one of the cabinets.

232 | KATIE REUS

Greer blinked once, and through the haze of her exhaustion realized Fiona was talking to her. "About what?"

The powerful, elegant dragon paused, her fingers wrapped around the neck of the bottle. "The...news report."

"What news report?"

"Ah." Fiona turned away and mumbled something as she grabbed a glass. The others wouldn't look at Greer.

Greer glanced around the island, then focused her gaze on Reaper. "What news report?" The last two days she'd been so focused on healing everyone that she'd managed to gather only snippets of what was going on around the world. Whenever she'd asked Reaper for updates, he'd given them to her.

And while she most definitely cared, at the same time she'd had to keep her focus on the here and now. On who she could help live. Which meant she hadn't been able to allow any headspace to worry about the rest of the world. On how many had truly died. On how many beautiful, bright lives had been snuffed out because of greed and evil.

Reaper looked unconcerned as he said, "You and I are apparently on the news."

"We are?"

Sighing, Ian pulled out his phone and a moment later slid it across the island to her. "You guys made quite the spectacle. Hell, you all did. It's a few minutes into the feed."

Greer pressed play and turned down the volume as a local newscaster, who she was pretty sure was supernatural, reported on what had happened in New Orleans and other places around the world. Only this broadcast included a warning that images would not be suitable for younger viewers. There were scenes spliced together showing various supernatural creatures working together to fight dragons burning everything in sight. Some places she recognized—Edinburgh, London, Rio de Janeiro. At the end of the first video, the woman came back on the screen and then announced that the next video had been filmed in New Orleans.

Greer stared as the video feed started showing Reaper destroying that first dragon. The angle was clearly from a rooftop, and though the image trembled a little, whoever had recorded it had done a decent job of capturing his savage beauty. His brilliant purples and golds showed up, making him appear otherworldly, beautiful, compared to the dull gray dragon intent on killing everyone. Oh—maybe that was why Ian had fist-bumped him. He must know they were related now.

The video shifted to Cynara and Justus in action—and Greer thought Cynara looked like a badass superhero. Next was the flaming blue female who Greer had recently learned was a phoenix. Apparently the female—Léonie—had lived here for over a hundred years and was very entrenched in New Orleans. She'd only half-shifted, something Greer hadn't realized was possible. Then again, she hadn't known that phoenixes existed to begin with. She'd thought they were myths—just like dragons.

The next image was taken from a rooftop with a steady grip on the cell phone or video camera. Flames and smoke licked high into the air, old buildings and new buildings burning, screams and shrieking sirens the background noise. Greer nearly dropped the phone when she appeared on-screen in dragon form. It was weird to look at herself. Her pale green and silver scales looked almost all silver against the backdrop of night and fire. Whoever was filming continued recording as she descended onto Decatur Street and shifted to her human form. Naked.

Welp, her breasts and other intimate areas were blurred out with little black stripes but she was very clearly naked. So...the whole world had seen her nude at this point? *Awesome.* The recorder zoomed in on her face as she glanced around in horror. Her every emotion was clear.

Suddenly Reaper was in the shot, whoever was filming having missed his shift to human, but they caught him as he strode directly toward her, his expression as fierce as she remembered it. What she didn't remember was that intense look that said he would destroy the world for her as he cupped her face before crushing his mouth to hers.

The kiss seemed to go on forever, though in her memory it had been over far too quickly. She'd barely gotten a taste of him, but watching them now, their bodies pressed up against each other was... Well, it was hot. She almost felt like a voyeur, and that was her on the screen. For all the world to see. Including her clan-mates.

She was a dragon shifter, so used to having to hide what she was that this almost felt like a violation. But it wasn't. Not really. As she watched Reaper and her-self...she felt her cheeks flushing. Clearing her throat, she said, "They sure gathered a lot of videos." She pushed the phone away, not needing to see any more. She had been there, after all, and it would simply be embarrassing if she got turned on and the others scented it.

"There are similar videos from Biloxi," Bo said. "Of the Stavros pack kicking ass, mainly. It's fucking bru-tal...and beautiful."

That sounded about right. As she sat there, a dull ache spread across the back of her skull. Sighing, Greer laid her head on Reaper's shoulder, not even question-ing the move. Leaning on him somehow felt right. She felt him jolt slightly but then he seemed to shift into it, kissing the top of her head once as she closed her eyes, trying to wrap her mind around all the news.

She was so damn exhausted and had so many ques-tions. She wanted to know what all the clan leaders were doing across the world, and knew she needed to check in with her own Alpha. She'd spoken to him twice in the last forty-eight hours and he definitely had things under control, but still, everything was different now. "How is King handling the city?" she finally asked,

opening her eyes again when there was a lull in the
conversation around her.

"As you know, there's a curfew in effect. Prima is
currently out there helping patrol the city and outlying
areas with a dozen other dragons," Rory said.

"No sign of Brennus or his cohorts," Reaper
growled, his annoyance clear.

The others started talking among themselves again,
and while she listened sleep started to push at the edges
of her mind. She would just close her eyes for a minute.

Reaper shifted slightly so she raised her head. "All
right." His expression was fierce as he looked at her.

She frowned at him. "All right what?"

Wordlessly he leaned down and scooped her up,
taking her off guard. She was so exhausted, in a bit of a
haze, that she let him manhandle her. At least that was
what she told herself even as she cuddled up against
him, not caring that he was doing this in front of her
friends. She was pretty much beyond caring about
much at this point. Especially after some fool had
filmed her naked and splashed it for the world to see.

"What are you doing?" she murmured.

"You need sleep. To recharge."

Ignoring the avid stares of the other shifters around
the island, she started to argue with him but he was
right. "Fine. But I can walk."

He simply snorted. "No one will bother her for at
least twelve hours," he tossed over his shoulder as he
left the room, his tone one of a general giving orders.

And he definitely expected said orders to be obeyed. "Make that sixteen."

"You're very bossy," she muttered as he reached the bottom of the stairs.

"Someone has to take care of you because you certainly are not taking care of yourself."

"I'm a grown female."

"Oh, I know you're grown." There was a wealth of heat in his words as he reached the first landing.

Whatever she'd been about to say died, because she wasn't playing with fire. Not now at least.

It didn't take him long to reach the third story and she realized that he'd completely bypassed her room and gone straight to his. "Your room?"

"Yep." He shut the door behind them. "This is where you will be sleeping."

Why wasn't she more annoyed by this? Why wasn't she fighting this? *Oh, you know exactly why*, that little voice in her head whispered. She wanted this. Badly.

He gently sat her down on the giant bed before heading to the en suite. A moment later she heard water start running. Then he popped his head out of the open door. "All your bath products are in there. You need to shower."

She lifted an eyebrow, tempted to forget the shower and just pass out on the bed right now. "Are you saying I smell?"

He gave her a dry stare. "You smell like heaven. But a shower will help you sleep."

She ignored the *heaven* comment. "You look smug when you're right."

"Then I must look smug all the time." His expression was deadpan, making her giggle.

The little joke surprised her, making him seem almost...not soft exactly, but not so rough around the edges. He cracked a hint of a smile as she laughed. "Fine. And thank you. I really am tired. I need clothes to sleep in though." While she preferred to sleep naked, that wasn't happening right now. Not in his bed.

He gave her a long, heated stare but simply nodded. "There's a robe for you to put on once you're done." Then he left the room, leaving her alone with her thoughts.

In the bathroom, she quickly stripped and stepped under the strong, heated jets. This house was probably over a hundred years old, but someone had renovated the bathroom—and most of the rooms, it seemed—and the jets were perfection for her tired body.

Once she was finished, she towel-dried her hair, pulled it back in a loose, damp braid and slipped on the robe. Since Reaper wasn't back yet, she just slid into the bed and curled on her side. She inhaled deeply, savoring his rich scent as she snuggled under the plush covers.

She was just going to close her eyes until he returned. Then she hoped he joined her, held her while she slept. Because the truth was, he looked as if he could use some rest too. They'd all been pushing themselves so hard. She wanted to find some peace in his arms and she hoped she gave him some too.

CHAPTER TWENTY-TWO

R eaper silently closed the door behind him, unable to tear his gaze away from Greer.

Asleep in his bed.

Her long hair was in a loose braid, stray wisps feathered out on the pillow behind her as she curled up on her side. She'd been working herself too hard and that was ending now. He'd been in and out of the house in between patrolling the city. Anything she'd asked for, he'd gotten for her. Now he realized what he should have been doing—taking care of Greer full time.

At least he could do that now. He was not leaving her side until she'd rested. And given what he knew about healers, she'd expended a lot of energy. Too much, likely. It was amazing she'd lasted as long as she had, giving up so much of herself. It said a lot for how powerful she was. And...about how kind she was.

He had been a fool to ever think he wanted a warrior like himself as a mate. No, she was everything he had never realized he wanted.

Needed.

She was a bright star in the world, one he wanted to see shine.

He set her suitcase—which was covered in stickers of odd-looking cartoons—at the foot of the bed. He hadn't

been sure what she wanted so he simply brought everything into his room. This was where she should be.

Presumptuous? Yes. Arrogant? Yes. But he would
make no apologies for who or what he was.

Instead of getting into bed with her as he craved, he
grabbed a rocking chair from the window and moved it
closer to her side of the bed. The position let him keep
an eye out the window as he kept watch over her. With
Greer being his priority. Though he wanted to slip into
bed with her, to pull her into his arms, he resisted.

Barely twenty minutes later, he saw Prima descend
into the yard, her movements short and jerky as she
shifted to human and sprinted for the house.

He went on high alert as he glanced at Greer. She
was in a "dead to the world" type of sleep so he quietly
slipped out of the room and met Prima at the top of the
stairs.

"I'm flying to South America. Now." She brushed
past him, not bothering to pause. The sharp scents of
her wild emotions were jagged, scraping against his
senses.

"What has happened?" Reaper kept pace with her as
she hurried to her room.

"I spoke to my sister about an hour ago and things
are fine. Well, fine enough for what's going on. Then
as I was patrolling the city, I felt our psychic link sever.
Mira had said they were investigating a gate to a Hell
realm, so if she entered one it is likely why the link severed. Our link does not stretch across realms. We have
to be in the same one. Regardless, I must go to her."

Reaper stopped at Prima's doorway even as she entered and pulled out her little suitcase. "I cannot leave Greer." Otherwise he would help Prima.

Prima paused, suitcase open, and gave him a half-smile. "I didn't expect you to come with me. I know you will not leave her. You *shouldn't* leave her. But thank you for thinking of it regardless. You are a good friend." She crossed the distance between them and sort of half patted, half punched him once on the shoulder before hurrying back to packing.

He wasn't sure if she was flying there herself or using one of those human planes but it wasn't his concern. She would do what would get her there fastest.

"Do me a favor?" she asked, tossing clothes into the brightly colored purple case.

"Of course."

"Tell Arthur I said thank you and that I apologize for leaving so abruptly."

"Should I thank him for having sex with you?" he asked dryly.

"That is not what I meant. Just tell him goodbye for me."

"Why not just text him yourself?"

"I don't have time." She hurried to the bathroom and came back out with a little bag that she shoved into her suitcase.

Reaper scented her lie—she could easily text Arthur. But that was not Reaper's business. "I will tell him that you have left when I see him again." He'd seen Arthur, Cale and Damari a couple times since the city had gone haywire. They had all been helping with the cleanup and keeping order under King's directives. It would be easy enough to relay the message.

Prima gave him another quick pat on the arm before she dashed down the stairs.

Reaper headed back the way he'd come and found Greer still sleeping. *Good.*

As he shut the door behind him, sleep finally dug its claws into him, telling him he needed to rest as well. He had not slept since everything had happened either. Though he was used to going without sleep, and after thousands of years in Hibernation, he should be fine. But...he needed to be at the top of his game.

He grabbed a little pillow with white ruffles along the edge from the rocking chair and placed it in between him and Greer as a sort of barrier as he stretched out over the covers. She did not stir at all, just snuggled deeper against her pillow.

He wished *he* was her pillow, that she currently laid her head on his chest. *Soon enough.* His dragon grumbled at that, not satisfied with waiting. Well too damn bad.

Stretching out onto his back, he closed his eyes and allowed himself to sleep.

* * *

Greer shifted against the soft sheets as she opened her eyes. Reaper's scent surrounded her, making her lightheaded as she inhaled. She wanted to roll around in that scent, bathe in it—roll around *with* him.

She stilled as she saw Reaper stretched out on his back, one hand under his head as he slept.

The male was as still and quiet in sleep as the predator he was. He was so preternaturally still that she could barely see his chest rising and falling. A soldier's nap, she believed it was called. Even in sleep, his arm muscles were defined, ripped.

Then she saw the little pillow tucked between them. For some reason the sight of it made her smile. Had he put it there? If he'd been trying to put a barrier between them, that was sort of…adorable.

No matter how obnoxious he'd been when they'd first met, she had come to realize he was simply arrogant because of his age. And, well, he was an ancient, skilled warrior. Of course he was arrogant. But she'd also seen the way he'd protected the city, and the way he was helping to patrol still, to keep people safe. He didn't have to either. He wasn't tied to New Orleans. He was not tied to *anything*. Least of all a wolf Alpha, yet he was more or less taking orders from King. Or at least not arguing with the male. And he did not need to. He was here because he wanted to be and he was a good, kind male.

She must have moved or made a sound because he suddenly opened his eyes and turned toward her.

"Greer." The way he said her name was a soft prayer, his deep voice dropping an octave and making her already frayed senses go just a little more haywire.

"Hey. Did you place the little pillow between us?"

"I did." He rolled onto his side, his eyes intense and glowing bright as he watched her. But he didn't move any closer. Just watched her.

"Why?" A little pillow wouldn't create any real type of barrier between them.

"I wanted to respect your space. And you should not be awake."

She frowned at him. "Why not?"

"You have only been asleep three hours. Not nearly enough time to recover."

She blinked. "How can you possibly know that?"

"I simply can. I can sense how much time has passed when I wake up."

"That's...impressive."

He shrugged it off. "Go back to sleep."

Her gaze drifted to his mouth, his very full lips, and suddenly sleep was the last thing on her mind. She was in that lazy, dreamy state and as she watched the way his chest rose and fell more rapidly now, sleep sounded boring as hell. She wanted to feel alive again. Wanted to feel him all over her. Inside her.

He growled softly in his throat as he rolled away from her, now staring up at the ceiling instead of keeping his gaze on her—where it should be.

Her dragon side did not like that. "What's wrong?"

"I am trying to be a good male. Close your eyes and go to sleep. I will not take advantage of your exhaustion."

Seriously? *Now* he was doing this? She wanted the arrogant Reaper who told her what to do.

As if he could actually take advantage of her. She was in full control of her faculties and she wanted him as she'd never wanted anyone else. Still, she laughed lightly as heat built up inside her. "Maybe I *want* you to take advantage of me—maybe I want to take advantage of you. I thought you said you wanted to taste between my legs. Was that a lie?" She wasn't sure where this bold side of herself was coming from but she embraced it. She would just blame it on lack of sleep. See? Lack of sleep was good for something.

He moved so quickly she didn't see his actual movements until he completely straddled her, caging her in with his forearms against the pillow by her head. "You are playing with fire."

"I like fire," she whispered. And she wanted to get burned by him. Her body ached, her nipples tight little beads as she stared up at him. When he didn't move an inch, she reached between their bodies and tugged on the tie of her robe. If this didn't motivate him, she wasn't sure what else would.

He sucked in a breath as she peeled it open. Cool air brushed over her bared skin, but the fire burning inside her was scorching.

"You should tell me to leave." His voice was all growly and sexy, his green-amber eyes wild and electric.

"Why would I do that?" she whispered. She arched her back slightly, brushing her nipples against his chest.

Yeah, she noticed that he'd gotten into bed without a shirt.

She imagined a male like Reaper was used to sleeping naked. Or maybe he'd done it to drive her crazy. Though she had a feeling he had no idea how insane he made her. The male had been in Hibernation for ages; he should be inside her right now, not fighting this.

He let out another soft growl and dipped his head to hers, biting her bottom lip—and not gently. Heat flooded between her legs.

"Robe, off," she rasped out, needing full-on skin-to-skin contact with him.

God, just a little nibble on her lip, and the friction of their bodies together, and she'd gone from zero to ready to orgasm now in mere seconds. She wasn't sure what it was about this male that made her so crazy. But there was no denying the incendiary attraction that sparked between them.

It took him literal seconds to help her tug off the robe and toss it to the floor before he caged her against him once again. She spread her legs as he settled in on top of her, his thick erection evident through the material of his pants. Material she wanted to burn right off.

"I'm going to make you come." A softly spoken promise that had tingles racing to all her nerve endings.

She was going to make him come too. Reaching between their bodies, she ran her hand over his covered erection, making him jerk against her. Good. She wanted to make him lose control, wanted him to come apart.

He growled again and dipped his head to her breast, sucking one of her nipples between his teeth as he cupped her other breast.

Pleasure erupted inside her as he teased and stroked her. It was heaven and yet not enough. And she wanted to touch him too. Everywhere.

She slid her hand down the front of his pants, grasping his thick cock as he lashed his tongue over her nipple.

He made a sort of rumbling sound as she stroked him, and the vibration sent all new sensations spiraling through her.

She slowly and probably too gently started stroking him, wanting to see what he liked. He allowed her to tease him as he teased her, as they learned each other's bodies.

As he moved down her body, she had to draw her hand away. She made a sound of protest until he settled between her legs.

"I've been fantasizing about this." He said the words straight against her pussy. Which was insanely hot.

Instinctively she rolled her hips, a silent plea for him to give her exactly what she needed. She was slick and aching for him, desperate for more. So much more.

He pinned her with an intense gaze as he slid a finger along her slick folds—watching for her reaction. She was already wet and wanting more and his teasing was ramping her need up even higher.

She wasn't sure when she'd started to really fall for him, but fall she had. The way he'd been checking in with her, offering to get her supplies or anything under the sun. He might be heavy-handed and arrogant, but he *cared*. It didn't matter that he was an ancient warrior used to killing and war—it was clear there was more to him than she'd originally thought. He was protective of her and completely focused on her needs.

And he'd never once tried to tell her what to do. Not truly.

When he slid two fingers inside her, she arched off the bed, her inner walls clamping around him.

Then he gave her an oh-so-wicked grin before he ducked his head between her legs.

"Reaper!" His name was a prayer on her lips as he lashed his tongue against her clit.

And that tongue? Pure magic as he teased her, over and over, with just enough pressure to push her right to the edge.

Her entire body jerked when bright purple flames swept over the bed and all around them, completely engulfing them. There was no heat, just beautiful, sparkling flames making everything glow.

The mating manifestation.

She jerked wildly at the sight and at the feel of what he was doing. She couldn't believe this was happening. She'd assumed that if they had been true mates, the flames would have showed up earlier since they'd kissed more than once. But there were no rules for how and when the mating manifestation showed up for dragons. It just did. And this…oh God. It was beautiful.

He looked up, saw their combined flames, then gave her a triumphant grin before ducking his head between her legs once again. As if he was completely satisfied at the sight of the manifestation.

Even though she couldn't believe this was happening, the pleasure of what he was doing took over all rational thought.

His tongue and fingers were magic, bringing her to the brink of pleasure until finally she couldn't stand it.

"Now!" she demanded.

"Now what?" She swore there was a hint of laughter in his voice as he flicked his tongue over her clit again. And again. And again.

"I'm…close…make me come." She sounded as if she was ordering him and she guessed she kinda was. But holy dragons, she needed to climax.

He laughed darkly and did just that, increasing the strokes of his fingers as he increased the pressure of his tongue. His magic, magic tongue that should be completely illegal.

Why hadn't they been doing this before? Oh right, she was an idiot.

She arched off the bed as her climax punched through her, singeing all her nerve endings even as the purple flames danced up the walls and across the ceiling, a beautiful blanket of fire surrounding them, encapsulating them. The climax seemed to go on and on as pleasure poured out of her.

As her body turned to jello, she let her legs fall against the bed. Moving like a predator, he crawled up her body, his fingers still buried inside her and his expression completely satisfied.

Then he kissed her, hard. It was a definite claiming. And the flames weren't dimming, simply flickering over everything as they grew brighter, bolder.

"I was right," he murmured as he nibbled on her bottom lip. "You do taste like heaven."

Beyond words at this point, she wrapped her arms and legs around him, savoring the feel of his hard body against hers.

He curled his fingers inside her. "Mine."

Heat surged through her, her toes digging against the sheets. Feeling frantic, she shoved at his pants, wanting to feel all of him. Thankfully he took over and tossed them to the floor—right on top of her robe—before he covered her once again.

She gripped his cock as he devoured her mouth, his kisses hungry, the fire in the room only growing, spreading outward so anyone on the street would see it.

Surprising her, he wrapped his fingers around hers, showing her exactly how hard he liked to be stroked. He kept his grip on hers as she teased him, bringing him to a hard climax that shot all over her stomach and breasts.

She wanted to feel him inside her, but loved the intimacy of this, of learning what he liked.

When he rubbed himself into her skin, she moaned into his mouth. For some reason it didn't surprise her that he was so raw and primal. Of course he was.

"Reaper—"

"Sleep now," he murmured as he pulled the covers over them. "And don't wash me off you," he continued, kissing her mouth even as he tugged her flush against his body. "I want you to wear my scent."

She loved being skin to skin with him, loved the heat of him. Vaguely she was aware that he was getting hard again but sleep was tugging her under with force.

The flames had died down, mere flickers now only covering them and the bed. That was a whole other can of worms she had to think about—was she ready to mate with him? The thought was too much to contemplate.

She couldn't think about that now. Definitely not now.

She was going to sleep and let the man she'd completely fallen for hold her in his arms.

Because she felt impossibly safe—which sounded insane even in her own head. The world had completely gone mad, but with Reaper, she felt protected.

Treasured.

Safe.

CHAPTER TWENTY-THREE

Greer opened her eyes into semidarkness, and stretched her arms over her head.

It took all of a second to realize that she was alone in bed. Frowning, she reached out and touched Reaper's side. It was cold.

She was surprised he hadn't woken her up. As she got up, she realized how refreshed she felt. And famished. It was still dark outside and something told her that it wasn't the same night she had gone to sleep—and been brought to climax by Reaper.

Fighting the disappointment that he wasn't still in bed with her, she searched for her cell phone. It was on the nightstand, and when she looked at the date she realized sure enough, nearly twenty-four hours had passed since she'd gone to sleep a second time. It was nine o'clock the next night and the house seemed very quiet.

No wonder she was starving. Even so, she could feel her energy burning bright inside her, warm and healing. She'd regained her strength.

After brushing her teeth and dressing, she checked in on the last two wolves who'd been at the house and found them gone and the beds stripped. They'd been so close to fully recuperating she guessed they'd left for good while she'd been asleep.

Downstairs in the kitchen she found it also empty—but the refrigerator was thankfully full. She wasn't quite sure what was going on with the city's food situation so she was grateful to not have to go out and hunt for food in dragon form. Still...she wondered where Reaper was.

As she started pulling containers out from the refrigerator, she called her Alpha.

"Hey, you're finally awake. You needing to sleep was the only reason I haven't called you," Conall said upon way of greeting.

"Really?" She'd forgotten to text Conall and let him know she'd be out of touch for a while. And that wasn't like her. But she'd also been dead on her feet and the world was burning right now so...she figured she was allowed a break.

"Yes. Reaper texted me and told me not to bother you." Conall's tone was dry.

"That sounds about right." She slid a plate full of pizza slices into the microwave—a nice little appetizer.

"I saw the news feed with you two." Again, his tone was dry.

"Is there a question you want to ask?" She opened the fridge again, looking for something cold to drink.

"What's going on with you and the ancient?"

If it was anyone else, she would have brushed them off but she had a feeling he was asking as her Alpha. "Reaper and I are having fun. Well, that sounds weird considering the state of the world right now but we are just..." Oh God, how did she explain what was going on

with Reaper when she didn't even understand it herself? The mating manifestation had revealed itself, leaving no doubt that they were mates if they chose to cross
that final line. He was kind and sweeter than she'd
thought to imagine. He was also fierce and protective of
her. "…ah, having fun," she repeated lamely. Even as she
said the words, she knew how pathetic they were. How
untrue.

It did a disservice to what she'd shared with him.
They were having more than just fun. But she wasn't
ready to open up to anyone about her growing feelings
for Reaper or the fact that the mating manifestation
had appeared. Not even to her Alpha, who she respected and had been friends with for a very long time.
Things with Reaper were too new and she wanted to
come to terms with this change before opening up. Unlike the younger generation of dragons, she didn't need
to open up about her every thought and feeling.

"All right." He paused, the silence growing as the microwave dinged once. "Look, I don't know if a male like
that will ever accept an Alpha. Me or *anyone*."

"Yes, I know." It was a simple truth about Reaper.
He was so ancient and capable, and unlike wolves who
needed packs, dragons were quite complicated.

She'd definitely thought of that too now that the
mating manifestation had made itself very clear. For
some reason she'd always assumed that when she got
mated, her mate would fit right in with her clan. In
hindsight that seemed like an obnoxious assumption to
make. She wondered *why* she'd never considered that

she might want to live with her future mate's clan. Maybe because she could be a little arrogant too? *Hmm.*

"Is there anything going on back home that I need to know about?" she continued, not wanting to talk about Reaper any longer.

"We have things under control. When are you coming home?" Blunt and right to the point.

And his question was fair. She'd just come down here to basically keep an eye on Reaper and Prima while Reaper looked for his friend. There was nothing keeping her here now. Well, nothing except Reaper. And she wasn't leaving him. That much she knew. "I don't know."

He sighed, the sound almost resigned. "Why do I have the feeling that you're never coming back?"

"Conall..." She struggled to find words to tell him that of course she'd be back. But things had changed. *She* had changed. Because of Reaper.

"If you decide to fly home, let me know. I'll make sure you're escorted by sentinels."

"If I do should I fly home in dragon form, or on the jet?"

"The jet should be fine. The skies are fairly wide-open right now."

His words were another reminder how much things had changed. Most commercial flights had been grounded because most airports were now nonexistent.

After they finished their conversation, she poured a glass of water then sat at the island with her food.

Before she'd taken her first bite, Reaper stepped into the kitchen from one of the open entryways, all silent and deadly.

"You're here." Joy burst inside her at the sight of him. He wore all dark clothing, right down to his black boots. Despite herself, she felt her cheeks flush as she thought of what they'd shared in his room—and what she hoped they got to do soon.

"I am here." His words and expression were flat, surprising her. And he didn't make a move to greet her.

Her dragon frowned, her fingers pricking slightly as her claws started to unsheathe. Oh, her dragon side did not like this. Before she could respond, she heard the front door open then close, and seconds later King stepped into the kitchen as well. So apparently people weren't knocking anymore.

King nodded politely at them. "Apologies for just stopping by. My wolves are home and I wanted to thank you in person for taking care of so many in my pack. I won't forget this, Greer."

"Oh…it's fine. And you're welcome." She felt weird receiving any sort of praise for doing something that simply came naturally, that was part of who she was. How could she not help others?

The sound of the front door opening and closing sounded again, causing both Reaper and King to turn. Cynara and Justus stepped into the kitchen seconds later. Cynara's purple eyes were bright and her movements fluid—as if she'd never been injured at all.

"Hey Greer, glad to see you up." Cynara rounded the island and wrapped her arms around Greer in a tight hug. "Thank you for all you did."

As she hugged the hybrid female, she scented Justus all over her—the mating bond. "You're welcome, and congratulations." She smiled as Cynara pulled back. "Glad you finally made the right choice."

"You and me both," Justus said, rounding the island. But when he made a move to hug Greer too, Reaper growled low and dangerous in his throat.

Greer's eyes widened at the primal display but Justus simply stepped back. "My bad, Reaper." Then he turned to King. "I got a lead on Brennus. I don't know if it's solid yet but someone from the local coven reached out to me and said he heard you were looking for the dragon and any of his clanmates. He gave me a couple addresses, said he thought Brennus's clan might own the properties but under a different name."

"Who told you this?" There was a bite to King's words.

Greer realized it was because this territory was his now. He would expect people to come to him directly with anything he deemed necessary. But...he couldn't expect change instantly though. People were too complicated for that, supernatural or not.

"Ah...look. I'm not telling you their name. Vamps have a ways to go before fully trusting you, and if you want to build bridges between shifters and my kind, you'll have to bend a little." Spoken as one Alpha to another. "I only see the trust truly happening when you take a mate." There was a slight questioning note in Justus's voice, no doubt because it was rumored that King was supposed to have taken a mate right before all Hell broke loose on earth. But he definitely hadn't or they'd have all scented it on him.

King nodded after a tense silence. "You're correct. So, do you trust this guy?"

"I do. He has no reason to give me bad intel. Everyone is pissed about what their clan did."

"Good, then." King glanced between Justus, Cynara and Reaper. "You three feel like going hunting?"

"You're not including me in that?" Greer asked.

King froze then looked at Greer. "Ah…you're a healer. I just assumed… You want to go hunting?"

"No. But I don't like being ignored." Okay, she was feeling a little snarky right now.

"Fair enough. So?" He turned back to the others.

They all nodded, except Reaper, who turned to Greer. "I will stay," he said to her.

"It's fine, Reaper. I'm fully rested. Besides, I'm sure Prima is around here somewhere."

"She left the country."

Uh, what? Greer would ask more on that later. "Oh, well, it's still fine. I'm a dragon and fully capable of taking care of myself. Go with them, find that traitor." She'd never thought of herself as particularly vengeful or violent but Brennus and all his clan deserved to die for what they'd done. They were responsible for the death of billions. They could rot in Hell.

It was clear Reaper was torn. "You will stay here?"

She frowned at him. "I have no plans to go anywhere."

"I'll keep her company," Cynara added, and while Greer appreciated the offer, she was annoyed. She was a grown-ass dragon. She didn't need a babysitter. Then again…it would be smart not to be alone right now. "Ian and the others said they would stop by later anyway. If anything changes or if you need backup, just text me," Cynara continued, looking at Justus.

The vampire nodded and headed out with King—but not before giving Cynara a searing kiss that would leave any female breathless.

To her surprise, Reaper hung back, though his distant expression and body language were crystal clear. What the hell was going on with him? "I will have my phone on me if you need anything." His words were stiff and stilted.

Despite the fact that Cynara was still in the kitchen, Greer pushed up from her chair and rounded the island to face him head-on. "Have I done something to offend you? Yesterday you couldn't keep your hands off me. Now…" He was behaving as if she were a stranger.

Cynara chose that moment to duck out of the kitchen, mumbling nonsensical words under her breath.

Reaper just watched Greer for a long moment, his dragon in his gaze. Finally he answered. "I will be back soon." Which wasn't an answer at all.

She wanted to stomp her foot in frustration but resisted the childish impulse.

He turned to go, but abruptly strode back across the expansive kitchen. Placing his hands on the countertop behind her, he leaned down, his expression no longer neutral. Now his dragon peered back at her, that bright electric amber gaze wild and angry. "What we did last night was more than *fun* for me. I'm in this for more than simple *fun*," he added again, his jaw tight, his words hard. Waves of potent, red anger rolled off him—and to her surprise, she felt the sense of his hurt more than anything. "You are my mate."

She slid her hands up his chest. Oh, she'd screwed up big time. "Reaper, I'm—"

He stepped back. "I've got my phone on me. Don't hesitate to contact me if you need me." Then he was gone, disappearing from the kitchen before she could blink.

Her stomach tightened as she collapsed back into one of the chairs. Clearly he'd overheard what she'd said to her Alpha about just having fun with Reaper. Inwardly she winced, not exactly surprised by his reaction. If she'd overheard him say that, it would have cut her up. Because what they'd shared went deeper than that. She simply hadn't been willing to talk to her Alpha about what was going on with Reaper.

Because she wasn't sure herself what was going on. Even so, she still felt like a giant jerk. When Reaper returned, she would make things right with him.

* * *

Reaper was in straight battle mode as they headed out onto the street, his dragon right at the surface, waiting to be unleashed. He tried to forget what he'd heard Greer say, but her words kept playing over and over in his mind as she'd told her Alpha that they were just having fun.

She had not said anything about him being her mate, about him being a worthy, capable male.

He wanted all of her. *Forever.* Perhaps she did not feel the same. But how could she deny what was between them? She'd *seen* the mating manifestation. The entire neighborhood would have seen it. She was his. He'd been pleased when it had finally revealed itself, but it hadn't mattered.

Because he had known deep down that she was his mate, with or without that manifestation. And even if they never took the final leap and fully mated, she was his. So to hear her dismiss what they had shared cut far deeper than any blade or claw, burned more than any dragon fire.

King's cell phone rang, interrupting his thoughts as they headed toward a darkly tinted large vehicle he believed was called an SUV. He was not sure what the acronym stood for though.

"Yeah?" the wolf said.

Whoever was on the other line spoke too low for Reaper to hear. Or maybe the Alpha had some sort of muffling mechanism on his phone. The more he learned about human technology, he figured that something like that was possible. Because his hearing was exceptional and he should have been able to eavesdrop easily.

King gritted his teeth as he slid his phone back into his pocket mere seconds later.

"We have a new problem," the Alpha said as they reached his vehicle. King slid into the passenger seat and Justus and Reaper got into the back. Reaper was not sure he cared for these vehicles—they were too small and stifling. He would prefer to simply fly everywhere.

The driver, another wolf, simply nodded at them in the rearview mirror, but did not speak otherwise.

"Head to Washington, near the cemetery," King ordered.

"What's going on?" Justus asked.

"A bunch of humans have broken curfew. They're pushing the boundaries intentionally, I believe. They aren't quite rioting, but they're not listening to my patrols or returning home."

"Or they are simply scared," Reaper said. For him change was inevitable and he was easily able to adapt, but he had learned that adapting was hard for some humans. Many had lost people they loved in an instant, their entire world changed in a massive way.

Now that he had found Greer, the thought of losing her was too much. So yes, these humans had a right to be afraid. Oddly enough, he felt he could relate to the humans.

King sighed. "True enough, but they're not getting a pass. Whatever this is, I'm putting an end to it tonight.

264 | KATIE REUS

Then we'll head to the address your contact gave you," he said to Justus.

The Alpha didn't ask if Reaper and Justus even wanted to go on this new mission so it appeared they were going. Which should have annoyed Reaper. But to his surprise, he kind of liked the wolf. The male was arrogant but that was not always a bad thing. And he had seen the male hold his own against dragons. The male was resistant to dragon fire—something that was impressive in itself. Only a few supernaturals had that gift, and they were very old and very powerful.

He rolled his shoulders once as they rode in silence down the cobblestone streets.

He forced himself not to think of Greer's dismissive words, of her tone. He knew what they had shared was more than just fun. He refused to believe otherwise.

If she decided she didn't want him as her mate? He…would not contemplate that thought now. He could not.

She was his.

He would soon claim her.

CHAPTER TWENTY-FOUR

Brennus answered the video conference call, even as he prepared himself to see his father on-screen. They had spoken many times over the last couple days as certain sects of their clanmates had gone into hiding—his own territory being one of them.

One of their younger clanmates had gotten trigger-happy and released dragons too early in London. So they'd been forced to release all of them worldwide before they had been completely prepared with each city.

At least they'd been able to disable all nuclear weapons.

His father didn't bother with any sort of greeting as he looked at him and the others in the room with Brennus. "Shenzhen, Moscow and Izmir are now in our clan's control." That was only three cities. Not that impressive. Brennus kept the thought to himself as his father continued. "I'm taking down Bayne today. We all need to make our moves."

Brennus nodded in agreement at his father's assessment. After the fires and destruction, only handfuls of supernatural-strong cities remained fully intact. Of course there were more rural areas that hadn't been touched. Areas his clan would claim soon enough. But first they had to take over the main supernatural strongholds. His father was currently in Edinburgh and the shifter in charge there was a dragon named Bayne. An obnoxious asshole.

"I'm ready to go. King will fall tonight." Brennus was prepared for battle with the wolf. The male might be fireproof—something he'd only recently learned—but he was no match for Brennus. He was a dragon after all.

His father nodded. "See that he does."

There would be no room for failure.

"What about Abana? Is she our ally?"

"No. She refuses to join with us." Rage filled his father's expression.

His father spoke for a few more minutes, directly addressing each of the clanmates on the conference call before he ended the feed. They'd been careful so far about their communications and now was no different. All their calls were encrypted. Human governments might have toppled but there were plenty of supernatural spies and hackers out there that couldn't be trusted.

Brennus turned to look at the others in the room, focusing on one male in particular. A male not part of his clan, but a dragon nonetheless. A powerful one. "I will take on King." It was important that he eliminated the wolf. He had to show the entire city that he was the true Alpha of this area. "You know what to do."

The male in front of him nodded. "I saw the manifestation last night. Reaper has claimed the female. I'll take her tonight and bring him to me. I'll make him watch her die. Is your distraction in place?"

Brennus nodded as anticipation filled him, coursing through his veins like the strongest supernatural drug, potent and exhilarating. Soon he would have everything he'd ever wanted. Everything he *deserved*. He was a fucking dragon. A god. He bowed to no one. "I'm leading King exactly where I want him to go." He'd had his dragons stir up some of the humans in the city and now they were in a state of panic and ready to riot. Brennus had no doubt that King would personally step up to ease their fears.

That was when Brennus would make his move.

"What if he doesn't accept your challenge?" the male asked.

"He will. If he has any pride—and he does—King will definitely accept my challenge. If he doesn't, I will kill him anyway."

But by officially challenging the Alpha, Brennus would have an easier time stepping into the role as the true leader of the city. That was how supernaturals operated. He expected to get pushback from the wolves in King's pack but they would be crushed easily enough. And all other supernaturals would either fall in line or challenge him. Simple as that. This was his territory now.

"Go. All of you." He focused on his longtime ally. "Take the female then do what you want with Reaper. Just make sure he dies." Because there was no room in this new world for Reaper. He was too powerful. Too much of a wild card.

The male nodded and left the room on silent feet.

Once he was alone, Brennus turned and looked out the huge window, watching the city spread out before him. The windows had a thin tinted covering over them so people couldn't see inside. But he could see out. He was still in hiding, still not out to the world. And he hated that. All that changed tonight. Soon he would claim what was rightfully his. What he was owed.

This was his territory and everyone in it would bow to him.

CHAPTER TWENTY-FIVE

"So…what's going on with you guys?" Cynara asked as she stepped back into the kitchen, not even hiding the fact that she'd been eavesdropping.

"I'm pretty sure I screwed up. Actually I know I did. I hurt his feelings." And Greer felt like garbage because of it. She might still be coming to terms with the fact that they were truly mates, but she shouldn't have said they were just "having fun." She should have told her Alpha that what she and Reaper had was none of his business.

"That man will definitely forgive you."

"It doesn't matter. I hurt him and…" *Ugh.* She pulled out her cell phone and called him, but he didn't pick up. Either he was ignoring her or he couldn't answer because they were hunting down Brennus. Which made her feel even worse. She shouldn't have let Reaper go at all without talking to him, without making things right.

"You're not perfect, girl. It's okay."

"Yeah…" Greer cleared her throat, unsure what else to say. Guilt ate away at her as she remembered his expression. It almost seemed impossible that she could hurt the arrogant, confident male. But she had. "Let's not talk about me. I'm so happy for you and Justus. When did this happen?"

"Literally as soon as I was fully healed and out of here. You were asleep but we headed back to his place and...we're mated." Cynara's smile was blinding. "And crazy enough, all my brothers are thrilled. One of them had the audacity to say it was good because I needed a male to take care of me."

"Javier?" The youngest, who loved to mess with Cynara.

Cynara laughed. "Bingo. I swear I can't wait till he gets mated."

"I'm so happy for you both. You and Justus deserve to be happy."

"Thanks. It still feels a little surreal but I'm trying to roll with it. I figure if the world is going to go mad, I'm taking this happiness with my mate for as long as it lasts."

Greer fully understood that, which was why she was kicking herself right now. "I feel kind of disconnected with what's been going on." That being an understatement. She felt as if she'd slept for a century. "Reaper said Prima left the country?"

Cynara nodded, her expression tightening. "Yeah. She felt the psychic link between her and her sister snap."

"Oh hell, that's not good. Is Mira okay? Or do you guys know anything yet?" Mira and Prima might be eccentric, but they were her clanmates and well loved.

"Well...sort of. Apparently Lyra and Vega's psychic connection severed as well. So Finn and Lyra are in South America now, the same as Prima. They hated leaving their baby, but he's with the pack and protected. Cell service is kinda spotty down there though. And from the gossip I've heard, Vega and some of the people she works with, including Gabriel, got sucked into some sort of Hell realm too. Prima, Lyra and Finn have gone after them."

The bombs just kept dropping. "Holy hell. Who's running the Stavros pack?"

"Solon, Ophelia and Gray are keeping things running. The pack already listens to Ophelia for pretty much anything and the other two are heading up security teams and keeping the city safe. Rory is really stepping up too but he's been back and forth between Biloxi and here thanks to Nyx's gift of travel." She paused as her phone buzzed and glanced at the screen. "Speak of the devil, Nyx just texted me. Prepare."

"Prepare for what?"

Before Cynara could answer, a cacophony of wind and noise burst through the kitchen, blasting out two of the glass-paned cabinets. Then suddenly four people stood in the kitchen. Bo immediately lifted his hand, freezing the glass in midair before guiding it back to its home.

Nyx's inky black hair was tousled with her arrival. She gave an apologetic smile. "Sorry about that."

"Don't apologize for who you are," Bo grumbled.

Rory and Ian straightened their shirts as they nodded at Greer and hugged Cynara.

As the daughter of a goddess, Nyx could transport herself and anyone touching her anywhere in the world she wanted, as long as she had been there before or had a clear image of the place.

"Everything okay?" Cynara asked as she squeezed Ian tight, looking up at her brother adoringly.

"We got a call that some shit was going down near here. Apparently humans are upset, and while it's not in straight riot mode yet, it could get there." Bo shook his head as he spoke.

"I just got a text from Justus saying the same thing." Cynara frowned at her phone screen as it buzzed again. "King, Reaper and the others diverted to the human mob instead. Who called you?" Cynara asked her brother, even as they all headed for the front door.

"The Magic Man," Bo said.

"Ah," was all Cynara said even as Greer nodded.

The Magic Man of New Orleans was Thurman, a human seer who ran a magic shop and had apparently been a little in love with Bo's mother many, many years ago.

For a moment Greer wondered where Fiona and Liberty were, but knew that Fiona wouldn't come if things were tense in the city—not when she was pregnant. And Liberty would be helping out with her pack.

Right now Greer was going to help out all she could. It bothered her that Reaper hadn't contacted her when Justus had texted Cynara, but things were very new with Greer and him. They had a lot of getting used to each other to do.

It didn't take long to get to Washington Avenue where at least two hundred humans and supernaturals alike filled the street and sidewalk that ran parallel to an old cemetery. It was late and all the shops across the street from the cemetery were closed, and from what she could see there was no actual rioting. But she scented fear.

So much fear from the humans that it was stifling to her senses.

"This is not good," she murmured more to herself than the others as they hurried up the street, coming up on the tail end of a cluster of humans.

Most of the humans had their backs to them, facing the huge wall where King stood addressing everyone.

A human woman who couldn't be more than twenty years old glanced over her shoulder, and when she saw Greer and the others her eyes widened. After the news, there was no way they could hide what they were.

And though Greer had over a thousand years of practice hiding what she was, she was actually grateful not to have to hide anymore. It was oddly liberating to just be herself. To embrace all of herself.

"Go on," she murmured to the others as she approached the woman and her friends—who had all turned around by now.

"What's going on?" she directly asked the first woman she'd made eye contact with. She wasn't going to ignore the woman when she was staring right at Greer.

The woman—hell, girl, really—cleared her throat as she continued to stare. She wore a ratty sweatshirt with

274 | KATIE REUS

the word Tulane on the front and her blonde hair was
pulled up in a messy bun.

"We heard that King's pack is going around and
dragging humans out of their homes and killing them,"
the girl next to her said. Her afro was short and she
wore a similarly sad-looking sweatshirt as her friend.
But she was a little braver or at least able to talk.

Greer snorted, the thought of that ridiculous. "Who
did you hear that from?"

Her friend with the blonde hair finally spoke. "We
all go to Tulane. We were in the quad and some guy
was telling my friend Nate about it. Said that the supernaturals were going to kill everyone in the city. That
New Orleans would end up like the rest of the world."
Tears filled her eyes then, but she dashed them away.
"My family was in Chicago and it's all gone now. I can't
get ahold of anyone because...they're gone."

Yeah, Greer had heard Chicago hadn't made it either. It was a fucking mess out there. A fiery, chaotic
mess. "You have no reason to believe me but King is
not killing humans. Whoever told you that is a liar and
wants to sow dissent." She glanced over their heads at
clusters of different humans, eyeing the males more
than anyone. Both genders could be violent, but in her
very long existence she had learned that human males
tended to be a lot more angry and violent in general
than females. And when they were together, a pack
mentality could take over.

She half listened to King talking to the humans, and while she trusted the Alpha to get things under control she would do what she could to help.

"I saw you on the news," the brown-skinned girl said. "You looked pretty cool." One of her friends nudged her and made shushing sounds but the girl lifted her shoulders. "What? She was cool."

"Thank you. Look, you guys need to head home. This will be taken care of tonight but I don't want you getting hurt in case some of those dumbasses over there start trouble," she said motioning toward the cluster of men who looked to be in their mid-twenties.

"All right," the first girl said after following where Greer had indicated. "But only because we saw you on the news. We saw what you did to kill those...dragons. It was scary awesome."

"My name is Greer. If you need anything, call me, okay?" She rattled off her phone number and the blonde quickly put it in her own phone. "Now go," she ordered.

The young women nodded and hurried off.

The others Greer had come with had already dispersed, slowly circling around the group of humans who were facing the wall along the cemetery where King still stood, continuing to talk to the humans there, trying to calm them down.

As he spoke in that rich, deep, melodic voice, she sensed some calmness settle over the crowd—but overall emotions were far too high. And it was no wonder. The people here might have survived what happened but they would almost all know people around the world and have family elsewhere. Family and friends that were now gone.

She saw the girls moving away from the crowd toward a side street and she was grateful they had listened. Now she just needed to convince more humans to leave—and to find Reaper. She scanned the crowd but didn't see him anywhere, and he was a male impossible to miss. At least she knew what had drawn the humans here. Someone was lying, and if she had to guess, it was probably Brennus and his clanmates.

It made sense. His endgame would be to take over the city, so how would he do that? Upset the people, then challenge those in charge. He and his ilk would be all about wreaking havoc and then taking over when people were weak and beat down.

She maneuvered her way through the back of the crowd, using her healer's energy to gently nudge people out of the way without them even realizing they were shifting for her. She more or less created a little barrier around herself as she moved through the throng of people. As she reached the middle, she saw Reaper far to the left of King on the wall.

Crouched down, he scanned the crowd, ever alert. He looked magnificent. Truly and utterly so. Just like the warrior he was. She needed to talk to him, to make things right. To apologize for the way she hadn't acknowledged what was between them. That wasn't how mates acted, and even if she'd been stunned by the mating manifestation…he deserved better than her response to her Alpha.

Hell, this was on her. As she stared at Reaper, she felt fire building inside her and looked away, not wanting the manifestation to start—because that would definitely scare the humans.

She wished she could talk to him right now and tell him what he meant to her—that she would live wherever he wanted. While she loved her clan and she still needed to get to know Reaper more, everything she knew, she liked.

More than liked.

She was on the hook for this male and it wasn't changing. Her dragon side was in full agreement too. He'd shown her exactly who he was. And once again he was down here watching over humans when he didn't have to.

She continued to scan the crowd for familiar faces and look for any potential danger. Justus was on the edge of it, and a whole lot of King's wolves were interspersed throughout the throng of humans. They were blending in well, ready to regulate the crowd if need be.

She glanced back over at Reaper and found him watching her intently.

He stood, his movements quick, his amber eyes pinned on hers. It was impossible to read his mood as he stared at her. Not taking his gaze off her, he reached into his pocket. When he pulled out a phone, she realized he was going to text her.

Sure enough she pulled her own phone out of her pocket, half listening to King explaining to everyone that they would be much safer inside their own homes.

Her phone buzzed. *You shouldn't be here.*

She frowned and texted back. *Why not?*

It's not safe.

She snorted to herself, but didn't respond. Hello, she was a dragon. Maybe she needed to get that tattooed on herself.

Go back to the mansion, he texted.

Oh, no. Anger flared inside her at his order, spreading out like a wildfire. Instead of responding, she shoved her phone back into her pocket and gave him a challenging stare. She'd been with one male who had tried to run her life, to tell her what to do. She wanted a future with Reaper but she wouldn't be with a male who tried to order her around. If he was truly worried, she would take precautions. But she was a *dragon shifter* and wouldn't deny who she was. If something happened here, she was going to help. She might feel bad about what she'd said, but that didn't matter. He better learn right now that she was literally never going to walk away from bad situations just because there might be danger.

"How the hell can we trust you?" a human to her right shouted out to whatever King had just said.

"Am I giving you a reason not to?" Frustration rolled off King now, his patience clearly running thin as his tone changed from patient to arrogant ruler in an instant. The real King was out now. The one who, she was fairly certain, was going to make a damn fine leader. "Where are these allegedly murdered humans? No one knows of anyone who has been killed or gone missing, do they?" He paused, waiting as silence spread, the crowd going still. "Why? Because it's all fucking lies. Someone wants the city to burn, to fall. I'm not going to let that happen. Neither will my pack or my allies." He pointed at Reaper, then Justus. "And I've shown you with my actions exactly what this place means to me." He slammed a fist against his chest once, his eyes ice blue and bright. "You can believe rumors without any basis in truth or you can use your damn heads."

She snorted at his rough words. There would be no sugarcoating or political-like speeches from this wolf. No way. He showed the world exactly who he was. A good male.

"Pretty inspiring," a familiar voice said next to her.

Blinking, she was startled when she turned and found one of Reaper's acquaintances next to her. He moved as quietly as Reaper did. Which made sense since he was an ancient too.

"He certainly is," she murmured. She glanced over at the wall but saw that Reaper wasn't there anymore.

The male reached out a hand toward her shoulder and she frowned, wondering what the hell he was doing, when she felt the pinch of something sink into her neck.

It happened so quickly she couldn't react, couldn't even move as pain exploded inside her, burning up her nerve endings. She tried to cry out but her throat wouldn't work. Realization dawned as her entire body went into paralysis.

Poison. She stared at the male in horror as he slipped an arm around her shoulders and leaned his head close to hers, holding on to her as if they were friends simply talking.

No! She screamed in her head, tried to struggle against him as she called on her energy. The spark of life tingled against her fingertips, but...nothing. She could barely move. He'd lifted her off the ground so her feet weren't dragging.

Oh God, Reaper! She tried to turn her head to see if she could find him, but this treacherous male continued hauling her through the crowd of people. Then another male was there, helping him guide her away. But she didn't recognize him.

Everyone was so focused on King they barely glanced at them.

She refused to be taken, refused to let this bastard kidnap her. She struggled to fight him, raging at her energy to work, but the poison was winding its way through her body. It moved out to all her nerve endings, sharp bites of pain carving a path through her body.

Dragon poison. It had to be.

She struggled to keep her eyes open, felt tears rolling down her cheeks as she opened her mouth in another silent cry of agony. Where were her friends? Where was Reaper?

Then she felt another prick against her neck and blackness dragged her under.

CHAPTER TWENTY-SIX

Reaper scanned the faces of all the humans who were now dispersing. *Finally.* He scented Greer but he could not see her. Had she stripped and then gone into camouflage mode? No, he did not think so. Her scent, so sweet and wild, like summer rain, lingered in the air, taunting him.

Damn it. He should not have sent her those abrupt texts. They had been "bossy," as she liked to say. But...he did not want her here. He wanted her back in the mansion, safe. Safe being a relative word. But she did not need to be around angry humans who might decide to turn violent.

He rolled his shoulders once as a group of male humans hurried past, giving him a sideways look. Fear and curiosity rolled off them and it took all his self-control not to snarl at them. Right now he needed to find Greer, not bare his teeth at humans. At least the humans had listened to King and were all going back to their respective homes. They'd all started to leave, fanning out in different directions, some seeming appeased, others simply afraid.

Five minutes later, the street was clear of humans and Greer was nowhere to be found. She had not answered any of his phone calls.

And he had called twenty-five times.

His dragon clawed at him, tugging at his barely there restraint, demanding he take to the skies and search for her.

King spoke with his wolves on the sidewalk, but Cynara and the others were talking in a circle near the high-gated entrance of the cemetery.

He approached them, not caring that he was interrupting their conversation. "Have you seen Greer?"

Ian answered him. "She came with us but stopped to talk to some human females. It looked as if she convinced them to head out." Frowning, Ian glanced around, as did the others. Reaper had recently figured out that they came from the same clan. It was strange to have family with him now, family he actually liked.

But nothing mattered at the moment. Reaper's agitation spiked, his claws pricking against his fingertips.

"She could have gone back to the mansion," Cynara said as she pulled out her cell phone. "Though I don't know why she would have." The hybrid made a call—to Greer, he assumed.

"I might have texted her and told her to leave," Reaper admitted.

Cynara snort-laughed. "She didn't answer for me… Did you phrase your text as an order?"

He lifted a shoulder. "My text might have been abrupt." *Translation, yes.*

"Well, then I guarantee she didn't listen to your dumb ass," Cynara said, rolling her eyes. "You don't order a dragon female to do anything." She looked around, concern growing in her expression. "She didn't answer my call but have you tried calling her?"

"Yes." And he felt like he was stalking her but he did not care.

King and his wolves approached then. "We've confirmed from every human that someone is spreading rumors that we are killing them," the Alpha said.

"It is obviously Brennus and his clan." Reaper knew he sounded exasperated and did not care. The only thing that mattered was finding Greer. "But I have a different problem. I cannot find Greer."

King straightened. "What do you mean?"

"She was here. I saw her—" His phone rang then, and relief punched through him when Greer's name appeared on-screen. These stupid phones were good for something, it seemed.

He swiped his finger across the screen. Prima had shown him how the camera function worked. So the night at the club before everything had gone crazy, he had snapped a secret picture of Greer when she hadn't been looking. She was laughing at something Cynara had said. Her hair was down around her shoulders, her eyes sparkling with laughter. He wished she was here with him now. "Greer. I apologize for what I said before—"

"You aren't sorry enough." A familiar male voice came across the line. "But you're going to be."

Ice filled Reaper's veins. "Damari? Why are you calling me on Greer's phone?" Even as he spoke, understanding sliced through him. There was only one reason for Damari to be calling from her phone, to be talking to him like this.

And now Damari would die.

"I have your healer. I thought you two had mated. But as soon as I poisoned her, I realized you hadn't. You're *pathetic*," the male spat. "Couldn't even get your mate to bond to you and now you never will. I'm going to kill your healer. Come get her. Maybe you can save her. Or maybe I'll let you watch while I cut her head off." He laughed maniacally right before the phone went dead.

He stared at the phone in his hand, paralyzed for the first time in his entire existence.

Kill Greer? *No.*

His phone buzzed and a picture of Greer flashed on-screen. Her arms and legs were bound and she was strung up from a tree branch. Her eyes were closed, her head lolled back, her copper-colored hair falling all around her. There was a weird tint to the picture, making everything look almost red.

Nausea rose inside him as he started to squeeze his hands around the phone. It started to crack before Cynara took it from him. It buzzed again, this time with an address. Before he could snatch it back, she clicked on it and a map pulled up. He read the words on the screen, recognized the area. It wasn't far from here. Which made sense; she hadn't been gone long.

His phone buzzed again so he grabbed it back from Cynara and read the next message.

Come alone and fight me for her. Five minutes. Tick tock.

Reaper tossed the phone to Cynara as he backed away from everyone.

"Dude, this is a trap!" Cynara said as he moved farther away until he was in the middle of the street.

Of course it was a trap. He didn't care. He let the shift come over him, let his dragon take control.

"We're going with you," Cynara snapped at his dragon even as King said, "You're not going alone."

He snarled at all of them, shoving out a burst of flames into the air. He didn't care if they came or not. He would save Greer and kill Damari.

Slowly. Painfully.

And he wouldn't wait for anyone. Ignoring them, he turned away, his wing slamming into a tree and big trash can, knocking them both over as he took to the night skies.

Find mate.

Stop threat.

Kill Damari.

Reaper's beast had almost completely taken control at this point, his rage wild and bright, fire bursting from his mouth as he flew, unable to stop himself.

He could not believe Damari had betrayed him. Had taken Greer. It made no sense. They had fought together, had been allies.

Treetops and homes flew by underneath him at a rapid rate as the wide-open cemetery came into view. Gravestones and statues covered the rolling hill, but so did huge oak trees, giving needed cover to anyone that desired it.

He had studied the topography and maps of the city over the last few days and now he was grateful for the foresight.

As he swooped downward, his wings skimming treetops, he spotted an unnatural red glow emanating from a cluster of trees. What the hell was it?

Oh, gods. It was Greer. Suspended from a tree in some sort of red, glowing cocoon. He had to get her out.

Right as he arrowed toward her, a red ball of fire flew past him, nearly hitting his left wing.

He rolled over midair before spiraling downward.

Another ball of red flames shot at him, lighting up the night.

He opened his jaw and released a raging stream of fire, unable to see the threat. His flames lit up the cemetery and he saw Damari surge up from the trees. Two dragons he didn't recognize sat guarding Greer. They didn't move even as Damari flew at him.

He tucked his wings in tight and started free-falling as Damari shot up at him. When they would have collided, Reaper let his wings unfurl, stopping his fall and unleashing a burst of fire.

He sliced through the softer scales of Damari's underbelly.

Damari snarled, and being the ancient he was, he veered midflight and arrowed straight for Reaper, blasting him with fire.

It rolled over his scales and body as he returned fire.

He would not be defeated. Reaper flew through the flames, straight at Damari.

They collided midair, their talons tearing each other to shreds.

Damari's dragon screeched as Reaper clutched onto the beast with his claws, digging into his scales and tearing wildly.

Ignoring the rush of pain as Damari bit into his neck, he blasted fire in the traitor's eyes and face.

Damari released his hold as they spiraled downward toward the trees.

Right before they would have crash-landed, Reaper released the other dragon from his grip. He flapped his wings hard, ignoring the agony streaking through him as he glided over the trees and swooped back toward his enemy. Toward the male who was about to die.

Damari was flying directly for him as well, his right wing injured.

Reaper let all his rage build inside him, the need to protect Greer an overwhelming force he had only experienced once—when he'd seen that dragon over Jackson Square about to attack Greer. He breathed out fire, the flames a bright, brilliant blue, so bright they decimated the trees and everything in between.

Damari rolled away, crashing down into the trees and out of sight.

Reaper didn't stop, but continued shooting fire through the foliage. It burned away, ash carrying on the wind as he dove straight at Damari, who was trying to run from him.

This male would never outrun him. Reaper would hunt him to the ends of the earth. And beyond. He would follow him straight into Hell and destroy him.

Damari turned, his claws digging up earth and gravestones as he tried to get away.

Reaper descended onto his back, breathing that same brilliant blue fire as he sank his jaw into the male's neck and tore through bone and cartilage.

With a stream of rage, he ripped his head off. Blood and fire erupted everywhere. But he wasn't done. He continued burning, burning, burning until nothing remained. No bones, just ash, carrying away on the wind.

CHAPTER TWENTY-SEVEN

Greer was aware of Reaper battling with that bastard Damari up in the sky. Damari was a fool if he believed he could take Reaper on. And the male thought he could. She knew because he had told her so before he'd stabbed her again, this time with a witch's nasty concoction.

Freaking witches.

So now she was wrapped up in a cocoon of fiery, dark magic. Too bad for Damari—her healer's energy would tear through this.

Eventually.

But he'd been a fool to think this concoction was strong enough for her. He clearly knew nothing of healers or their energy. He should have tranqued her a hundred times more than this dosage if he'd wished her to remain unconscious. Of course she had to deal with the two big dragons on either side of her, guarding her.

That was simply semantics. Because she was going to get out of this alive. And she was going to mate with Reaper as well. She refused to die like this, to die right after she'd met her mate. Right after the entire world had been destroyed and reshaped. No, she wanted to be around for at least another thousand years with Reaper by her side. She wanted to have dragonlings and see what this new world would bring. She. Would. Not. Die.

Her rage fueled her energy, tingles spreading up her fingers, her arms, and throughout her entire body as her own magic worked, pushing back against the darkness trying to take over.

Through the red haze she could see war raging in the sky but couldn't actually hear anything. It was like this cocoon was insulated.

The dragons were watching the battle as well, their bodies tense. They weren't paying attention to her at all. *Fools.*

She needed to get out, to help Reaper. She pushed out with her power, her own energy a soft green glow, eating away at the interior of the cocoon, inch by inch, destroying the insidious darkness.

Out of the corner of her eye, she thought she saw shadows moving. It could be help or it could be nothing—or more enemies. She ignored the shadows peeling away from the trees. Right now she was going to depend on herself. And Reaper.

Her energy created a force field around her body, shoving against the strange, witchy magic somehow keeping her suspended and separate from the world.

Closing her eyes, she took a deep breath, focusing hard before she shoved outward, sending her power streaming from her fingertips.

The cocoon exploded, remnants of it turning to sharp, jagged glass, raining down all around her.

The dragons screeched as the glass punched into their thick scales. Without thought, she held her hands out on either side, blasting both of them with her healer's power.

They barrel rolled, knocking down trees and gravestones. Then they stopped moving.

Holy shit. She'd never done anything like that in her entire life.

No time to dwell on it, however. She had a mate to find. She refused to accept that Reaper might not have survived. Couldn't even let her mind go there.

Fire erupted from the trees at least a hundred yards in front of her. Instead of shifting, she ran straight for it, calling on her supernatural speed to empower her.

She heard movement behind her, and glanced over her shoulder.

She wasn't exactly surprised to see Cynara, Bo, and the others killing those two dragons.

Good.

As she raced into the cluster of trees, she jerked to a halt, nearly crashing into Reaper.

Who was alive. "Reaper!" she shouted, her joy limitless. Ash floated on the air around him as he moved toward her.

He shifted to human, the flow so seamless it was one of the most incredible things she had ever seen. She'd been a fool to ever think she could walk away from him, to even question if they should complete the mating. He belonged to her.

He cupped her face, pulling her to him. "You're okay," he said, breathing out the words.

She needed to tell him everything she knew. "The other two dragons are dead. He poisoned me with dragon venom at first, then used some sort of witchy magic to keep me contained. I think he was just working with those two dragons and Brennus. He was the one who spread all those rumors about you and Prima. He told me that he hated you—it's why he was in league with Brennus even though he didn't agree with everything he was doing. He didn't tell me why, but it sounded personal. And he told me Brennus would be going after King. Brennus's extended clan is taking over cities around the world and New Orleans is his. His clan has been killing the ancients."

In response, Reaper simply crushed his mouth to hers, desperate and hungry to taste all of her.

Maybe she should care that he was naked and bloodied and dead dragons were scattered throughout this cemetery but all she cared about was kissing him back. Bright purple flames spread out everywhere, including the entire cemetery, licking high into the treetops as she wrapped her entire body around him. She wanted to jump him right now, to take him right on the grassy earth. Somehow she pulled her head back, and knew her eyes were as bright as his. "We are going to mate," she said.

He simply growled in response, their flames licking up even higher.

There were things to take care of, dragon bodies to burn, and other shit to figure out—like if King and the others were okay—but all she cared about was mating with him. Feeling him sink deep inside her as he officially claimed her for his own.

She kissed Reaper back with a hunger she felt bone-deep. She wanted to imprint herself on this male so the world knew he was hers. That he was taken and would always be taken.

"Guys," a familiar voice interrupted them. Greer ignored it. "Guys!"

Reaper and Greer both growled, turning to look at the interloper.

Cynara held up her hands. "I am so sorry to interrupt. Like, *so* sorry. But you guys are creating quite the show. And we have two dead bodies to take care of."

Reaper looked back at Greer, his dragon bright in his eyes. "We could leave right now."

Oh how she wanted to. Desperately. "Damari has more clanmates," she forced out instead. And they could be a threat to all of them. He hadn't implied they were but...who knew.

"And King is battling Brennus," Cynara said.

Greer snapped her gaze back to her friend. *"Right now?"*

"Brennus attacked King as we followed after Reaper. We chose to come help you."

Oh, hell. Greer looked at Reaper. They couldn't just leave now. They had to help.

CHAPTER TWENTY-EIGHT

B rennus would have sneered if he'd been in human form. King was alone with his wolves as Reaper flew away in a fruitless effort to save his mate.

Everything had come down to this. This was his due. King, a fucking wolf, thought he could rule this city? Thought he had the stones to take on other supernaturals?

Fool.

He let his camouflage fall as he descended on the now nearly empty street. King and his wolves scattered as he shot fire at them.

That's right, run, little wolves!

He released another stream of fire along the wall, burning the treetops as he arrowed down toward the cemetery.

They— Where the hell was King?

His clanmates swooped down with him, landing on two opposite walls of the cemetery as he circled, looking for the Alpha.

He had to kill him. Had to do it now. Had to take over the city.

There! A shadow peeled off one of the gravestones. A wolf.

He flew downward, his wings flapping sharply as he descended.

A piercing pain sliced into the tip of his wing. He twisted midair and saw King standing on a gravestone, shirt off and sword out. A fucking wolf who used a sword?

He changed direction and flew back, breathing out fire as he dove. The wolf brushed it off, not bothered at all by it. No one could withstand it forever though.

The male shoved the sword into the ground and...ripped off a headstone. With impressive strength he threw it at Brennus.

He dodged to the left, barely missing a blow to the face. The huge headstone slammed into his wing, however.

He screeched, falling onto a cacophony of headstones. They shoved against his underbelly. Immediately he jumped back up, taking to the air when another headstone slammed into his face.

It broke in half against the hardness of his scales.

Hell no.

He released another stream of blazing hot fire and dive-bombed King. He'd thought to play with this wolf, to rip him to shreds. Now he would simply destroy him.

Fire-resistant or not, this wolf would not withstand his teeth and claws.

Closer, closer, he zeroed in on the wolf, flying fast.

King jumped off the gravestone, grabbed the sword with wicked speed. Before Brennus could pull up, the male tossed it at him.

He heard the soft singing of the sword as it swished toward him.

When it pierced his underbelly shock and pain tore through him in simultaneous blows. *No!* This sword should not have been able to hurt him.

Gritting his teeth through the pain, he continued his descent and released another stream of fire.

King dodged it, shifting to his wolf midair with a quickness he'd only ever seen in other dragons.

Unable to stop his flight, he slammed into two gravestones, ripping them up with his claws.

Fire and agony punctured his neck as a heavy weight slammed into him. Claws and teeth tore into his back. He twisted, fighting the attack.

A sharp, piercing pain sliced down his spine. He couldn't move, couldn't breathe fire for the agony that shot down his entire body. He couldn't move his limbs. Couldn't do anything. The wolf had...ripped out his spine.

Wait...no! This wasn't how it was supposed to happen. He was supposed to be victorious.

He was a dragon.

A fucking dragon.

"Just die already" were the last words he heard before death consumed him, her sharp talons reaching up to drag him to the afterlife.

CHAPTER TWENTY-NINE

Greer scaled the giant wall to Cale's house with her friends, and King and his wolves. Apparently while Reaper had been killing Damari, King had killed Brennus. And it had been quite the show, according to some of King's packmates—who had finished off Brennus's New Orleans' clanmates. They hadn't made it in time to help, but it seemed King's pack hadn't needed it after all.

If Brennus had any clanmates left in the city—and King didn't seem to think he did—they would eliminate them. For now, they had to tackle a different problem.

She just wished Reaper had agreed to come with them in human form. Instead he was…well, he was in a rage. A full-on dragon rage.

As Greer landed on the soft grass, she winced as Reaper's huge dragon slammed into the third story of Cale's house.

She'd tried to tell him they should go subtle and catch the other male off guard, but he was beyond subtle at this point.

"Your man certainly knows how to make an entrance," King murmured, a hint of a smile curving up his normally hard mouth.

"He certainly does."

Greer heard shouts from inside even as Reaper turned right back around and dove straight for the house again, slamming into the second story. Seriously, he could have just set the place on fire, but he was in pure destructive mode. One of the little turrets flew off as wood and brick splintered through the air, landing in chunks against the ground.

"What the fuck are you doing?" Cale shouted, racing out of the front door shirtless as he looked skyward at Reaper. "You crazy motherfucker!"

The fact that he hadn't shifted and attacked Reaper was potentially a good sign. Maybe he hadn't been involved in her kidnapping. For his sake, she hoped he hadn't. Greer didn't want Reaper to have to kill another ancient. Damari had been on a tirade, telling her how Reaper had taken from him and how he was going to take from Reaper—meaning her. But he'd never mentioned his half-brother being involved.

Cale spotted the rest of them stalking across the lawn then. He froze, his gaze sweeping over all of them. All in all, including Reaper, there were about twenty of them that had invaded his land.

Yep, not a social visit.

Reaper landed on the ground next to him, tearing up dirt and grass with his claws—and breathed fire right in Cale's face.

Once he finally stopped, Cale's clothes were gone, turned to dust, but his claws were now out. He slashed out at Reaper's nose. "Shift to human so we can talk, you lunatic!"

Reaper growled low in his throat.

Greer thought he showed a lot of restraint but he had sworn that he wouldn't simply kill Cale until after he'd talked to him. He wanted answers as much as Greer did. Especially since she was the one who had been kidnapped and shot full of poison. If Cale was guilty...he would die.

Reaper shifted, magic sparking into the air, a waterfall of colors. He stalked toward Cale and shot out his hand, wrapping it around the other male's neck.

Cale was just as fast, wrapping his own hand around Reaper's neck. Greer started to step forward but King held up a hand as if to stop her.

"He needs to do this. You are his mate."

"Yeah, well he's my mate too." Even if they weren't technically mated, she was claiming him as her own. She stepped around King and hurried forward. "Let each other go. Now."

Reaper didn't take his eyes off Cale as he released him. Wincing, Cale looked between the two of them, then everyone else. "Anyone want to explain why you just dive-bombed my house? You're going to fix it, by the way. Jackass."

"Did you know Damari was going to kidnap Greer?" Reaper snarled.

Cale flinched back in shock, his expression one of concern as he looked at Greer. "Wait, what? Are you okay?"

Before he could answer, Reaper snarled again, stepping in front of him so that Greer was completely behind him. "You don't ask questions. You answer
truthfully or you die. If by some miracle you manage to
get past me, King and the others will finish you off. But
I won't fail in killing you. Then when I'm done, I'll kill
anyone you've ever loved." Reaper's voice was pure
beast now, barely any human at all as he growled at the
other male.

"I will answer your questions." Cale said, his voice
calm. "Stay back!" he continued, ordering his clanmates
who had spilled out of the house. They would naturally
want to defend their clanmate, but thankfully they listened. And if any of them had been assisting Damari,
they would die too.

Greer placed a calming hand on Reaper's back,
wanting him to know that she was here. That she
wasn't going anywhere. Ever.

"Do you have any plans to overthrow the city?"
Reaper asked.

"No."

"Have you ever been in league with Brennus to kill
humans?"

"No."

"Were you involved in any way in the kidnapping of
Greer?"

"No."

On and on Reaper went, asking the same question
five different ways as he made sure Cale was not lying.

Greer scented Cale's truth too. Well, truth and anger.

When Reaper was satisfied the male was telling the truth, he shoved out a sigh. Then he said, "Your brother is dead. He kidnapped Greer, and I killed him."

Now pain washed off the other male, but it wasn't potent, it was more...just resigned sadness. Cale looked at Greer now as she stepped around from behind Reaper. "I'm sorry. He...did he hurt you?"

"Yes. He poisoned me. It was a weird concoction of dragon poison and witch magic. It was very dark. It bound me, but I'm stronger than a witch."

Something like resignation flickered over Cale's masculine features as he closed his eyes. "Damari, you stupid fool."

"Why do you say that?"

"He liked to play with fire." Cale's eyes snapped open. "He never really got over the death of Abria."

Reaper stared at him blankly. "I do not recognize the name."

"She was from the O'Dea clan. Ring any bells?"

"Why would I ring a bell?"

Cale blinked, his mouth curving up ever so slightly, but there was no humor in his eyes. "She was a red and yellow dragon, and part of a surprise ambush against one of Bayne's strongholds. I don't even remember how many thousands of years ago that was. Her clan thought to take over property that was not theirs. So...you stopped them."

"Ah," Reaper said slowly. "I remember now. Why was he angry about that?"

"She and Damari were lovers...would have been mates if they'd ever gotten the chance. The manifestation was there but they didn't fully mate before you killed her. He always held a grudge but the kill was justified. And he never mentioned anything about hating you. Not truly. He just didn't like you. He...mentioned his loathing of you after you came to visit us recently. Said you were still an arrogant asshole. But I never suspected anything like this."

"I do remember now. I went into Hibernation not long after that kill." Reaper's tone was neutral, but his body was tense as if he expected to fight Cale.

"So did Damari. And that is a long time to hold on to a grudge, especially in sleep." Cale shook his head.

Reaper ran a hand over his face, suddenly looking exhausted. "There were some other dragons with him. I have saved their heads but only temporarily, so you may identify them. I believe they were your cousins as well."

"I probably know who they are—were. Two young dumbasses who idol-worshipped him. Fucking Damari," he muttered, anger spiraling off him in waves now.

"You need to clean out your house." Reaper's words were spoken softly for only Greer and Cale to hear.

Greer understood completely. If there were more like Damari living with him, Cale would have to take care of it. Especially if he wished to live in New Orleans

under King's rule. For all Greer knew, however, Cale
and his dragons would be leaving soon.

"I will." Cale's answer was just as quietly spoken.

"Are you and I going to have a problem? Are you going to hold a grudge?" Reaper asked, at a normal level
this time.

"No. Never." Cale held out a hand and clasped
Reaper's hand once, hard. "You are honorable. I know
you would not have killed him unless you had to." Then
he looked at Greer. "My family owes you a blood debt.
You are a healer and therefore—"

She shook her head. "Nope. You don't owe me anything, and I'm not going to take it. The actions of your
family have nothing to do with you. If you weren't involved, then we are good. If you come after me or my
mate or my friends, then we'll have a problem." Greer
let her healer's energy loose, two twin balls of green
flames hovering in both her hands to drive home her
point. "Understand?"

"Yes. Still, I am sorry, and we *do* owe you. We will
most definitely repay you."

She wanted to argue with him, but dragons and
their traditions were so long-lived, especially dragons
as ancient as Cale. It wasn't as if she would ever call on
the debt anyway so she let it drop.

"We leave now, then." Reaper turned to her, his
dragon wild and beautiful in his eyes.

"What about my fucking house?" Cale growled.

"I'll take care of that." Bo stepped up, but Greer only
had eyes for Reaper.

306 | KATIE REUS

In that moment, she only cared about leaving with Reaper.

Her mate.

She simply nodded at him and stepped back, letting the shift come over her. She didn't bother taking off her clothes either, just shredded them. Because who cared about clothing right now? Maybe she should feel bad about leaving the others to clean up the damage but she didn't. Not at all.

As she shifted, Reaper did the same. Before he could take off, she took flight first, practically daring him to catch her. They were mates, and if he wanted her, he would have to catch her first.

That was the dragon way.

She flew high into the sky, her wings stretching as she arched higher, higher until she darted into a set of thick clouds.

There was so much she and Reaper needed to learn about one another, but she'd never been so sure of anything in her life as she was of mating with Reaper.

The clouds were pea-soup thick as she dove through them, the moistness in the air refreshing.

Not wanting to hide for too long, she burst through the clouds and wasn't surprised when moments later Reaper appeared at her side, his waterfall of colors glittering under the moonlight.

She dove downward in a tight spiral, completely showing off her flying skills—her dragon half was in full-on preening mode right now. Greer had never imagined that she would care what a male thought of her but right now she wanted Reaper to love what he saw.

Because he was beautiful to her in dragon form, a magical work of art against the near full moon suspended above them.

He dove down after her, mimicking her spiral until they almost hit Lake Pontchartrain. Almost as if they'd choreographed it, they both pulled up at the last second, their wings stretching out as they glided over the water, sending ripples out everywhere. She felt completely free as they stretched their wings.

He took her cue when she turned upward, joining her. Their wings flapped in unison as they pushed higher and higher, a kaleidoscope of brilliant colors under the full moon.

As they flew, losing themselves under the night sky, she spotted a couple familiar dragons against the moonlight, flying in beautiful dips and arches.

It was strange to see dragons out with no camouflage.

Free.

She had very rarely risked it in the past because of human satellites, but to see her own kind free, if she had been human, she would have cried out in joy. There was no more hiding, and while it was a little terrifying, it was also liberating. She might hate what had gotten them here but...dragons and other supernaturals were truly free to be themselves.

She released a short burst of fire, signaling to Reaper, and banked back north. No more flying tonight.

It was time to claim her mate. She put on a burst of speed, knowing he would follow. That was another strange thought—to have no doubt that this male would follow where she went.

He was hers and she was his. Talk about being free.

CHAPTER THIRTY

Reaper had never flown so fast or hard in his life as he chased after his mate. As they landed on the mansion's grounds, they both tore up dirt and grass as they skidded to a halt.

She shifted before he could, and by the time he had turned human, she was racing for the back door, her rich, throaty laughter and long hair trailing behind her in the breeze.

He caught her on the top landing of the stairs, scooping her up as he raced to the nearest bedroom on the second floor.

He didn't care where they did this, outside, inside, on a hard or soft surface. A bed of grass or inside a shower. He simply wanted her.

But he wanted to do this right for her.

He crushed his mouth to hers as they fell onto a fluffy, giant bed with far too many pillows. As she wrapped her arms and legs around him, he shoved the pillows out of the way. Brilliant purple flames erupted everywhere, bathing everything in their wake.

"Do you want this?" he growled against her mouth, barely sounding human.

"Yes. Yes!"

He would not ask twice. She was a female who knew her own mind. His mouth was on hers again as he reached between their bodies, sliding one, then two fingers inside her. She was slick, completely soaked. All for him.

She rolled her hips against his hand as she ran her hands up his chest and around his body, digging her fingers into his back. He savored the bite of her nails against his skin.

Everything about this female had him twisted up in knots. She eclipsed every single fantasy he had ever had of what his mate would be like.

No fantasy could compare to reality. To Greer.

His erection was heavy between their bodies, and when she wrapped her fingers around his cock he shuddered. She widened her legs and he guided himself inside her without any help.

Sweet heaven, she was perfection.

As he thrust once, then twice, the flames seemed to consume everything, eating up everything in their path but not actually burning.

The only thing that existed in front of him was Greer.

He cupped her breasts, teasing her nipples as she grabbed onto his ass, urging him to go faster. Harder.

Part of him wanted to slow down, to savor this moment, but he felt possessed. He couldn't stop. She was just as hungry as he was, her kisses wild and harsh. Her need as sharp as his.

He wasn't sure how long they mated, but when he felt her inner walls tightening around his cock, he knew she was close.

So was he, barely balancing on a razor-thin edge. All his muscles were pulled taut as he continued thrusting inside her. He reached between their bodies and barely grazed her clit, teasing the sensitive little bud.

That was all it took to push her over the edge. Her climax surrounded him, and going on instinct, he bit down on her neck, marking her.

Surprise and pleasure punched through him as she did the same, sinking her canines right where his neck and shoulder met. Then she came even harder, her head falling back as her climax crested.

He let go of his control, losing himself inside her as he sought out her mouth again.

Even as he came down from his high, it was too much and not enough. He wanted more.

So much more. All of her. Forever.

"I'm not done," he rasped out as he rolled onto his back, taking her with him.

Her hair was long and wild, draped around her breasts and face. "Good. I'm not close to done either." To reiterate, she tightened her walls around his already growing cock.

He'd been asleep for thousands of years. He had a feeling he wasn't going to be done for at least a week. Maybe longer.

Maybe never.

CHAPTER THIRTY-ONE

Three days later

Greer stretched her arms above her head, enjoying the feel of the warm sunlight bathing the bed she shared with Reaper. Over the last three days they had mated over and over, only taking breaks to eat and sleep. Barely. Some of her friends had checked in but she'd made it clear that unless there was an emergency or someone needed help—she didn't want to see anyone else.

She'd even lost weight, but didn't care. She'd never felt so energized, so alive, in her life. "I'm hungry," she murmured as she rolled over, cuddling up against his side.

"I am too." There was a wicked note in his voice as he stroked his fingers down her spine.

Though she was very tempted to give him exactly what he wanted—what she wanted—she nudged at his chest. "Food first. Real food."

He made a sort of grumbling sound that was way too adorable before he rolled off the bed and grabbed her robe.

They'd eventually made it back to the bedroom that he had claimed as his own. As far as she knew they weren't going anywhere anytime soon, so this room was as good as any.

As she thought of that, she realized that they did need to talk about the future. Talking wasn't something they'd done a lot of in the last three days.

Unless dirty talk counted.

She slipped into her silky robe as he grabbed a pair of pants and tugged them on. No shirt of course because he wanted to make her crazy. The wicked look he gave her as they left the room had heat rushing between her legs.

This male.

Eventually they made it downstairs to the kitchen—but not until after a quickie on the stairs.

After the first twelve hours, she'd realized that the mating bond was no joke. The need she felt for him was still growing.

"I seriously never expected you," he murmured as he opened the refrigerator.

"Right back at you. But I wouldn't want this any other way." It was weird, but she couldn't even picture her life without him now, and she'd only known him such a short time compared to her very long life.

"I can't believe my awakening never hinted at you." He shook his head as he pulled out a carton of eggs someone had dropped off. "You are the only thing that even matters.

She had no idea where the food was coming from— *Wait, what?* "What do you mean?"

He paused, watching her carefully. "When I woke up, my blood told me that there was fire and destruction on the horizon, that things would soon change. That...fire would bathe everything."

Hurt punctured her chest as she digested his words. "Why did you not say anything before?"

He rounded the island supernaturally fast, cupping her cheek with one hand. "There was nothing anyone could have done. It was simply what I knew, what my dragon half knew bone-deep. There was nothing I could have changed."

"You still should have told me."

He watched her carefully. "You are right. I'm not used to sharing anything with anyone. I used to operate on a need-to-know basis with my subordinates."

She narrowed her gaze. "I am not your subordinate."

"No, you're not. You are my mate. My very forgiving mate," he murmured, leaning forward so that his lips almost touched hers.

She couldn't help but smile. "We're definitely going to need to work on our communication skills. That means we talk about stuff. Heck, we talk about *everything*. I don't want secrets between us. If you have a weird feeling, please tell me. And I will do the same."

"I don't want secrets between us either." Then he kissed her, his mouth featherlight against hers before it deepened into something more.

But she gently pushed against his chest even as her dragon grumbled. "No way. *Food.*"

He grinned wickedly but actually stepped back. "We will eat quickly."

"Have you ever had any other weird feelings?" she asked as he started pulling out different things to cook with.

"Occasionally, yes, before my Hibernation. I don't know another way to describe it but my blood simply tells me things."

"Hmm."

"What does that mean?"

"I don't know. But you gave me something to think about."

"What are you doing on your phone?"

"Texting Victoria, who is a giant research nerd."

"I do not know what this word 'nerd' means. I don't think there is a translation for it."

Greer simply snorted and continued texting Victoria. If Reaper's blood had "told him" of this coming fire and destruction, she wondered if there were perhaps any prophecies about all of this.

It didn't hurt to check.

* * *

Greer heard her phone ringing on top of the island countertop, and when she made a move to grab it Reaper wrapped his arms around her, his fingers digging into her bare ass.

"No moving," he grumbled against her neck as he nibbled her sensitive skin.

She giggled against him. After they'd eaten, they'd had more fun on the kitchen floor. Twice.

"Come on, I recognize Victoria's ringtone."

He sighed as if she was asking him to lift the entire world on his shoulders, but eventually he loosened his grip and helped her to her feet.

"Hey," she said to her friend and fellow healer.

"Hey yourself. I've dug up a bunch of interesting information on a prophecy after your text. That was a good thought and I'm pissed I didn't think of it earlier."

"So you found something?"

"Maybe, yeah, I think so. And this prophecy mentions your new mate. I'm assuming he's with you?"

"Yes. Want me to put you on speaker?"

"Yes. Though I'm sure he can hear anyway, but this will just be easier."

Greer put her clanmate on speaker and then hit the video capability.

Victoria grinned and waved at the two of them. Her jet-black hair was pulled up into a messy bun with two pencils sticking out of it. Greer could see Drake in the background, poring over some giant tomes that they'd clearly laid out in the clan's library. It looked as if he was her research assistant. Something Greer was certain the kind dragon did not mind. She also saw their little baby boy in a bassinet, swaddled and soundly asleep right next to Drake.

As if she read her mind, Victoria pointed over her shoulder. "Drake helped me with the research."

Drake half grunted, but didn't glance over at them as he flipped a page on a huge tome.

"Basically what I've got is that there is this prophecy about the entire world—the Nahom prophecy. It's a ridiculously old one. There are various mentions of different leaders rising up, including..." She frowned once. "Ah, I'm not sure how to pronounce this but my translation says that it means Reaper. I'm pretty sure it relates to you." Victoria looked at Reaper so Greer slightly moved the phone.

Reaper simply nodded but did not respond.

Victoria didn't care about his non-response because she kept going, talking about various leaders around the world, including Finn, Lyra, the twins—who were thankfully alive and healthy in South America right now after closing the door to a Hell realm. She also mentioned some Alphas that Greer knew of in Mauritius, Japan, Australia and Italy. The others mentioned Greer wasn't familiar with, but Victoria assured her that they were all current leaders of supernaturally strong territories. The places that had survived. "There's also a reference to Reaper working with a king. It probably means the Alpha, King."

Greer turned to Reaper, surprised. Then she turned back to her friend. "Will you send us everything you have?"

"Definitely. I'm actually compiling a file and sending it to all supernatural strongholds around the world. The more information we share, the better. So far all of the supernatural cities are more than just surviving, they are thriving. It's giving everyone hope for a future."

Greer nodded because she had heard the same thing. "Thanks," she said.

"Unfortunately there are mentions of the Zmey clan. Even with Brennus and his father dead, his clanmates have taken over a few territories, which is right in line with this prophecy."

Once they disconnected, she turned to Reaper.

"So...this prophecy says that you work with King?"

He lifted a broad shoulder. "It doesn't mean I have to. I'm not tied to the male."

"Well...we haven't exactly talked about where we're going to live. Do you want to stay here or move back to where my clan lives?"

"I only want you to be happy. I do not care where we live as long as I'm with you."

Smiling, she reached for him, wrapping her arms around his back and pulling him close. "That's not exactly an answer."

"It is the only answer. And it is the truth."

"I don't see you ever truly submitting to an Alpha. Especially a wolf you don't know well."

"That is also true. But I like King and I like what he is doing here. I could work *with* him."

"I'm sure you will butt heads."

"I butt heads with everyone. I am arrogant after all," he murmured.

Laughing she leaned up on tiptoe and kissed him. "True enough."

"Tell me what you want, my mate," he said. "We can stay or go. I simply want to be with you."

Though she would miss her clan, Greer already knew the answer. "We will stay here. This place needs more help than where my clan lives. I think we can do a lot of good here." She felt that calling deep in her bones, just as she'd felt the calling to be with Reaper. This was where they needed to be.

He kissed her in response, long and hard. And for the next hour she didn't think of anything other than losing herself in Reaper.

CHAPTER THIRTY-TWO

"**I**gnore it," Reaper said to Greer as someone banged on the front door of the mansion. Sunset had fallen not long ago and after almost four days alone with his mate, he was not ready to give up their privacy.

"It could be important."

"*This* is important," he said, reaching between her legs and cupping her. Sometime in the last few minutes she had put on underwear, a useless material he did not understand. She should be naked all the time.

Another knock followed, this time harder.

Reaper grabbed a pair of pants and tugged them on before storming out of the living room. They had just gotten settled in front of the fire and he'd planned to taste his mate again. He was completely addicted to her.

Whoever had interrupted them would pay.

He practically ripped the front door open. "What?" he growled.

King stood on the front porch, along with Arthur, Cynara, Justus, Cale and four females he did not recognize. Well, he recognized one as the phoenix but he did not know her.

"I'm sorry to interrupt. I can come back later." King raised an eyebrow in question.

"Good." He slammed the door in the Alpha's face.

"Reaper," Greer gasped, surprise rolling off her as she pulled the door back open. Her robe was tied securely around her, but her hair was down in soft, tousled waves.

He wasn't sure why she was surprised. His dragon was close to setting all of them on fire, even his friends.

"Why don't you all come in? Is everything okay?" she asked as Reaper stepped back, wrapping an arm around her shoulders and keeping her close. He resisted the urge to snarl at everyone.

"Things are good," the Alpha said. "Stable at least. But I want to talk to both of you, actually. I'm in the process of setting up a system around the city where different supernaturals have different roles. I love this city, and what I'm proposing is more of a roundtable type of ruling."

Reaper was vaguely familiar with the reference. *Fuck.* It seemed as if they would all be staying for the near future. Well, he certainly wasn't going to offer them food or drinks. He couldn't even feign civility. "Come on." Turning, he stalked to the kitchen, but didn't take his arm from around his mate.

He heard Cynara snort and mutter something about his hospitality but he couldn't even smile.

"What has brought this on?" Reaper asked once they were all standing in the spacious kitchen. Even though he simply wanted everyone gone, the appearance of these supernaturals was curious.

"After some soul-searching, I realized that right now I need to concentrate on the greater good. I can't do that if there is infighting among supernaturals. And the vampires will never follow me unless I mate with one of their own. Not truly anyway. And I refuse to have a mate of convenience."

Reaper could respect that. A mating like that was destined to fail anyway. He nodded at the wolf. "I understand. Greer and I have talked and we have decided to stay in New Orleans. Depending upon what you need of us, we are more than happy to help rebuild and keep the city safe." He looked at his mate for affirmation. He did not want her to think he was speaking for her.

She smiled at him and then at King. "It is as he says. I need to talk to my Alpha but I am here to stay. I'm not swearing complete loyalty—that is earned. And as of now, Conall is my Alpha but...if you prove you're worth it, I'll call you Alpha one day."

King nodded once, his mouth curving up slightly. "That is more than fair."

"We want to rebuild the world," Greer said, her words impassioned.

"Rebuild it better than it was before," the phoenix— Léonie—said, her skin shimmering a faint blue as she spoke.

There were murmurs of agreement all around the island. Reaper was inclined to agree. He hadn't been awake long, but from what he'd seen the world had been on a dark path. This was a time for rebirth.

"Then if we are all in agreement, I will figure out which sectors of my territory each of you will be in

324 | KATIE REUS

charge of." He looked at Greer." "With you being the exception. As the healer, you will help wherever you are needed, whenever you choose."

"I would love to get together with more of the healers in the city," she said. "I actually work with a network of healers around the globe. Most of them survived, and we've always shared information."

King smiled, nodding. "Good. Once we've figured all this out, I will be hunting down two of Brennus's clanmates who escaped New Orleans."

"There were two more?" This surprised Reaper as he thought that King had killed all of the ones in this city—unfortunately many of Brennus's clanmates still lived in other places around the globe. But he had not left Greer's side in almost four days so he was not up to date on everything.

"It would appear so. Justus's intel on his clan's hideouts turned out to be correct, and two of those bastards escaped my wrath. They might only be two dragons, but I will not allow them to escape to another one of their clan's holdings. They have abandoned all their properties, which is just as well. I'm repurposing their properties into homes for people in need. We've already started working on a food collective—there are farmers and mages more than willing to help increase the food supplies. No one will go hungry in the city. And everyone will pitch in and work."

Reaper nodded in approval. That was as it should be.

Leaning back slightly, he wrapped his arm around Greer's shoulders. She was giving up a lot to be here with him and he would never take her for granted.

He had woken up expecting fire and war. But he had not expected her.

Thankfully the fates had given him this perfect female.

EPILOGUE

"Thank you so much for this," Greer said as they all basically crash-landed into a giant snow-covered field on her clan's land.

Nyx, who had transported Greer, Reaper, Bo and their sweet little baby, Thea, smiled. "It's no problem at all. We had been planning to come up here anyway. Especially since Ian is visiting with Arya and Dragos."

"Well, I'm still grateful. I'm going to head to see my Alpha. Do you know where you're going?"

Nyx and Bo nodded, with Bo plucking Thea from Nyx's arms and cuddling her close. Seeing the half-demon cuddle his daughter would have warmed anyone's heart. "We've been here enough to know the layout," Bo said. "Go on. Just let us know when you're ready to leave."

Greer linked her arm with Reaper's, their boots crunching in the snow. He kissed the top of her head as they walked in silence, the simple action making her feel secure.

But as they reached her Alpha's neighborhood, he said, "Nothing is set in stone. You do not need to move to New Orleans. I like this Montana just as well. In truth, I don't care where I live as long as I am with you."

He had told her the same half a dozen times. She looked up at him. "Can you trust that I know my own mind? We need to be in New Orleans right now. I feel it in my bones."

"All right, my smart, beautiful mate."

She smiled at the compliment, basking in it and him. It didn't take long to reach Conall's house and, to her surprise, the door swung open before they'd even reached the front stoop.

Rhea raced out, a big smile on her face as she practically launched herself at Greer, pulling her into a hug. "I've missed you!"

Laughing at the welcome, Greer hugged the smaller wolf shifter, holding her tight. Unexpected tears stung her eyes as she released her friend. She might be leaving but this would always be a place she could return to if they decided. These were her people.

"Don't cry." Reaper sounded panicked as he gave the order.

Laughing, she dashed away the wetness on her cheeks. "It's fine. I'm just happy. And...you have news." She eyed Rhea carefully, unsure if the Alpha female had told anyone.

Rhea blinked, then her cheeks flushed. "We literally just found out. We haven't told anyone," she whispered.

"Then I won't either, but congratulations." Greer kept her tone just as low, as she could hear and scent many others inside. Rhea being pregnant was *huge* news, but news they would definitely need to share on their own. And no matter what, Greer would return

when her friend gave birth. No way would she miss
something like that.

"Thank you. So...you're not back for good, are you?"
Rhea looked between the two of them, only frowning a
little bit as she eyed Reaper. "I guess I can't get too mad
that you're stealing her away since my clan stole me
from my pack."

Reaper simply wrapped his arm around Greer's
shoulders and they headed inside.

Greer was pleasantly surprised to find not only Conall in the living room, but Keelin and her mate Bran.
Then there was August, Prima, Mira, Finn, Lyra, Vega
and Gabriel. And a couple shifters she didn't recognize.
"What's all this?"

Conall had already risen to greet her and pulled her
into a hug. "They just returned from South America.
We were simply talking about the state of the world."

After hugging those she knew and introducing her
new mate to everyone, she found herself pulled into
Reaper's lap as he sat on an uncomfortable high-backed
chair Conall seriously needed to get rid of.

"So you made it out of South America." Greer looked
at Mira and August, who were sitting *very* close to each
other. She couldn't scent the mating bond between the
two of them but something had definitely happened between those two. And she would get answers later. She
was a nosy dragon after all.

"That is a story for another day," Prima said, looking
at August and Mira.

"We've heard about all that you guys have done for New Orleans," Vega said, speaking up. "Soon we'll be headed back to Biloxi, where we're going to stay put for a while." She reached out and linked her fingers with Gabriel, her mate.

"I hope we get to see more of each other, then," Greer said. Biloxi was not a far flight from New Orleans.

"Count on it."

Greer leaned back, listening to the others talk, and realized that the world was in good hands. At least Cale had not been involved with Damari's treachery—and Damari had not been involved in the killings of ancients. Not directly anyway. Supernatural hackers had ferreted out that the Zmey clan had been behind all of that, targeting strong ancients they thought would be a threat to them. They'd spent decades planning everything. Soon their supernatural strongholds would fall, Greer knew.

There weren't many, and the world was beyond angry at what they'd done. Supernaturals everywhere were united in the desire to destroy them. When she heard Prima say she would be returning to New Orleans with them, Greer wondered if it had anything to do with Arthur, but she certainly wouldn't be asking the ancient female. As she listened to her clan speak, she also discovered that Alma had left, at least temporarily, to be with two Alpha wolves in another territory. Something Greer found interesting—and would be following up on. When she heard that Judoc—an Alpha

330 | KATIE REUS

wolf—had survived, along with his whole pack, she was glad. It seemed many supernaturals had worked together to help each other and humans alike.

She was surprised when barely ten minutes later Conall motioned for her and Reaper to follow him. In that moment she almost felt like a dragonling being summoned to her Alpha's office.

"You've come to tell me you're staying in New Orleans," Conall said as he shut the door behind them.

"For now, we are. The two of us are needed in New Orleans, and King is a good male."

Conall snorted. "He's young and arrogant."

"Well, he's young compared to you," she said. "And I think arrogance is probably a necessary quality for an Alpha. Or at least confidence."

Her Alpha smiled, then looked at Reaper, his expression hardening. "Do you have anything to say for yourself?"

"If you expect me to apologize for claiming my mate, you are delusional."

Conall barked out a laugh. "A perfect answer." Then his dragon flashed in his eyes, sharp and deadly. "You better take care of her."

"We will take care of each other." Reaper squeezed her hand once.

"Okay, then."

"Will you guys be okay with one healer, truly?" Greer asked, going to sit on one of the chairs in front of Conall's desk.

"We will be more than fine. This area was not hit hard and we are keeping all communication open with allies. We're not far from Keelin and Bran's clan either. Relatively speaking. And apparently August has had a plan in place for a long time in case anything should ever happen."

"He has?"

Conall nodded. "Apparently. He said he would rather be prepared than be sorry."

She would expect nothing less from a black ops operative. Still, it was impressive. "Wow. Okay, then… I'm going to miss you guys but I'll be available by phone or we can fly here if needed. Or Nyx can bring us."

"Don't worry about that now. Just know you'll always have a home here. You'll always be one of mine. Always." Conall turned to Reaper then, held out a hand. "So will you."

Reaper grasped Conall's hand tightly. "Thank you."

Damn it. Tears spilled over now, freely and unabashedly. She was going to miss her clan so much but she was excited about starting a life with Reaper.

"Take a moment with your mate." Conall moved to the door as she wiped her tears away. "Because we have a little going-away party planned for you tonight. Right now, the clan needs a reason to celebrate so don't say no. They all want to say goodbye properly. I'm including myself in that. It'll be held at Victoria's place, six o'clock sharp."

She could be mistaken but she was pretty sure there were tears in his eyes too.

"My sweet mate," Reaper murmured as he pulled her into his arms. "I do not like these tears."

She sniffled against his shirt. "I'm going to miss my clan."

"They will always be your people."

"I know. Still."

"We will stay, then." Now he full-on growled.

Surprised, she pulled back and cupped his cheek. "No. I'm simply sad, but it changes nothing. I'm excited to start a new adventure with you."

"As I with you." His eyes flickered to his dragon for a brief moment. "Do you think we could sneak out the window in here and head to your house? It should be empty, yes?"

She blinked as laughter bubbled up inside her, eating away the melancholy threatening to undo her. "Seriously?"

"Seriously. Either that or I'm going to make you come right here on this desk."

"You're serious."

"I will never joke about making you come." His tone was deadly serious.

Laughing even harder, she threw her arms around him and kissed him. There was so much uncertainty in the world right now and a lot of grieving, but she sensed a desperation from every supernatural and human alike to hope.

Hope for a new future, hope for better.

She was filled with it too, so much it was bursting out of her, and right now she was going to take every single moment of joy she could with her mate. With her Reaper. "Let's sneak out the window, then."

Her clanmates would definitely understand.

Mates came first. Always.

Dear Readers,

I know some of you are asking... is that it? And the answer is, yes and no. Darkness Rising is the end of the Darkness series but not the end of this particular world. Since things shifted so dramatically at the end of this book, I decided it was time to do a spinoff that will start right where this one ends. You're going to see new characters and more of the same characters very soon. So this is not goodbye, just "see you later".

I'd also like to say a great big thank you to all my wonderful readers who have been with me since the launch of this series. It has been a wild ride and my pleasure to bring these characters to life. I hope you've enjoyed every second of this series! Saying goodbye to a series is always difficult, but thankfully it's not as hard this time because I know there is more to come.

Katie

ACKNOWLEDGMENTS

Whew! This has been a wild ride and I owe a lot of thanks to some incredible people. Kaylea Cross, I'm so grateful for all your insight and for our plotting trip to New Orleans. Julia, thank you for your edits and insight. Sarah, thank you for all the behind-the-scenes work you do in general and on this book in particular. Jaycee, I'm grateful for another beautiful cover. For my wonderful, wonderful readers, thank you for joining me on this journey. To my family, thank you for keeping me sane. And of course, I'm grateful to God.

Darkness Series
Darkness Awakened
Taste of Darkness
Beyond the Darkness
Hunted by Darkness
Into the Darkness
Saved by Darkness
Guardian of Darkness
Sentinel of Darkness
A Very Dragon Christmas
Darkness Rising

Deadly Ops Series
Targeted
Bound to Danger
Chasing Danger (novella)
Shattered Duty
Edge of Danger
A Covert Affair

Endgame Trilogy
Bishop's Knight
Bishop's Queen
Bishop's Endgame

Moon Shifter Series
Alpha Instinct
Lover's Instinct
Primal Possession
Mating Instinct
His Untamed Desire
Avenger's Heat
Hunter Reborn
Protective Instinct
Dark Protector
A Mate for Christmas

O'Connor Family Series
Merry Christmas, Baby
Tease Me, Baby
It's Me Again, Baby
Mistletoe Me, Baby

Red Stone Security Series
No One to Trust
Danger Next Door
Fatal Deception
Miami, Mistletoe & Murder
His to Protect
Breaking Her Rules
Protecting His Witness
Sinful Seduction
Under His Protection
Deadly Fallout
Sworn to Protect
Secret Obsession
Love Thy Enemy
Dangerous Protector
Lethal Game

Redemption Harbor Series
Resurrection
Savage Rising
Dangerous Witness
Innocent Target
Hunting Danger
Covert Games

Sin City Series (the Serafina)
First Surrender
Sensual Surrender
Sweetest Surrender
Dangerous Surrender

Linked books
Retribution
Tempting Danger

Non-series Romantic Suspense
Running From the Past
Dangerous Secrets
Killer Secrets
Deadly Obsession
Danger in Paradise
His Secret Past

Paranormal Romance
Destined Mate
Protector's Mate
A Jaguar's Kiss
Tempting the Jaguar
Enemy Mine
Heart of the Jaguar

ABOUT THE AUTHOR

Katie Reus is the *New York Times* and *USA Today* bestselling author of the Red Stone Security series, the Darkness series and the Redemption Harbor series. She fell in love with romance at a young age thanks to books she pilfered from her mom's stash. Years later she loves reading romance almost as much as she loves writing it.

However, she didn't always know she wanted to be a writer. After changing majors many times, she finally graduated summa cum laude with a degree in psychology. Not long after that she discovered a new love. Writing. She now spends her days writing dark paranormal romance and sexy romantic suspense.

For more information on Katie please visit her website: www.katiereus.com.

21970657R00203

Printed in Great Britain
by Amazon